On *The Boy in His Winter*

"[Lock] is one of the most interesting writers out there. This time, he re-imagines Huck Finn's journeys, transporting the iconic character deep into America's past—and future."
—***Reader's Digest***

On *American Meteor*

"[Walt Whitman] hovers over [*American Meteor*], just as Mark Twain's spirit pervaded *The Boy in His Winter*. . . . Like all Mr. Lock's books, this is an ambitious work, where ideas crowd together on the page like desperate men on a battlefield."
—***Wall Street Journal***

On *The Port-Wine Stain*

"Lock's novel engages not merely with [Edgar Allan Poe and Thomas Dent Mütter] but with decadent fin de siècle art and modernist literature that raised philosophical and moral questions about the metaphysical relations among art, science and human consciousness. The reader is just as spellbound by Lock's story as [his novel's narrator] is by Poe's. . . . Echoes of Wilde's *The Picture of Dorian Gray* and Freud's theory of the uncanny abound in this mesmerizingly twisted, richly layered homage to a pioneer of American Gothic fiction."
—***New York Times Book Review***

On *A Fugitive in Walden Woods*

"*A Fugitive in Walden Woods* manages that special magic of making Thoreau's time in Walden Woods seem fresh and surprising and necessary right now. . . . This is a patient and perceptive novel, a pleasure to read even as it grapples with issues that affect the United States to this day."
—**Victor LaValle**

On *The Wreckage of Eden*

"The lively passages of Emily [Dickinson's]'s letters are so evocative of her poetry that it becomes easy to see why Robert finds her so captivating. The book also expands and deepens themes of moral hypocrisy around racism and slavery. . . . Lyrically written but unafraid of the ugliness of the time, Lock's thought-provoking series continues to impress."
—***Publishers Weekly***

On *Feast Day of the Cannibals*

"Lock does not merely imitate 19th-century prose; he makes it his own, with verbal flourishes worthy of Melville."
—***Gay & Lesbian Review***

On *American Follies*

"*Ragtime* in a fever dream. . . . When you mix 19th-century racists, feminists, misogynists, freaks, and a flim-flam man, the spectacle that results might bear resemblance to the contemporary United States."
—***Library Journal*** (**starred review**)

The

Caricaturist

The

Caricaturist

Norman Lock

Bellevue Literary Press
New York

First published in the United States in 2024
by Bellevue Literary Press, New York

For information, contact:
Bellevue Literary Press
90 Broad Street
Suite 2100
New York, NY 10004
www.blpress.org

Cover Photo © North Wind Pictures / Bridgeman Images

This is a work of fiction. Characters, organizations, events, and places (even those that are actual) are either products of the author's imagination or are used fictitiously.

Library of Congress Cataloging-in-Publication Data
Names: Lock, Norman, author.
Title: The caricaturist / Norman Lock.
Description: First edition. | New York : Bellevue Literary Press, 2024. |
    Series: American novels series
Identifiers: LCCN 2023036369 | ISBN 9781954276277 (paperback ; acid-free
    paper) | ISBN 9781954276284 (epub)
Subjects: LCSH: Cartoonists--United States--Fiction. | Crane, Stephen,
    1871-1900--Fiction. | United States--History--19th century--Fiction. |
    LCGFT: Biographical fiction. | Historical fiction. | Novels.
Classification: LCC PS3562.O218 C37 2024 | DDC 813/.54--dc23/
eng/20230828

LC record available at https://lccn.loc.gov/2023036369

Bellevue Literary Press would like to thank all its generous donors—individuals and foundations—for their support.

 This project is supported in part by an award from the National Endowment for the Arts.

 This publication is made possible by the New York State Council on the Arts with the support of the Office of the Governor and the New York State Legislature.

Book design and composition by Mulberry Tree Press, Inc.

Bellevue Literary Press is committed to ecological stewardship in our book production practices, working to reduce our impact on the natural environment.

♾ This book is printed on acid-free paper.

Manufactured in the United States of America.

First Edition

10   9   8   7   6   5   4   3   2   1

paperback ISBN: 978-1-954276-27-7

ebook ISBN: 978-1-954276-28-4

For my cousin and friend David Moore,
Our grandmother Helen Ida (Barrett) Hub,
And our great-grandfather Franklin Barrett

A man walked into the Night.
"What must I do?" he asked of it.
"There is nothing you can do," Night replied.
The man would have seen its teeth
Had there been light to see by.
"What must I say?"
"There is nothing to say."
He would have heard Night snigger
Had it not been for distant thunder.
"Will I be allowed to remain here?"
While he waited for Night to reply,
Darkness roared down the vast jetties of Space,
Engulfing him.

—Written by Stephen Crane on board
the *Three Friends* and pocketed
by Oliver Fischer, June 10, 1898

The
Caricaturist

Fiasco

If there is a witness to my little life,
To my tiny throes and struggles,
He sees a fool . . .

—Stephen Crane

Philadelphia and Croydon, Pennsylvania

The tassel on my Turkish fez fell across my nose each time I nodded over the bubbling hookah. The attic room, packed like a portmanteau with the necessities of the undiscovered artist, was heavy with the languid smoke of hashish, which loosened, if not my tongue, which felt like a lump of India rubber in my mouth, then the muscles that combined to keep my head erect. In plain words, I would fall into a drowse until a sneeze returned me to a kind of consciousness, causing the tassel to swing madly like the tail of a horse harassed by an imperialist fly, its tiny bulb of electric jade beyond the skill even of Lalique to imitate.

"It smells like burning mummies in here!"

Robert Pearson threw open the windows. He had arrived unceremoniously while I was in a Pre-Raphaelite garden, admiring Swinburne's golden bird.

"What do you call that thing on your head?"

"A fez."

"Makes you look an ass!"

I bowed my head over my Persian slippers, which had been crushed under Pearson's big boots. The tassel swung across my face, and I swatted it furiously.

"You're a first-class clown, Ollie!" The result of a derisive snort, snot bubbled up in his nostrils, which he wiped on his sleeve. The sleeve, I noted, was frayed.

"Pearson, that's a filthy habit," I said as I lighted the gasolier, which cast a sickly gloom.

Settling noisily on my couch, he set to picking at the ravelings.

I drew on the hookah with a force sufficient to make the water boil madly in the blue glass bottle. "No doubt you've read Baudelaire's *Les Paradis artificiels* concerning his use of hashish. . . . No? Well, I'll lend you my copy if you promise not to wipe your boots with it."

"I don't sling the lingo," said Pearson, who looked as if he'd sucked a sour pickle.

"By jingo, you should! Or maybe you think a Baldwin locomotive is more beautiful than Manet's *Le Déjeuner sur l'herbe*?"

Pearson looked for a place to spit his contempt for the Old World and settled on an empty tomato tin in which I let my brushes steep.

"I have in mind a boating trip to Croydon," I

said like a nabob proposing an expedition down the Ganges.

"Are you inviting me?"

"We're friends, aren't we?" Despite our sniping, we were friends, and would be still, had he not been perforated by Spanish shrapnel. "Every Algernon needs his Jack. We'll enlist Teplov in the business."

Michael Teplov painted icons in the Russian style of such exquisite tininess as to elude criticism by the faculty of myopic old men at the Pennsylvania Academy of the Fine Arts, where we sniffed turps and linseed oil and dreamed of fame. His father, Mikhail, after beginning life in America as a sidewalk "puller-in" for the downtown department stores, had attained the enviable position—in our eyes—of wine merchant, supplying Philadelphia's restaurants with French and German tipple. We could usually put the touch on the old man for several bottles of *vin ordinaire* to fuel our revels, so long as his bashful son was invited to sit among the sots.

Pearson stroked his beard. "What's so special about Croydon?"

I was about to lay out my scheme when "Salome" let herself in. I had given her a key to my room in recognition of our *alliance,* spoken as the French pronounce it. I'd given her the handle "Salome" in praise of her sensuality. We had met the previous summer at Asbury Park, a resort town on the New Jersey seacoast, where I had set myself up as a boardwalk caricaturist. I have hers to this day, done in crayon, although the woman herself got away. Her name, front to back, was Anne Neel.

"Hello, you two scrags!" She unpinned her hat, and with a carelessness that always drove me mad, she tossed it on the bed.

Coloring to the roots of his reddish beard, Pearson said, apropos of nothing, "Gee rod!"

"We're not the least scragged," I said, waving my hand as if to dismiss the universe.

"You, my love, have been at the pipe."

"Which is not to be scragged, tanked, or otherwise soused." I leaned toward her and said, "I am drunk in the manner of a man whose senses are deranged by beauty."

"What an idiot!" grumbled Pearson, who could be counted on to become a fool in Anne's presence. (Yes, old friend, I was every bit of one in those days. Nearly ten years later, as I look back on them, I see little in my favor, except your affection for me.)

She drew on the hookah to no effect, since the hashish was dead and past reviving in the bowl.

Pointing to the rubber gas hose drooping from the wall, I invited her to take a draft.

"Maybe later," she said as she unbuttoned her shirtwaist with a slowness that would have aroused a sloth.

"Not tonight, Salome."

"I thought you wanted to draw me in the raw," she said, her pretty lips gathered in a pout.

Pearson held his breath as I let the seconds pile up in a silence broken only by the popping of the gas fixture.

"Can't you see I have a guest?"

A strangulated noise could be heard coming from Pearson's throat.

"Oh well." She buttoned up her blouse and fetched her hat. "Another time."

"Stay awhile. I'm organizing a trip up the Delaware on my grandfather's boat."

"I'm fond of the old boy; he's right off the square."

"There's something you can do for me."

"In Croydon!" said Pearson, scowling, since he could think of nothing intelligent to mark his presence in the room. Sensing his inadequacy, he began to smoke a cigarette at a furious rate.

"Croydon is a charming place," she said, recalling, I hoped, the afternoon when we had chased her windblown hat into the japonica bushes.

"I'll have one, Robert."

Pearson took a cigarette from the pack. She parted her lips. His hand shook; she steadied it with her own. His face turned incarnadine, but he managed to light it with a Diamond match.

"Thanks." Her eyes narrowed in an uprising of blue smoke. "You were saying, Ollie?"

My eyes glazed with smoke and memory, I saw once more the japonica blossoms caught in her long hair.

"Oliver!"

A hand organ playing in the street abruptly cut memory's ever-lengthening cord.

I laid a hand on Anne's arm and my eyes on her breast. Had she read my thoughts?

Irritated, Pearson took a loose piece of wallpaper and yanked it. A little cumulus of dust arose and mingled with the smoke of tobacco and stale Turkish hashish.

"Damn it, Robert, I was fond of those fronds!"

Shamefaced, he tried to rehang the torn paper with a paste of spit and powdered plaster.

"Oh, shut up, Oliver!" said Anne sharply.

I muzzled the droll, incorrigible Algernon Moncrieff, whom I had idolized ever since I saw a Mask and Wig production of *The Importance of Being Earnest*.

The floor being hard and pillows scarce, we sat our derrières on books—Pearson on *The Idiot* and Anne on *Anna Karenina*. I plumped for *Crime and Punishment*. Russian novels tend to be more commodious than the slender volumes of the Symbolists. Reverently, I opened a secondhand edition on French art to a reproduction of *Le Déjeuner sur l'herbe*. "I want to paint this!"

"Manet's *Luncheon on the Grass*," I said.

"In Croydon?" asked Pearson skeptically.

"Yes."

"Whatever for?" asked Anne.

"Does an artist need a reason?"

"It's a damned queer picture," said Robert, fingering his Adam's apple.

"Paris went berserk in '63 when it was shown at the Salon des Refusés. The critics called it 'scabrous'—all but Zola, who mocked them."

There are some leaves, some tree trunks, and, in the background, a river in which a chemise-wearing woman bathes; in the foreground, two young men are seated across from a second woman, who has just exited the water and who dries her naked skin in the open air. This nude woman has scandalized the public, who see only her in the canvas. My God! What indecency: a woman without the slightest covering between two clothed men!

Referring to the reproduction of the *Luncheon,* I assigned our parts in the *tableau vivant.*

"You, Robert, by virtue of your reddish beard, will take the role of the gentleman at the center of the painting—this handsome fellow dressed in a chestnut-colored coat, white flannels, and a dark tie knotted at a soft collar. You're completely at ease, sitting slightly behind Anne, who sits with one leg drawn up, her chin resting in her hand as she gazes unabashedly at the viewer."

"Why am I smiling?" she asked.

"We don't know. It's one of the aspects of the painting that makes it enigmatic. Another is why neither gentleman takes the slightest notice of a naked young woman in their midst."

"And what is *she* doing?" asked Anne, pointing to a dark-haired woman dressed in a chemise, whose gaze is lowered and hand partially submerged in the river in which she stands.

"Admiring her reflection."

"Don't be such a mug!"

The second man in the picture leans on a hummock, one hand raised like a bishop's, the other clutching a walking stick. He is the very image of the boulevardier. "The part of this gent dressed in gray trousers, dark coat and vest, and a pasha's hat is mine to play. A false beard is all that's needed for the impersonation to be complete."

Pearson and Anne studied the picture, she pulling at her lower lip, he the lobe of his ear. The organ-grinder and his monkey had gone elsewhere in search of kindness; the plaster dust had settled; the room had entered a peaceful phase, though rich in expectation, as if awaiting another outburst. It issued from Anne.

"You must be tanked to think I'll sit naked on the grass to be ogled at by two dime-novel dudes! Holy Roller Wanamaker would have me exorcised and thrown out on my ear if he were to hear of it."

"Look at the picture, Anne; our eyes aren't on you. Besides, it's Croydon, not Fairmount Park or Bartram's Garden. It's a secluded spot, *if you recall.*" I may have winked.

Turning to Pearson, she said, "Ain't he smooth?"

"Oh, he's an awful chump!"

"I'll say!"

We sat in moody silence broken only by the retort of Pearson's swollen knuckles as he cracked them twice.

"I'll be *her*," said Anne, cigarette smoke leaking from her lips. "The one in the shimmy."

I glanced at Pearson, who appeared unsure of

his place in the universe, never mind in the fête champêtre. He went to the washbasin and splashed water on his face.

"Not that!" I shouted as he was about to dry his dripping beard on my bathrobe. "There's a clean towel in there." I indicated a coal box. Empty coal boxes are the principal furniture in an artist's garret. (They are useful precisely because they're empty, an absence keenly felt in winter, when a fellow is inclined to stay in bed and shiver. In a pinch, a large coal box will do for one.) "I thank the household gods that he spared the lambrequin," I said, smoothing the damascene cloth draped over the mantelpiece, on which several scandalous volumes in French leaned like cocottes against a wall.

"You're a peacock, Ollie! I don't know how you stand him, Robert. I really don't."

"He talks through his hat!"

Perhaps I do, but you, friend of mine, can't take your eyes off Anne's breast.

"A dub who wears lavender trousers and an idiotic hat is a— What did you call him?"

"A chump."

She nodded her head as if a wisecrack were wisdom. "He takes the cake all right."

"And where are we to find a young woman unencumbered by the morals of the Sunday school?" I asked mockingly.

Anne stuck out her tongue at me. Pearson

carefully folded the damp towel as if it were cloth of gold. The atmosphere was electric with sex. Pearson and I were a pair of lightning rods poking up into the ether and begging for a consummation though it burn down the house. Even as the effects of the hashish wore off, I felt elated—no, elation is what children feel at Christmas with a package on their laps. I felt such ecstasy as I have seen on the wimpled faces of nuns after eating the body of Christ.

"Sarah Jenkins models in my drawing from life class," said Pearson just as I was thinking that he'd fallen into a swoon or out the window.

"Excellent!" I rubbed my hands like a fly contemplating a choice bit of filth.

"Her hair is something like hers. I mean, the girl in the picture. The naked one."

"Will you ask her, Robert, old fellow?"

"I might." His attractive face expressed all manner of warring emotions as he took great drafts of the night air into his lungs.

"Tell her that she will be lolling boldly between two swells dressed to the teeth. Here." I sketched the scene quickly in crayon, mindful to capture the entanglement of limbs as seen in the reproduction of the Manet. "Show her this."

"Say, I've got an idea!" exclaimed Pearson, bearing down on us as the *Merrimack* did the *Monitor*, or Theseus the Minotaur, if your imagination runs to the Greek. "Take a photograph instead." I would have looked at him in mystification, because he went on to say, "Instead of painting the thing, which Manet already did, take a picture."

"Well, I don't know about that. I've been thinking all along that it would be a painting."

"Old hat! I like Robert's idea!" declared Anne, laying a comradely hand on his shoulder, a gesture that made his cheekbones rise.

"You can hand color the thing, if you're set on daubing," said Robert.

"That's a swell idea!" said Anne, whose compliments were giving Robert false hopes.

I dithered a moment, pulling at the end of my skimpy mustache. "I won't kick, dammit!"

After the two of them left, I stood at the window and watched as a shabbily dressed man, his face caught momentarily in the shimmering blue light cast by an arc lamp, made his way to a five-cent flophouse—or so I imagined as I hummed George Gaskin's "Down in Poverty Row."

Had that midwife variously named destiny, accident, or chance delivered him into the lap of Paris instead of Grubbtown (at the time of his birth and childhood, a village on the outskirts of Philadelphia), my grandfather Franklin Barrett would have been one of the renowned eccentrics of the City of Light, a companion of Toulouse-Lautrec and Henri Rousseau, Stéphane Mallarmé and Charles Baudelaire, and as execrated as any other radical who wore the disgrace of *le mal du siècle* like a military decoration on his lapel. Not that Franklin felt "the sickness of the century." His was an American sort of decadence: He arranged the particulars of his character into a being that had no need of God to complete it. He was, he liked to say, drunk on Whitman. Franklin behaved in a manner that industrious, respectable Philadelphians judged either wicked or lazy, depending on their state of grace. Baptists, Methodists, and Presbyterians condemned him to their picturesque hell, while Lutherans and Unitarians tended to commend him to God's mercy, with provisos.

Franklin painted voluptuous nudes wearing little more than an egret feather and their own skin, which could be white, black, or high yellow. The frank products of his brush were gawped at by gents as they combed beer suds from their mustaches in taprooms from the river wards to the waterworks. Dives and drinking holes were the Salon des Indépendants, where he hung his canvases bearing titles like *Lily on the Divan, Mathilda in the Bath,* and, my favorite, *Ida Lets Down Her Hair.* Embellished by gilded frames shaped by a soused carpenter's rococo fancies and transformed by hissing gaslight into objects of reverie, his painted ladies established my grandfather's reputation as an artist of the Philadelphia demi-monde and a society portraitist for the déclassé.

A young man during the 1873 panic and depression, he had painted flowers on old glass-plate negatives, whose original images—many of Civil War carnage—had faded till the ghostly figures strewn on roads and in ditches vanished. Franklin sold them door-to-door for twenty cents apiece to people hungry for color and the emblems of summer, which, in those saturnine days, seemed never to arrive. Man does not live by bread alone, as God's plump ministers say over greasy plates of meat and fried potatoes.

"I like your grandfather," said Anne. "He's a peach."

"I'm damned fond of him myself," I said, admiring the glister on the brass ferule of my sword stick in the high-summer light. I'd bought it at a theatrical supply store on Arch Street to scare the bejesus out of those willing to suspend their disbelief. (Although the sheathing stick was made of hickory, the rapier hidden inside was rubber.)

Anne and I had come out from the city on the Philadelphia and Germantown Railroad. At Nicetown, we had climbed aboard a Philadelphia Traction Company trolley and sat on a rattan-covered seat, surrounded by passengers quietly ripening in the August swelter, as the electrified car jounced and jolted along rails laid down on Wyoming Avenue.

To get her goat, I took a silk handkerchief from my breast pocket and held it to my nose.

"Don't be an ass, Oliver!" Snatching the article from my hand, she tossed it out the car window.

I watched it flap uncertainly on yellow wings until, caught in a freshening breeze blowing from an ash heap, it assumed its possibility of form and, like a bird, flew into the yard of a dye works whose effluent was, at that moment, turning Tookany Creek Prussian blue.

Taking my hand, she held it in her lap, and we communed in a silence undermined by the rattle of wheels across the points and the rasp of the steel pantograph mounted on the roof, which conducted electric current from the wire overhead to the whining electric motor on the chassis.

"Pop Barrett taught me to paint." I called him "Pop" to spite my father, who is, in every way, his opposite. (Although I haven't seen my father since 1897, I doubt that he has changed even after a decade has elapsed. Such men are seldom visited by an epiphany.)

"According to Robert, you paint like a child with a corn broom."

Although she had spoken lightly and smiled, her remark rankled.

"Pearson is a stick-in-the mud when it comes to painting. He thinks fine art is what you see on a biscuit tin or a can of olive oil. Mark my words, Anne, one day your Robert will be the rage of the galleries of this provincial town. Why, last week he flourished a check for six dollars under my nose, paid by one of the illustrated weeklies for some black-inked trifle! The man has no pride."

"He's not *my* Robert," said Anne, making a face, whose meaning was lost on me. Even artists of renown find the subtleties of a woman's expression baffling.

"He thinks the eyes of you, you know."

"Does he?" She seemed surprised. Women can be remarkably obtuse to the havoc they wreak on men.

I reminded myself to keep unencumbered by passions of the flesh and blood variety. It's one thing to give a woman a key to your room, quite another to give her an open sesame to the heart. I was on the boil; my head was turned by ambition as frenzied as a steam calliope. I will be remarkable, I told myself, if not as a painter, then as a character. I will read *The Yellow Book,* drink green absinthe, and revel in the corpse light shed by the paintings of Gustave Moreau.

Abruptly, the trolley began to slide down the rails as the motorman let out sand from the bottom of the car to assist in an unscheduled stop. My head shot forward into an arrangement of stuffed birds nesting on a lady's hat. On the tracks ahead, a man stood beating a horse harnessed to a wagon whose rear tire had caught in a narrow gap between two sets of converging rails. The junkman was behaving in response to Newton's second law of motion, abetted by a passion for strong drink, of which his red-veined nose gave ample evidence. Exasperated by a universe over which he had no control, he was flaying his dray, an entitlement conferred by a notarized bill of sale. The lady whose hat I'd crushed had flown out the trolley door and was engaged in beating the man with her parasol.

"Oh, the poor horse!" whinnied Anne. "Won't somebody do something?"

I jumped from the trolley's vestibule, unsheathed the sword, and set about to thrash the two-legged brute.

"You cunt!" he shouted, enraged by my weapon, which was nipping at his bare arms like a maddened mosquito out to draw blood. "I'll bust your fucking head."

The man's obscenities strengthened the fury of the woman, who broke her pink parasol over his bullet-shaped head, which, if pickled, would take pride of place in the Mütter Museum of medical oddities. The blood having left her vital organs, the doughty lady fainted and was hauled into the shade by two young black men dressed in the uniform of the Pythian Baseball Club, Philadelphia's contribution to the Negro leagues, who'd been wheeling toward a nearby baseball field on Columbus bicycles.

"En garde!" I said, bending my right knee and flexing my arm in prelude to a lunge.

The passengers had evacuated the car to see the show, leaving only the motorman to lay on the bell strap in a show of exemplary devotion to duty. I stole a glimpse at Anne, whose face semaphored her admiration for me and detestation of the bully. I was where I liked to be: at the center of attention, though never before had I anything sharper to fence with than words. I had the brute on the ropes, so to speak, and was savoring my advantage, when he jumped backward and picked up a length of pipe. He glowered, and I was shocked to see that he was dead sober and in deadly earnest. His teeth looked as though they had been filed.

"I'm going to stick this pipe up your ass and light a match!" he snarled rudely.

Rendered speechless, the crowd waited to see what would happen next.

I could do nothing against an iron pipe. I looked appealingly at the trolley driver, who no longer beat the gong. I glanced wistfully at the two Negro base-ball players, but they wanted no part in this white man's business. They mounted their bicycles and pedaled off around a bend in the road. I gazed tenderly at Anne, who appeared to be assaying the temper of my spine to see whether it was steel or rubber, like my sword.

Anne, won't you beg the brute to spare my

life—on bended knees, if you must? Tears would not be ill spent, nor a little hand-wringing and hair-pulling to appease the enraged lout.

I had put my head in the lion's jaws, lain under the upraised foot of a circus pachyderm, climbed into the barrel of a cannon and dared the clown to light the fuse. For twenty years, I had managed to escape the ethical dilemmas that shape or break us. I had been, in my father's words, a "scapegrace" and "ne'er-do-well." Privation I knew not; sacrifice I had made none. I was the lucky son of a prosperous father whose own father had hired a substitute to fight in his place during the Civil War. Suddenly, on a hot August afternoon in 1897, I was being asked to give an accounting of myself. If only Anne had not been there to see my humbling!

"I'm going to part your hair right down to your dingleberries." The junkman's voice was low and steady, his composure as cool as a bullet in a chamber waiting for the hammer to fall.

He swung the pipe; I jumped; he missed. "Your head is next," he said "with menace," as the news of my death would be reported in tomorrow's editions. I pictured my father, glancing up from the *Inquirer,* his spoon stopped on its way to decapitate a soft-boiled egg. "Oliver got his comeuppance!" he'd announce to my mother and sister. His satisfaction would be as evident as a crumb of toast on the immaculate tablecloth.

I was about to lay down my sword and beg for mercy, when a policeman on horseback appeared, followed by the two Pythian wheelmen, who had decided to meddle in white men's business after all. So beside himself and in such a lather was my would-be assassin, I doubt that he noticed the policeman who collared him and sent him flying. The stunned man landed in a heap. The pipe struck the car tracks, which rang like a bell at a boxing match tolling defeat.

"He come at me with a sword!"

"It's not a sword," I objected. "It's a theatrical prop."

"He stabbed me with the fucking thing!" The junkman showed off the welts on his arms raised by the rapier's stiff rubber blade.

"He was beating his horse!" I croaked, my throat parched.

"I weren't!" protested the bully.

"Yes, he was!" cried Anne, again with a piteous whinny in her voice.

"That right?" asked the copper of the others standing in the road.

"It's true!" they called in unison across the space of Belgian bricks that separated them from the scene of my ethical crisis.

"He gave the old lady a smack in the teeth!" cried an outraged citizen, pointing to the woman who held her broken parasol like a regimental flag. The others did not dispute this false accusation, considering it beside the point. Their sympathies were with the horse, as were those of the mounted policeman. He went over to the poor animal. Seeing that its leg was broken, he put a bullet through its head.

A citizen produced a rope from God only knows where. The crowd was all for hanging the man from the trolley car's pantograph, but the motorman argued that the pole belonged to the Philadelphia Traction Company and might suffer harm. The policeman tied one hempen end of the rope to the villain's wrists and the other to his saddle horn. "And you," he said, pointing a white-gloved hand at me. "Give it here."

Lee did not surrender his sword to Grant at Appomattox Court House more elegantly. (I prefer exaggeration to plain speaking, which is commendable in notaries and grocers.)

The policeman turned his horse and headed down Wyoming Avenue, the malefactor in tow, cursing sotto voce an unjust universe bent on his destruction.

The motorman rang his gong. The passengers boarded. I noted that the stunned woman's hat was torn, and the birds had flown the coop. The trolley crept up on the wagon and the dead animal and shoved them aside with the delicacy of an elephant dandling a circus girl from its trunk, then continued on the avenue, sparking like Phaethon's fiery chariot from the pantograph overhead. (Similes are the glaze on the doughnut and the shine on the thorn.)

Anne and I continued on foot to the Burk estate, where Franklin Barret lived, along with his wife and eldest daughter, in the caretaker's house.

As we walked into the yard through a gap in the trees, Anne and I heard horselaughs and loud voices. My grandfather Franklin, Henry Burk, and two other men were exchanging "stories in doubtful taste," a euphemism for the racy tales enjoyed by men in shirtsleeves while their wives cooed over morning glories and delphinium, or smoked cigarettes behind a boxwood hedge.

"Hello, Ollie!" called Henry Burk. "You're just in time to eat."

Crossing the lawn, I caught my foot in a croquet hoop and fell headlong into the asters. Sprawled in the flower bed, I recalled that Manet had painted a picture of a croquet game. For a reason known to alienists, the fact lessened my embarrassment. I stayed where accident had put me, long enough to prepare a witticism appropriate to the game: "I'm well and truly pegged-out."

"Hard luck!" said Burk, who escorted Anne to a pergola, where a small party of men were taking the air—or shooting the breeze, to speak like one of Whitman's roughs.

Burk had made his fortune in sewing machines

and tanning. As fortunes stood in the days of railroad, coal, steel, and munitions barons, his fortune was tiny. But it was sufficient to start a meatpacking company by the Delaware River, which Henry did in the 1880s, along with his four brothers. He acquired a large tract of land to the north of Philadelphia, had a stone house built for his wife and six children and a smaller brick house to let. Hired by the "meat king" to oversee his estate, Franklin Barrett moved his wife and three daughters into the brick house. In time, the two men became friends.

I stood and brushed off my clothes, then followed the pair to a rustic table furnished with potato salad, pickles, pitchers of beer, and sundry meats whose provenance was a Hampshire hog—in other words, a table set for men who like to eat with their collars off.

"You young folks, have some lunch," urged Burk, playing the genial host. We may have called the house Pop Barrett's, but the whole shebang belonged to the meat packer.

"Hello, Mr. Barrett!" said Anne brightly to my grandfather, who was sitting back in his chair, his thin face hidden in the shade cast by a navy blue yachting cap.

"Nice to see you again, Anne! Good of you to join us, Ollie. I was telling Connie about that damned seed thief Burpee. Have you met Connie?"

I shook my head. "Nor this fellow, either." I languidly waved a hand toward a man built like a barrel.

"Oliver Fischer, meet Connie Mack and Trupert Ortlieb. Connie manages the Athletics Baseball Club. Trupe owns the Ortlieb brewery in Northern Liberties."

We rumbled greetings at one other. Ortlieb, who was hard of hearing, played his part in the antiphony with the aid of an ear trumpet.

"And this young woman is Ollie's lady friend, Anne."

I glanced at her to see if she would bridle or smile, but she did neither.

"I wrote Burpee last week, and he as good as told me to go to hell."

I knew the history of my grandfather's wrangle with Washington Atlee Burpee, who had grown a mail-order chicken business into a successful seed company. Pop claimed that W. Atlee had stolen his Barrett's Delicious. Waged in an endless back and forth between the two men, the dispute was as long and tedious as *Jarndyce and Jarndyce,* the legal case in Chancery at the heart of Dickens's novel *Bleak House.*

"You're beating a dead horse," said Burk, whose profession entitled him to speak of meat.

"I bought some seed last week at Burpee's store at Fifth and Buttonwood. When I asked the counter girl if it came from the original corn produced by Franklin Barrett, she went into the office to look it up, came back, and said, 'It did.'"

"For Christ's sake, Franklin, let it go!" said Mack.

Rakish in appearance, he was puffing on a fifty-cent Havana cheroot, whose smoke made his bushy eyebrows jump.

"It's time you took the son of a bitch to court!" shouted Ortlieb, who seemed inclined to bellicosity as well as deafness. "Forgive an old soldier his language, miss." A foot soldier in the Thirty-first Pennsylvania Volunteer Infantry, he had been concussed at Gettysburg.

"I'll do it when I'm good and ready!" shot back Franklin, who, I suspected, would never be ready to go against the Burpee Company and its lawyers. He may have enjoyed the feud with W. Atlee, although by Franklin's lights, his Delicious seed corn would have made the erstwhile Grubbtown native rich.

"That's just what 'Mother' McClellan used to say soon as the gray bellies showed up to the ball. He was scared stiff of a fight with Johnny Reb and had no business being a Union general!"

"Damn it to hell!" cried Burk, slapping his meaty hand on the table. "Why can't you lunkheads get along? I apologize, Miss Anne, for the contrariety of my two friends."

Like a locomotive coming to a stop, the argufiers grumbled awhile before cooling their boilers with pitchers of lager.

"Some sausage, Miss Anne?" asked Burk attentively. "What about you, Ollie—sausage, or maybe a pig's foot in jelly?"

My stomach revolted as he held a trotter, stuck on the end of a fork, under my nose.

"No thanks." My face, I sensed, was turning the color of a cadaver's. I had seen several in various stages of decomposition, laid out on the medical college's dissecting table for us to draw.

"I'll try it," said Anne—to spite me, I thought.

"There's a girl with spunk!" said Burk, setting the pinkish object on her plate.

"I'll have a sausage." I did not want a sausage, but I felt obliged to profess an appetite for entrails or forfeit my place among men and be forever a disgrace in Anne's lovely eyes.

"Righto! Franklin, get off your bony ass and take care of your kinsman."

Pop took a rope of sausages from a skillet on the brazier and wound them on my plate.

"You look sickly, Ollie. You look like you couldn't hold up your end in a conversation. What do say, Miss Anne? Is he up to snuff?"

She put a morsel of jellied meat into her mouth and chewed. We waited to hear what she would say when she swallowed. "On the way here, he stabbed a drunkard in the road who was beating his horse."

I'd have thrown her a kiss had I not been conscious of my greasy lips.

Burk put down his knife and fork with a clatter of astonishment. "What's that you say?"

"Attaboy!" bellowed Ortlieb. His blood up, he dashed a glass pitcher to pieces with his ear trumpet.

"Good for you, Ollie!" Franklin held the smoking skillet as if it were a pistol he had just discharged.

"What did you stab him with?" asked Mack.

"A sword stick," said Anne before I could reply.

"Well, I'll be damned!" said Burk, for once confounded.

"And you say he was abusing a horse?" asked Franklin indignantly.

"He was beating the poor animal with a whip," she said. Her amber eyes welled up as she saw the scene play out again, a sympathetic reaction that increased the story's verisimilitude and my fondness for her.

"What happened to the sword stick?" asked Burk, a note of dubiety coloring his voice.

"A cop took it when he arrested the drunken brute."

"And the horse?" asked Franklin, who liked all creatures great and small.

"The cop put it out of its misery," Anne replied. I marveled that she could speak at all as her teeth crunched what sounded like cartilage.

"Damned shame!" said Mack, taking off his boater to mop the damp headband with the napkin tied around his neck. Beads of sweat stood out on his brow. It might have been two outs and bases loaded, with Joe Kelley at bat for the Orioles.

"Was it a dago anarchist did the deed?" asked

the rambunctious veteran, bellowing into the ear-
piece of his trumpet.

"I don't know!" shouted Anne down its bell.

"I'm proud of you, Ollie!" exclaimed Franklin.
"Damned if I'm not!"

I had the odd sensation of being present at my
funeral luncheon. Anne was my eulogist and principal mourner. I took a turn around the lawn, careful
of the croquet hoops, and sat back down in my chair
in time to hear her say, "Mr. Thomas Eakins called
Ollie his most promising student."

He had called me no such thing. We'd never
even spoken, although I had seen him in the hall-
ways, walking to the lecture theaters and studios and,
once, had blundered into his drawing-from-life class,
where a scrawny old man was leaning on a plinth.

"Eakins, you say?" This piece of erroneous intelligence impressed Franklin, who, as a lesser practi-
tioner, knew of the painter's fame. "He's a great artist.
What he doesn't know about anatomy isn't worth spit.
He used to pal around with Walt Whitman before
the poet passed."

"Eakins is a sodomite and so was Whitman!"
hissed Ortlieb, showing surprising animus and bad
teeth.

"Walt Whitman was the truest poet in America, and Thomas Eakins is the truest painter!" Pop
declared, hammering his palm with a meat mallet as
resolutely as a centurion on the Hill of Skulls. "You,

of all people, should revere Whitman for his devotion to the sick, wounded, and dying soldiers laid up in the hospitals of wartime Washington! 'From the stump of the arm, the amputated hand, / I undo the clotted lint, remove the slough, wash off the matter and blood . . .'"

Before my eyes, the various meats piled on platters and plates began to ooze. Fascinated, I watched a rat gnaw on my sausages, its teeth the size of piano keys, while congregations of flies hymned jubilees as they feasted on gore.

"I was not to know," responded the chastened brewer.

"You forget your manners, gentlemen," said Burk sternly.

Ortlieb bowed his head to Anne, his pocked nose coming close to the potato salad. "I beg your pardon, miss."

Anne waved away his apology.

Their attention on the little comedy, I spirited the rest of my sausages under the table.

Regarding me once more, Franklin asked, "Have you been to see Eakins's painting *The Clinic of Dr. Gross*? It's hanging in Jefferson Medical College, not far from the academy."

I hesitated to answer in case Anne should wish to speak for me again. She said nothing, however. She may not have known whether the picture was one to praise, condemn, or pardon.

"No, Pop, I haven't." It was said that Eakins's paintings were too scientific. I upheld the opinion, although, to be sure, I didn't understand it.

Franklin shuddered. "A ghastly scene! The surgeon Gross, scalpel in his bloody hand, is addressing the medical students, while his two assistants lay open a boy's putrid femur. They say it's a great picture. Well, by God, it is! Though I prefer Eakins's river paintings, *Shad Fishing at Gloucester on the Delaware River, Mending the Net,* or *The Swimming Hole,* where boys are larking naked as jays." The table bucked, upsetting several pitchers, whose contents seethed in a golden foaming tide across the oilcloth. We jumped up in time to escape a wetting—all but Ortlieb, who got it in his lap.

"Christ! What's that almighty raging and ramping?"

The answer came in the shape of Henry Burk's redbone coonhound, which trotted from beneath the table, my sausages dangling from its mouth.

Mack mopped the oilcloth while Franklin continued his reminiscence: "I saw *The Gross Clinic* at the Centennial Exposition, hung in a room fitted out like a Civil War field hospital. The selection committee refused to display it in the main exhibition hall. You'd think it had measles! Ollie, I don't understand why you haven't seen it yet—not with Eakins on the faculty."

"He's been busy with his own stuff," said Anne,

resuming her place at the table and her part as my advocate. "He's painting John Wanamaker's portrait."

"That so, Ollie?" asked Franklin, much impressed.

"Pop, I've been up to my elbows in paint."

"Always do a thing right up to the handle!" shouted Ortlieb.

"What other things do you paint when you're not pandering to big-shot department store owners?" asked Mack.

"Oh, you know, this and that." I liked his old-fashioned high collar and ascot scarf, which he insisted on wearing, along with his boater, at the ball games, instead of a manager's uniform.

"Does he paint naked ladies, like his grandpop?" asked Ortlieb, leering at Anne.

"He paints scenery," she said. "And he draws the most tremendous caricatures."

"Caricatures, you say," said Mack. "The boys always draw me with a head like a pickle. I look a prize dope in the sporting news."

"Say, Ollie, why don't you draw us?" asked Burk.

"Sure, that's the ticket!" concurred Mack. His smile flashed a few gold teeth.

"I don't have my drawing things."

"No matter," said Burk. "Franklin, get your grandson something to sketch us with."

"Leave me out of your shenanigans," said Ortlieb, pulling at his scraggly goatee.

"While you're at it, Pop, get me a jigger of rye whiskey."

"There's a girl with ginger!" exclaimed Burk. "You're better than a Gibson Girl, Miss Anne. Are you a painter, too?"

"I should say not! I work in a stockroom."

"A stockyard?" cried Ortlieb, fumbling for his ear trumpet.

"*Stockroom*, you bag of tripes! Say, you ought to get yourself a sousaphone to stick in your ear, you deaf old stick!" said Anne in a voice pitched high enough to make the dog bark. "I work in Wanamaker's stockroom, where I do twice what men do for two-thirds the boodle."

"Why, she's a goddamned suffragist!" shouted Ortlieb. "Ain't that so, little miss hussy?"

"Hooray for Susan B. Anthony and Elizabeth Cady Stanton, you dried-up pig's pizzle!"

"Hot dog!" cried Burk.

Her slam took the tucker out of Trupert. He sputtered like a damp firecracker before it goes out.

Franklin set down a glass in front of Anne. "There's nary a fume of rye in the house. Will gin do?" She nodded. "I have Angostura bitters, if you'd care for some."

"Three drops," she said, treating him to a smile that would have beguiled Saint Simeon Stylites to climb down from his pillar or Sampson to put his head on a platter for Salome.

I watched the dog bury a few uneaten sausage links in the raw-umber earth beneath the cobalt blue delphiniums. (For chemists, the world is constituted of elements; for mathematicians, integers; for philosophers, first principles; for theologians, sin; for hangmen, knots; and for artists, pigments.)

"Damn! I forgot the drawing things," said Franklin, starting once again for the house.

"Damn Susan B. Anthony!" growled Ortlieb. "Double damn Elizabeth Cady Stanton!"

Connie Mack broke into a suffragist's anthem, sung to the tune of "Goodnight, Ladies":

> Good news, ladies, good news, ladies,
> Good news, ladies—we're going to let
> you vote.
> Merrily we'll go along,
> Go along, go along,
> Merrily we'll go along,
> Down to the polls with you!

Anne banged her glass of gin and bitters on the table. "Don't expect us to curtsy and say thanks! You dubs better get wise to yourselves!"

Ortlieb shied a pork chop at her. She ducked, and the hound dog caught it in midair.

"I need that red dog at shortstop," said Mack, fanning himself with his boater.

"Sign 'em up, sign 'em up!" barked Burk.

Always a good sport, Anne trilled, in a passable

contralto, "Der Deitcher's Dog," a popular song by Philadelphia lyricist Septimus Winner, whose mother was related to Nathaniel Hawthorne:

> Oh where, oh where ish mine little dog
>   gone;
> Oh where, oh where can he be?
> His ears cut short und his tail cut long;
> Oh where, oh where ish he?
>
> I loves mine lager 'tish very goot beer,
> Oh where, oh where can he be?
> But mit no money I cannot drink here,
> Oh, where, oh where ish he?
>
> Across the ocean in Garmanie,
> Oh where, oh where can he be?
> Der deitcher's dog ish der best
>   companie,
> Oh where, oh where ish he?

Burk and Mack threw back their heads and bayed like two hellhounds.

> Un sasage ish goot, bolonie of course,
> Oh where, oh where can he be?
> Dey makes um mit dog und dey makes
>   em mit horse,
> I guess de makes em mit he.

"You're a real ball of fire, Miss Annie!" cried Burk.

"I'll say!" said Mack, wiping tears from his eyes with the heels of both hands.

Hopping mad, the brewer croaked, "Miss pudding pants is making fun of Germans!"

Grandmother Gertrude and Aunt Myrt, bearing a hamper between them, made a timely entrance. Gert could scald the bristles off a pig with the acid of her tongue. "The alligators are hungry, you old piece of shoe leather, so behave yourself, before Burk takes a sledgehammer to your thick skull!" Turning to Mack, she said, "The stockings are finished."

"Thanks, old girl."

"Gert, I don't give a snap pea for your alligators!"

"You give me the jinks, Trupert Ortlieb!"

Franklin kept a pair of alligators in a cement swimming pool. They summered in sight of consternated visitors and wintered with his orchids inside a steam-heated enclosure. The boldest of the children tossed beef shanks down their gullets, supplied by Burk Brothers slaughterhouse.

Gertrude turned to Mack, her anger trailing after her like a lighted fuse. "Connie, don't you want to see the stockings?" Her words were sharp as serifs when her patience was tried.

"Accepted sight unseen!"

My grandmother, along with her daughter Myrtle, embroidered dark blue *A*'s onto the Philadelphia Athletics jerseys and stripes on their stockings. I suspect that Mack cared more about carousing with

Franklin and Burk than he did for the quality of the needlework. She shrugged her broad Teutonic shoulders, as if to say, No skin off my nose, and went back into the house, followed by Myrt, as quiet as a fizzle.

Franklin returned from the house with a sketch pad, pencil, sandpaper, and a lump of putty rubber.

"All right, which of you gents wants his mug immortalized?" asked Anne, brassy as a sidewalk huckster.

"Do your worst," said Burk.

With quick, assured pencil strokes, I pulled and pushed and twisted Henry Burk's fleshy face into a shape that was instantly recognizable and, at the same time, grotesque, but not in the spiteful way the papers draw William Jennings Bryan and Charles Darwin. I made him look like a bighearted Falstaff.

"Pretty fair likeness, I'd say," said Franklin, giving me a wink.

Taking a toothpick from between his teeth, Mack leaned across the table. "You look a treat, Henry. What do you think, Trupe?"

Trupe had nodded off, his forehead resting on a plate of pickled tongue.

"Let the old crank sleep," said Burk.

"Have a go, Mr. Mack?" asked Anne.

"I'm game!"

I exaggerated the length and narrowness of his face and gave him a Neanderthal's jutting brow.

"What do you think, Connie?" she asked, hand on hip in that impudent way of hers.

"I look like a delegate to Barnum's Ethnological Congress of Strange and Savage Tribes."

"That'll be a dollar."

"For two cents, I can see myself in the paper and read *The Yellow Kid* while I'm at it."

"Don't be a cheapskate!" Burk rebuked him. "Here, Anne—one dollar." He took a bill from his wallet and pressed it into her hand. "Buy yourself a kid glove." He gave her another, saying, "Buy yourself a pair."

"Mr. Barrett?"

"No thanks, I'm feeling bilious."

Endowed with the fine sympathy of its kind, the redbone coonhound walked into the irises and was sick.

"Gentlemen, we thank you for your patronage. Ollie, it's time we shoved off."

"Gents, it's been swell. Oh and Pop, if it's all right with you, we'd like to take the *Myrtle Jane* out on the river next Sunday."

"Fine by me."

We went into the house to get the fitting he would pull from the boiler to foil thieves.

"I like that young woman, Oliver. I hope she doesn't slip through your fingers."

Night had fallen when Anne and I caught a Fifth Street car at Wyoming Avenue, which rattled south toward Franklin Square, located at the heart of the old city. Along with two other women engaged by Wanamaker's department store, she had rooms in Osler's boardinghouse, near the square. Six blocks past the Nicetown stockyards, the motorman slowed his trolley. Echo Park blazed up beside us like a fire balloon.

"What is it—a revivalist meeting?" I asked the motorman.

A sprawling tent in the middle of a field shone blue in the electric rays of the park's arc lamps. Smoking smudge pots burning alongside the path leading from the street put me in mind of secret conventicles of dubious intent where black-hooded members carried little nooses in their pockets. From inside the tent, yellow light would sweep out over the grass like a brush fire each time a knot of people passed through its canvas flaps.

"It's a convention," explained the motorman. "They've been at it all day, hammer and tongs. On my last northbound trip, Sousa and his band were giving a concert. Since the car was empty, I stopped awhile and ate my supper."

"Let's get off!" said Anne impulsively.

Passing beneath an ornamental arch, we entered the park. The wind had turned, bringing the stink of the stockyards with it. As we drew near the tent, we heard a man's voice raised to an unseen audience, in a tone favored by gasbags, bunco steerers, brimstone preachers, and wattled congressmen. Wearing the tin badge of the Women's National War Relief Association, a woman rattled a collection can at me. Her face—what I could see of it by the gleam of the smudge pots—was fierce. I emptied my pockets of change in return for a lithographed broadside showing a militant Lady Liberty armed with a shield and a spear. An eagle squatting at her sandaled feet, she smiled benevolently on two barefoot Cubans dressed in tattered cotton clothes and straw sombreros.

Anne and I stood amid a clot of men and women that had formed inside the vast tent's yawning mouth. A thin man dressed in an old-fashioned coat and topped by a fiery mop of hair was introducing a Cuban insurrectionist, Juan Padilla, to a multitude no miracle of fishes would feed nor inexhaustible jug of Cana intoxicate. Not that the mob needed stimulation; it had been driven half mad by patriotic sentiment.

Padilla stood at a makeshift podium, and with a passion no amount of repetition could diminish, he addressed us in the words of his deceased compatriot Carlos Manuel de Céspedes, author of the October the Tenth Manifesto, written in 1868, at the time of the first Cuban revolt against Spanish occupation, which was brutally suppressed.

"Spain governs us with iron and blood. She keeps us in ignorance of our rights under Spanish law, while my people are seized, exiled, and executed without lawful proceedings. We are excluded from the administration of our island and are forbidden to assemble peaceably, unless in the presence of the military. She denies us political, civil, and religious freedom."

Padilla's face darkened as he swayed in and out of the orange light cast by the electric globes suspended at intervals from the greater darkness of the canvas high above him. With one hand clutching a small table, he steadied himself; with the other, he yanked at his old-fashioned wing collar.

"Spain has promised to improve our condition, but she has deceived us and left us no recourse but to take up arms to defend our properties, protect our lives, and save our honor. We want to remove the yoke of Spain and become a free and independent nation. If Spain recognizes our rights, she will have, in Cuba, an affectionate daughter; if she persists in subjugating us, we resolve to die before surrendering to her domination.

"We appeal to God, your conscience as Americans and as brothers and sisters of the same hemisphere, and to the good faith of all civilized nations."

The Cuban bowed his head under the thunderous applause of the patriots sweating in their shirtsleeves. He sat in a chair placed at the back of the platform as Albert Beveridge, a Republican politician from Indianapolis, took the stage. In an impassioned speech that would come to be called "The March of the Flag," he harangued us concerning our "special destiny":

"Fellow citizens. It is a glorious history our God has bestowed upon His chosen people; a history whose keynote was struck by Liberty Bell; a history heroic with faith in our mission and our future; a history of statesmen, who flung the boundaries of the Republic out into unexplored lands and savage wildernesses; a history of soldiers, who carried the flag across blazing deserts and through the ranks of hostile mountains, even to the gates of sunset; a history of a multiplying people, who overran a continent in half a century; a history divinely logical, in the process of whose tremendous reasoning we find ourselves to-day."

He appeared to choke on his words, croaked, poured a glass of water from a pitcher on the podium, drank, washed away the sand from his throat, and went on with greater vigor:

"The ocean does not separate us from the lands of our duty and desire. Steam joins us; electricity joins us—the very elements are in league with our destiny.

"President McKinley and the vested interests object that Cuba is not contiguous with the States and territories. That Puerto Rico is not contiguous. Neither are Hawaii and the Philippines contiguous! I say that American speed, American guns, American heart and brain and nerve will make and keep them contiguous forever!"

Sousa turned on his heels and, with his baton, launched the Marine Band into a racket of screeches, skirls, and brassy shrieks while the voice of a buxom woman dressed as Lady Liberty soared into the stuffy atmosphere, only to droop like a bird that has lost its feathers to the greed of the millinery trade. When the spirits of the crowd had fallen like a barometer predicting rain, she let out all stops and, with a heave of her astonishing bosom, hurled her voice upward into—one might have supposed—the ears of the Anglo-Saxon God. She sang:

> Hurrah for the flag of the free!
> May it wave as our standard forever,
> The gem of the land and the sea,
> The banner of the right.
> Let despots remember the day
> When our fathers with mighty endeavor
> Proclaimed as they marched to the fray
> That by their might and by their right
> It waves forever.

Amplified by five hundred pairs of hands, the crowd's approbation might have blown the fairground tent into the upper atmosphere, if not for the manila guy ropes driven home by the sledgehammers of the roustabouts. Dressed in Roman drapery, the blond chanteuse staggered under the weight of the aforementioned bosom.

Sousa had gotten ahead of Beveridge, who had not finished his oration. I saw annoyance on the latter's flushed and sweating face, like that of a man who has prematurely left a moment unfulfilled, its potential energy discharged. Having downed a second glass of water to compose himself, he started in on his peroration:

"Shall the American people continue their march toward the commercial supremacy of the world? Shall free institutions broaden their blessed reign as the children of liberty wax in strength, until the empire of our principles is established over the hearts of all mankind? Have we no mission to perform, no duty to discharge to our fellow man? Has God endowed us with gifts beyond our deserts and marked us as the people of His peculiar favor, merely to rot in our own selfishness?"

"No!" replied the multitude. That single syllable expressive of absolute negation sent a galvanic current through our common nerve. Like a man recumbent in a dental surgeon's chair, his mouth open to a metal prod whose sole purpose is to find the root of corruption by inducing an exquisite agony, we jumped, as one, and screamed again, "NO!"

In a coup de théâtre worthy of a Broadway melodrama, Annie Oakley, standing atop her horse

Target, trotted through a heretofore unseen entrance, trilling in a surprisingly tiny voice:

> Freedom's battle once begun,
> Bequeathed from bleeding sire to son,
> Though baffled oft, is always won!

Her unruly crinkled hair escaped her cowgirl's Stetson and fell about her shoulders. She did not meet the standard of comeliness set by the bathing beauties of Asbury Park, New Jersey. But she would lend herself readily to a caricature. For a moment, I forgot myself and imagined sidling up to her to ask, in the patter of the boardwalk trade, to let me immortalize her face and figure in pastel crayon.

"I have written to the president, offering my services as a sharpshooter on behalf of the downtrodden Cuban people in their war against the murderous Spaniards! Some of you may have seen me perform as Peerless Lady Wing-shot in Buffalo Bill's Wild West Show, when I shot a dime from between Frank Butler's fingers and a cheroot from his mouth. I promise you, I'll shoot the eyeteeth out of any Spinacher who gets in my way!"

"Hip, hip, hooray!"

"God bless Annie Oakley!"

"God bless America!"

"God bless Uncle Sam!"

Sousa struck up the band, and the crowd bellowed "The Yankee Message, or Uncle Sam to Spain":

I hear across the waters,
From out the southern sea,
The wail of sons and daughters,
In woeful misery;
If you must act the butcher,
And helpless ones must die,
I swear by the Eternal!
I'll smite you hip and thigh!

Suddenly, the prut and pop of rifles were heard at the four corners of the tent. Concealed by the crowd and thick smoke—the air tasted of gunpowder!—armed assassins seemed to be everywhere.

"¡Muerte a los norte americanos!"
"¡Fuego!¡Fuego!¡Fuego!"

Bewildered by shouts in a language some would have recognized as Spanish, the crowd stampeded toward the entrance, where a bottleneck soon formed, which the crescendo of gunfire soon stoppered entirely. The blood-curdling cries continued:

"¡Viva Chucho el Roto!"
"¡Disparar sus armas!"
"¡Enviarlos al infierno!"

The staccato of bullets resounded beneath the expanse of canvas and numbed our ears.

"¡Viva España!"

The bottleneck broke, the bottle uncorked, and the crowd spilled onto the grass.

Anne and I stood among fragrant black locust trees behind the tent, which looked like a sagging circus balloon, all hot air spent. I put my arms around her and felt her tremble. How insubstantial she seemed at that moment, this woman who had often embarrassed me by her strength of will; how small were her bones. I felt puffed up. Young men can be fatuous and fatheaded.

In the grotesque shadows cast by the locusts, I kissed her. Pearson and the others may have believed that we were intimate, but that was only an illusion I fostered, a male display of plumage meant to excite their envy, though not her lust. In truth, I had never seen Anne nude, although I painted her thus after she had put on her shirtwaist, pinned up her hair, and left my room. Invoking my imagination, which was my more virile part, I filled in the portions of her anatomy left hidden by her chemise. Modesty was the reason she had refused to pose naked at the luncheon that I had cavalierly proposed.

"Ollie," she whispered, her head buried in the collar of my summer coat.

"What is it, dear girl?" I murmured, feeling the lion waking in my loins.

"You must go!" Her head was thrown back by the force of a powerful emotion, bringing her face, unexpectedly serious, into view.

"I'm sorry," I said, believing that she wanted me to leave her, having regretted the kiss, the embrace, the revelation of yearning.

Sensing that I had misunderstood her, she shook

her head violently. "To war! If it comes, you really must go to Cuba!"

I had mistaken excitement for desire, a woman's passion for the thrill of surrender to a common, electric purpose.

"Will you go?" she asked, her pretty mouth practically frothing.

"Yes, yes, yes!" I cried. I thought then that the price she was asking for a box seat at the opera was a small one.

"Take me home with you." Had I an ear trumpet more sensitive than Trupert Ortlieb's, I might have heard, beneath her whispered words, a sound like melting snow.

My memory of that night is vague. I have an impression of awkwardness, a fumbling at buttons and straps, a clash of teeth, an embarrassing grumble of my unfed belly, and, at a climactic point in the proceedings, a debilitating leg cramp. I can say this much with certainty: Amplified by the aforementioned ear trumpet, the noise of my deliverance would have been that which ice makes burning on a sunlit windowpane, if not an avalanche.

I do recall what Anne and I said on the morning after the encounter, which was much less of a fiasco than the one being prepared and soon to be unpacked like a hamper of costumes for a Goldoni farce in which I would play Pierrot and she Colombina.

"I dreamed that Susan B. Anthony chopped off your finger," said Anne, brushing her hair in my shaving mirror, which was too small to contain its luxuriance. "The little one."

"Did she say why?" I was at the window, gazing at the street, while she dressed.

"She may have. I can't remember."

"What do you think it means?"

"My dream? I don't know. Maybe nothing."

Finished dressing, she joined me at the window.

I looked at her face—quite a pretty one. She was not smiling, nor was she frowning. If anything, it bore a puzzled expression, which, as young as I was then, I knew to be better than a bored one.

"You're really sweet, Ollie, and not the cynic and scoffer you put on."

Although I didn't need to shave, I went to the washstand and stropped my razor.

"Say, you wouldn't have a safety pin, would you? I've got a button on my shirt about to fall off."

"No, sorry," I replied, stropping to beat the band.

"No matter. I'll borrow a needle and thread from one of the girls."

"Will you . . ." I felt my face turn red. Whether scarlet or carmine, I couldn't have said, since the mirror had misted.

"Let you make love to me again?"

I was glad to hear it called so, for it had seemed to me a shambles.

"Well?"

"We'll see," she replied. "What will you do today?"

"I thought I'd go to the Mütter Museum and draw. Care to come along?"

"I'd rather see a dogfight than the malignant tumor removed from Grover Cleveland's hard palate. Besides, I work for a living, unlike some duffers I could name."

Down below in Lombard Street, a pair of brawny teamsters, their rolled-up shirtsleeves peeking from leather aprons, were manhandling a butt of pilsner brewed by C. Schmidt & Sons at the old Robert Smith Brewery in West Philadelphia. They had stood it upright on an elevator that, as one of the men turned a crank, slowly descended into the aromatic darkness of proprietor Winston Ensor's cellar. Up above it, one of the barroom's smoke-stained walls was graced by a reproduction of an English hunting scene, *Shooters Going Out in the Morning,* and not, as I had hoped to find there, one of Franklin Barrett's recumbent nudes.

As the two men carried on, a pair of urchins staggered along the curbstone, imitating, I would guess, their fathers arriving home "with a brick in their hats," as the Irish say. The man who was not engaged in lowering the oversized barrel into the bowels of the establishment had struck an attitude of profound immobility, like that of the Belgian king Gambrinus, grand patron of brewers, looking down on his subjects from the taproom roof. So still did the teamster stand in contemplation of his own idea of beauty that a mangy dog of no recognizable strain stopped its zigzag hunt for smells on the pavement to lift its hind leg. "Goddamn son of a bitch!" shouted the teamster, giving the dog a swift kick in the bollocks.

The boys fell over each other in snickers and guffaws until the man of the sodden trouser leg went after them in a fury. "I'll tear your ears off, you little bastards! I'll pull your arseholes out through your noses!" Still laughing, the urchins beat it up the alleyway, jumped a fence like steeplechasers, and were soon gone.

"Time to shove off, Ollie," said Anne, whose gaze had been on the burlesque outside the window, if not her thoughts, which, I guessed, were already lost in the orangey gloom and swirling dust of John Wanamaker's stockroom. (I was not such a fool as to imagine she was dwelling on the night just past.)

"Shall I stop for you after work?" I asked.

"Let's go to the chop suey joint on Race Street."

I nodded and cupped her chin, but she turned her head before I could kiss her mouth. I kissed her cheek instead. She shut the door behind her as she left.

Pearson, glowering like a Puritan, barged into my room. "I just passed Anne on the stairs. What gives?"

The day before, I would have delighted in teasing him with broad winks and innuendos. But on that morning, I was respectful of a mystery that had partly been solved. (I think I knew then that I would never penetrate its core, which is a woman's mind.) "She stopped on her way to work to ask about Sunday. Pop will let us have the boat. What about the girl in your life drawing class? Is she game?"

"She is, but she wants five dollars. Did you lay your hands on a camera?"

"Harry Owens has a Blair Folding Hawk-Eye," I replied.

"Do I know him?"

"Maybe not."

Owens had made a platinum print of the dreadnought *Maine* when she was docked at the naval shipyard, which had been displayed at the Philadelphia Photographic Salons. Members of the city's Charcoal Club burned with resentment. Luks, Sloan, Glackens, and Shinn declared that artists must find their subjects in Dock Street flophouses and not in instruments of imperialism. Robert Henri, the son of a riverboat gambler and an instructor at the academy, beat his drum for an art as real as mud and snow studded with horseshit. It must convey the reek of human sweat from toil and not the scent of a dandy's handkerchief or a lady's hair.

"I'm heading to the Mütter to sketch the abominations. Want to go along?

"I haven't had my breakfast yet."

"So I gathered when your stomach started talking in Low German."

We walked downstairs and into the street, then went our separate ways.

The daubers at the Pennsylvania Academy of the Fine Arts sneered at my visits to the Mütter Museum. They declared, in the doctrinaire way of the young, that an artist's proper study is anatomy. Pathology, pursued for its own special glories, indicates a "peculiar" temperament. I was drawn to the medical oddities assembled, in the 1840s, by the preeminent surgeon of his day, Thomas Dent Mütter, of Jefferson Medical College. The macabre exhibits spoke to me of unnatural, forbidden things—the stuff of decadent art.

The cysts and tumors, the conjoined liver of Siamese twins Chang and Eng, a piece of thoracic tissue removed from John Wilkes Booth, or a section of the brain of Charles Guiteau, President Garfield's assassin—they were tentative daubs on a provisional self-portrait. The fact is, I liked to be seen going into the museum, but often as not, I'd hurry past the various horrors hung in cabinets and pickled in jars to the Chevalier Jackson Foreign Body Collection of objects that had been swallowed: buttons, pins, nuts, coins, bones, screws, dentures, and small toys. An amazing quantity of jacks had been ingested since 1747, the year inked in delicate calligraphy on the oak tag below the earliest specimen. Their number testified to the popularity of the schoolyard game and to the appetite of children for the inedible.

As I walked south on Thirteenth Street toward the College of Physicians building, my gut began to grouse. At Chancellor, I stepped into a beanery patronized by us students of the paint pots. Annexing a table in the corner, I stowed my linen coat and Ecuadorian straw on the chair opposite to discourage interlopers. I wished to be left in peace to eat and ponder the meaning of the previous night. (One should never ruminate on the meaning of anything so important as love or desire on an empty stomach.)

I had pan-fried rabbit, a savory dish of corn mush, pork scraps, and trimmings favored by the Amish. Still hungry, I ate a slice of "breakfast pie," as my long-suffering mother called the treat she served me after my father, the sobersided banker, had left the house to catch the trolley car to the vaults on Walnut Street. A boy came in to hawk the morning edition. As I made the two-penny purchase, I asked him, "Aren't you ashamed to be selling tales told by idiots?" The roughneck looked at me as if I'd coughed up the ruins of Carthage, to the delight of Chevalier Jackson. "I don't care a fart!" he replied with a fleer. Turning on a steel-clad heel, he left me, rudely, as becomes a boy of the streets.

I opened the paper to a slew of typographical exclamations of a kind not seen in print since John Brown captured the Harper's Ferry engine house in '59.

FREE CUBA RALLY ATTACKED!

HUNDREDS FLEE FOR THEIR LIVES!

ooooo

BOYS CHARGED WITH COMMITTING A PUBLIC NUISANCE!

MORTIFIED PARENTS VOW TO SKIN THE SCAMPS ALIVE!!

The commotion and rout following the singing of "The Yankee Message" were caused by boys from nearby Feltonville who had acquired a few truculent imperatives in Spanish from the popular dime-novel *The Generous Bandit*. The book recounts the true adventures of Chucho el Roto, a Mexican Robin Hood, venerated by the poor, who died of dysentery in San Juan de Ulúa Prison. What most of us in the tent believed to be bullets fired from Spanish Mausers turned out to be firecrackers. Miraculously, the only injuries sustained during the stampede to the exit were to the women's hats, although Peerless Lady Wing-shot fell off her horse and broke her trigger finger.

I balled up the paper in disgust. By now, Anne would know that the threat of imminent death at the hands of Spanish agents, which had thrown us into each other's arms, was only a Tom Sawyer prank.

At the table nearest mine, two student painters were wrangling over contemporary art.

"Seurat is a fraud—a geometer—a pedant. You can't woo the muse with science."

"Seurat represents the most advanced art of Paris, which is to say, the world."

"His figures are stiff as sticks!"

"They are formal organizations within the space of the canvas! They emerge from it as figures do from an ancient frieze."

"They are decorative!" No harsher criticism could have been leveled.

"Every work of art is, or comes to be seen as, decorative!"

"His compositions dissolve into pretty colored dots!"

"His compositions are architectural—the 'frozen music' that Goethe spoke of!"

"Liar! It was Friedrich von Schelling who said it!"

"Your ignorance is abysmal!"

"Yours is the bliss of a complacent man bloated with self-satisfaction!"

"From this moment on, Mr. Bostick, you are dead to me!"

"And you, Mr. Stoddard, are even deader to me!"

"You're the deadest of everything that creepeth upon the Earth!"

Exhausted, they subsided into their chairs. Their eyes were glazed, their mouths parched. They drained their water glasses in one noisy go.

Bostick looked at his watch and said calmly, "Frank, we're going to be late for old man Egan's color theory class."

Stoddard confirmed the lateness of the hour with his conductor's watch, a bequest from his father, who had worked many long years on the railway, only to be crushed in the street by a runaway brewer's truck. He snapped the lid shut and returned it to his pocket. "Shall we be off?" he asked his friend pleasantly. I watched them walk up the street like two Romans on the way to Trajan's Baths.

I finished my lunch and went on to the museum.

To strengthen my character, I chose a ghastly memento mori to sketch: a skull that had been split by an ax. I could just as well have selected a kidney put up like Mother's piccalilli, a pair of severed hands shiny as lacquered wood, a spine twisted by rickets, or "Jim and Joe," the green-tinted corpse of a two-headed baby sleeping in a broth of formaldehyde.

"I've seen you here before, young man."

I looked up from my sketchbook in time to see Thomas Eakins step out from the light slanting through the window.

He took a chair next to mine. "Why draw such a thing?" He stubbed his finger on the charcoaled bone as casually and emphatically as he would have put out a cigarette. His eyes betrayed the weariness of someone who has looked too closely at life and acknowledged its sadness. His nails were clean, I noticed, while mine were flecked with paint—a badge of the young artist, like a fancy vest or a flower in a buttonhole.

Eakins dressed like a man of business—dark brown coat, vest, and trousers, small black tie knotted at a plain collar, clay-colored brogans, and an ordinary hat, which he had placed on his knee. To pass him in the street, one would think he was on his way to an exhibition of farm machinery or a baseball game. He would hate to be taken for a gentleman, one of the Newport swells—"a guilt-edged shitter of gold bricks," as I'd hear Stephen Crane describe them in Key West.

"You're free to draw a pig's ass," he said. "But unless you know why you're doing it, it's pointless. You're a student at the academy?"

"Yes, sir."

"What year?"

"The first."

"What's your name?"

"Oliver Fischer."

"How old are you, Mr. Fischer? Eighteen, nineteen . . ."

"Twenty."

"I don't expect that you've had to wrestle with the

devil, or with an angel, either. Gnat-sized quandaries and conundrums; the elephantine will come later."

Had the duffer been any other than Thomas Eakins, I'd have told him to go play marbles. He could have had his pick from the Chevalier Jackson collection: aggies, immies, alleys, clouds, bumbos, cat's eyes, corkscrews, or peewees.

"I'm interested in the effect this object has on you to make you wish to draw it."

I looked at the sketch as though it might hold the answer. I nearly shrugged my shoulders, the gesture of a humbled man or a bewildered one, which my father had taught me to suppress as indicative of a weak character. "I don't know."

"It were better to have drawn the man whose brain it was. Men and women living in the world— neither a literary nor a lurid one—should be the inspiration of the painter, sculptor, and photographer."

"What do you think of Manet's *Luncheon on the Grass*?" I asked slyly.

"*Le Déjeuner sur l'herbe* is one of a number of troublesome paintings by an artist I admire for his realism. *Le Suicidé*, *The Café-Concert*, *Le Bateau goudronné*, showing two men tarring their boat on the beach at Boulogne-sur-Mer—marvelous pictures! The four people he studiously posed in *Luncheon on the Grass*, however, could exist nowhere but in a painting. Their world is not ours. I doubt it was anyone's."

He didn't look to me for comment, and I was glad

to let the matter drop. "My grandfather is an artist," I said for no other reason than to put the conversation on familiar ground.

"Might I have heard of him?"

"I don't think so."

"What's his name?"

"Franklin Barrett."

"I've seen his work," said Eakins, a wry smile raising the cheekbones of his handsome face.

I was astonished. Pop is a dabbler and doesn't pretend to anything more.

"A great jolly nude hanging in Kelsey's saloon!" I had gone red in the face. "Don't be embarrassed, Oliver! Not every painter is lucky enough to have his work viewed by an audience in such an excellent frame of mind. I'll tell you this, as well: Many an artist I could name in this town would be happy to have a painting seen by so many eyes. My own canvas—*The Gross Clinic*—was put in a corner during the Centennial Exhibition, where only the man who swept the floor could see it."

The bell at St. Luke's pealed the hour. Eakins looked at his watch.

"I've got a room full of young artists champing at the bit." He stood and shook my hand. "I'm glad to have met you, Mr. Fischer. Give Franklin Barrett my regards." He put his hat on his head and winked. "You'll have to introduce me one of these days. And know this, Mr. Fischer: Affectation is not the expression of freedom you suppose; it is a restraint on the natural man."

I decided to take a look at Eakins's painting of Dr. Gross in his clinic. I walked east on Market, past the vast eight-story Philadelphia & Reading Railroad depot, a hymn in brick and iron to industrial progress. I passed the *Inquirer* building, where Linotype machines and steam presses were stoking the town's war fever with extra editions.

At Snellenburg & Co. department store, loafers, strollers, and lunch-hour oglers had gathered on the pavement outside the display window, behind which two young women dressed in bathing costumes sat on a blanket, eating sandwiches. A pair of blue parasols, a red shovel of the sort that children dig with, a pink starfish, flotsam festooned with green weed, and a basket of cherries completed the illusion of a picnic on a beach. The basket, need I say, resembled that in Manet's *Luncheon*.

I went into the store and, catching a salesgirl by the sleeve of her yellow shirtwaist, drew her to the display window. "I would like that basket," I said in the tone of voice of someone not to be denied.

"They're out of stock, sir," she replied, admiring her reflection in the window, the perfect oval of her face and the heap of chestnut-colored hair.

"I'll take that one, then." I waved my hand at the basket on the tartan blanket.

"I'm sorry, mister; it's part of the display."

I declared my intention not to leave without it.

Evidently, the young woman had had no previous experience with obstreperous customers. At a loss, she sucked on the imitation pearls of her necklace until, taking heart at the sight of a passing floorwalker, she called, "Mr. Larkin, do you have a moment, please?"

I explained to Mr. Larkin the urgency of my purchase—that it was for the sake of art and the world would be the poorer for its lack.

"The basket would be missed by Mr. Snellenburg if I were to authorize its sale." He spoke as if his nostrils were pinched.

I claimed the customers' right and prerogative to have their wishes honored.

"I'm afraid that I cannot oblige you in this instance," said Mr. Larkin, swabbing, with a handkerchief, the Macassar hair oil running down his cheek.

"I'd like a word with Mr. Snellenburg or the tail of the dog constituting 'and Co.'"

"Impossible."

"How so?" I leaned toward Mr. Larkin; he leaned away. The action was reiterated several times. Were we a pair of lumberjacks, we could have felled a sequoia.

"Absolutely impossible!"

Without wasting another word, I yanked the basket from the window. The two bathing beauties screamed, as though harried by the formidable claws of a famished crab. The salesgirl chewed through the string of her necklace, sowing the sand with pearls.

On the pavement, a trio of smart alecks, derbies pushed brashly back, toothpicks between their teeth, spurred us on, as they would have bantams at a cockfight.

"Attaboy!"

"My money's on the peacock with the yellow socks."

"The kid's already winded. Grannie Landis will mop the floor with him."

Evidently, the two bathers, who had spent the lunch hour on display to passersby, caught a sudden chill of modesty. Commencing to shiver from head to toe, they covered themselves with blushes and with the parasols before beating a hasty retreat into the interior of the store.

Mr. Landis sold me the basket. He drew the line, however, at the waxed cherries inside it. No, he would risk his situation before letting go of the cherries. I slipped out the door leading to a side street in case the police had been called.

I walked on to Jefferson Medical College, where I studied the colossal canvas *The Clinic of Dr. Gross*. I was glad not to have lunched at Sweeney's on Market Street, where typographers and pressmen from the

Inquirer gorged on pigs' ears and porter. My gut had not yet settled after my tussle with Mr. Landis.

An old man shambled up to me. He was wearing one of Samuel Jewett's artificial legs, a common accoutrement for Civil War veterans. "It's a good likeness," he said, turning from the somber oil painting to regard me through lenses thick as mica peepholes on a furnace.

Thinking he meant Dr. Gross, I agreed, although I had no idea how the eminent surgeon had looked in the flesh. He had died before I first laid eyes on his painted self.

"Yes, and the mother—see how she covers her face with her arm. The poor woman! Eakins painted her that way to conceal her suffering, which would have belittled the majesty of the great Dr. Gross. You, young man, would have been turned to stone if you'd seen her face. Poor, poor woman!" He stood there, eyeing the work for several minutes more, then quaintly bowed and lumbered from the room on his wooden leg.

As I walked toward the exit, I paused at a deal table piled with pamphlets, prints, and postcards showing the famous artwork, and a stack of books whose cloth covers were gold-stamped with the unsensational title *Reminiscences of an Army Surgeon,* by Edward Fenzil, published by E. Goldman & Company of Brooklyn.

"In his youth, Mr. Fenzil was a curator of Dr.

Thomas Dent Mütter's collection," said an odd little man whose antique brocaded vest had been pierced by glowing embers of tobacco. His beard was scraggly, his eyebrows bushy, and his face of a greenish hue.

"I often visit the museum," I said. "I'm an artist, you see, and I find it useful to sketch the anomalies."

"An artist, you say! I wondered why you were so interested in Mr. Eakins's picture. Most people shy away from it."

"We're both at the Pennsylvania Academy of the Fine Arts. You could say that I'm his protégé."

"Then you must read Mr. Fenzil's book," said the man, who may have been a docent, a concierge, or a codger come about his gallstones. "He knew Eakins, and the painter's friend Walt Whitman. He knocked about town with Edgar Poe. Look here." He slid a postcard reproduction of the famous oil under my nose. "Eakins placed Fenzil among the medical students." He tapped a tobacco-stained finger on a blurred face looming in the gallery of the operating theater. "That's him. I think you'd find his book interesting."

I asked the book's price and, considering it reasonable, purchased it. Then I asked if he knew the crippled man to whom I had spoken.

"He claims to be the young fellow whose leg was operated on by Dr. Gross. The mother, he says, is his.

She died years ago, and he comes once or twice each week to have a look at her, though her face is hidden."

"You say he's the patient on the table?" I asked, feeling a curious excitement.

"He's a bit mad. He lost his leg in a street-car accident. It left him with a screw loose. Oh, he's harmless, though he does sometimes annoy the visitors, especially the ladies. He lives over at the Irving House, on Sansom Street, and clerks at the Thomas Edison Electric Station next door to it."

I left the old man to his thoughts, which appeared to be focused on his dingy cuff.

Back in my attic room, I read a little of Fenzil's *Reminiscences*:

> Thomas Eakins's painting, accounted famous by those who can appreciate it, of Dr. Gross's clinic at Jefferson Medical College in Philadelphia has always given me the horrors. Not the reeking hands of the surgeons nor the raw, ensanguined flesh exposed on the young boy's thigh disturb me—by 1875, I was inured to gory scenes, having served in the Union army medical corps during the War of the Rebellion—no, it's not the blood, but the general murk above the harshly lit operating theater where the students sit, in attitudes of boredom or indifference, observing the removal of the diseased portion of the boy's femur, that makes

me anxious. To gaze at them, at the death masks of faces rendered brutal by smears of paint, calls up in me a sensation of dread, as if I were straining to raise something repellent from the lightless depths of memory—a thing too blighted for the light of day.

After seeing Eakins's painting with its bloody knife and femur, who would be moved by a drawing of gallstones the size and color of a clinker, which are no more tragic than the marbles that boys play with and sometimes swallow? A pickled human brain that resembles browning cauliflower, a skull bearing a cutaneous horn—they are dead things and deserving of nothing but our morbid interest. Measured on the scale of human pain, *The Clinic of Dr. Gross* is an elephant, my dreary doodles a gnat, as Eakins would have said.

As Anne and I entered Franklin Square, I looked up at William Penn standing atop City Hall and gazing toward the famous elm beside the river, where the good Quaker had made peace with the Lenape Turtle Clan. "Have you seen the view from underneath Billy's big boots?" I asked her, pointing upward to Alexander Milne Calder's gargantuan bronze presiding over the here below. I had been to the observation platform, once or twice, to see the city's rooftops, docks, and parks as a bird would, its tiny eyes on the lookout for a puddle or a worm.

"Not likely!" The sight of Penn's outsized hat encouraged her to fiddle with her own. "What's he blowing about? I wonder."

A man of formidable appearance was hurling thunderbolts from a bandstand where, on Sunday afternoons, John Philip Sousa would sometimes conduct his shrill military marches.

"Let's go, Anne! I'm too hungry to dawdle."

She shook off my arm. "I want to hear what he has to say."

She weaseled her way into the crowd. I trailed after her.

"Look who it is, Ollie! William Jennings Bryan! Get a gait on!"

As we drew near the bandstand, words knitted into sentences shaped by his spellbinding oratory. "The individual is but an atom; he is born, he acts, he dies; but principles are eternal . . ."

The crowd showed its enthusiasm like farmers at a county fair, hurrahing a blue-ribbon ox, or workingmen cheering for Napoléon "Nap" Lajoie, the batting king, standing at the plate, unencumbered by decorum, spittoon, or a copy of Mrs. Humphry's *Manners for Men*.

Bryan's scorcher of a speech at the 1896 Democratic National Convention at the Chicago Coliseum—"you shall not crucify mankind upon a cross of gold!"—earned him the admiration of liberal Democrats and Populists and made him the abomination of the "Bourbon" Democrats and Republicans, who took up the cause of William McKinley and the gold standard. The Nebraska firebrand's mug had glared like that of a pop-eyed, Medusa-haired messiah at readers of eastern newspapers championing gold, beloved by financiers and their flunkies. Bryan lost to McKinley in the November 1896 election, and the farmers howled.

The Populists demanded that the federal government mint more silver coins to put money back into circulation—the nation's bank vaults having been drained of gold specie by the panic of 1893 and the ensuing depression that rolled over the people and, even at the time of which I write, was rolling still. Of the million thrown under the juggernaut emerged a mass of beaten, broken, half-starved men, women, homeless children, beggars, tramps, prostitutes, thieves, and—squeezed dry of all that nourishes body and soul—suicides. (I tell the hard facts of the harshest of realities, from the vantage of 1907.)

Franklin Barrett loved Bryan and his attacks on gold, robber barons, the idle rich, and the bigwigs of commerce. "Bryan's the people's man," Franklin liked to say before quoting from a letter written to Bryan by an Indiana farmer that had been printed in a socialist rag: "God has sent you amongst our people to save the poor from starvation, and we know you will save us."

My father—wing-collared, stiff-necked parishioner of Zion Lutheran Church, whose pew none dared take even in his absence—despised Bryan, the Free Silver Movement, Populists, Democrats of every stripe except the conservative Bourbons, advocates of a progressive federal income tax and the regulation of the railroads—anyone, in fact, who lacked the wherewithal to put money in his bank. He judged Bryan a demagogue, an anarchist, a secret Roman Catholic in the pocket of the pope, and an enemy of capitalism and America's Manifest Destiny.

In Philadelphia's Franklin Square, the silver-tongued orator pulled at his suspenders, rocked on his heels, and let fly words that seemed to flock in the air above us like small birds gathering against their mortal enemy the hawk.

"There are many, today, who argue that the United States has come of age and can do what it pleases; it can spurn the traditions of the past; it can repudiate the principles upon which the nation rests; it can employ force instead of reason; it can substitute might for right; it can conquer weaker people; it can exploit their lands, appropriate their property, and kill their people. There are many who argue that it is our duty to protect the Cubans and the Filipinos from Spanish tyranny."

The people in the crowd looked about

suspiciously, as if to discover an imperialist in their midst. I have no doubt that they would have stoned him, or—there being no stones at their feet—hanged him, or—no rope to hand—crushed him as casually as a steamroller over a hill of ants.

"But duty is not an argument; it is a conclusion," said Bryan. "To ascertain what our duty is, in any emergency, we must apply well-settled and generally accepted principles. It is our duty to avoid stealing, no matter whether the thing to be stolen is of great or little value. It is our duty to avoid killing a human being, no matter where the human being lives or to what race or class he belongs."

"Isn't he wonderful, Ollie?"

"I'll say!"

"Benjamin Franklin, citizen of Philadelphia, whose learning, wisdom, and virtue are a part of the priceless legacy bequeathed to us from the revolutionary days, expressed the same idea in even stronger language when he said, 'A highwayman is as much a robber when he plunders in a gang as when single; and the nation that makes an unjust war is only a great gang.'"

Had it not been for Susan B. Anthony flanked by a squad of Germantown suffragists, the crowd would have rushed the "Great Commoner," torn him from the bandstand, and carried him on its shoulders through the streets of Philadelphia. Children would have laid palms in his path, while Judases in striped trousers plotted against him in bank vaults and gentlemen's card rooms. As worked up as anyone else in that crowd, I would have kissed Anne on the mouth had she not thrown back her head in ecstasy and yawped.

Bryan's finely tuned instrument modulated into reverence as he invoked the first of our nation's martyred presidents: "Lincoln said that the safety of this Nation was not in its fleets, its armies, or its forts, but in the spirit which prizes liberty as the heritage of all men, in all lands, everywhere, and he warned his countrymen that they could not destroy this spirit without planting the seeds of despotism at their own doors."

As did my grandfather, Bryan feared that we would replace the Spaniards in Cuba and the Philippines with ourselves.

The crowd took up the Great Emancipator's 1860 campaign tune, unsung for nearly forty years, as though it had been put away in one of memory's drawers, to be brought out again for an occasion like this:

> We'll finish the temple of freedom
> And make it capacious within
> That all who seek shelter may find it
> Whatever the hue of their skin!
> Success to the old-fashioned doctrine
> That men are created all free
> And down with the power of the despot
> Wherever his stronghold may be!

To this day, I can't explain how the words came to me, who had never heard them sung, unless "the mystic chords of memory," as Mr. Lincoln called them, had been struck and the song ascended to the heavens on the summer air.

Father Abraham—his craggy, careworn face gazing down from the sky pityingly at us—appeared, as though he were riding Elijah's fiery chariot, or so it seemed to me. I stood silent and amazed until a whirlwind jumped up from the grass, the evening sun slipped into a mountain of clouds, and Lincoln vanished into the western sky, followed by a flock of pamphlets denouncing the cross of gold.

Feet shod in red-white-and-blue socks, a man leaped onto the bandstand, shouting, "We must free the Cubans from the House of Bourbon and the Spanish regents! We must educate the poor peasants in the articles of faith in democracy! We will take Cuba from the tyrants and hold her in the palm of our hand lest she fall into barbarism! We will do this in God's name!"

"Imperialism finds no warrant in the Bible!" shouted Bryan, his voice wobbling under the strain like an Adam's apple gone mad. "The command 'Go ye into all the world and preach the gospel to every creature' has no Gatling gun attachment."

The militarist attempted a martial air by Bolgiano, in the upper register of his untrained voice:

Hurrah, hurrah, we'll wave the banner
     there;
Hurrah, hurrah, for old Havana fair.
We wouldn't do a thing to Spain,
But fight with all our might and main . . .
With cannons pointed in their face,
Which threaten to destroy their race,
The Red, White and Blue!

Raising himself up, Bryan delivered his rebuttal swiftly and decisively: "When the desire to steal becomes uncontrollable in an individual he is declared to be a kleptomaniac and is sent to an asylum; when the desire to grab land becomes uncontrollable in a nation we are told that the 'currents of destiny are flowing in the hearts of men.' . . ."

He was attacked by fusillades of rotten fruit that had been secreted in the pockets of the warmongers. A woman whom I recognized as Lady Liberty from the previous night in Echo Park produced a melon from beneath her dress (I had believed her to be with child) and tossed it at the People's Man. It hit him squarely on the nose, which commenced to bleed. Anne retaliated with a hat pin, which pierced the woman's bottom. They fought like catamounts as the crowd broke into two factions, each intent on battery. In the western sky, painted rose and gold, the shade of Abraham Lincoln reappeared and wept a shower of rain onto the rough-and-tumble below.

"It's time to vamoose before the boys from the

First Regiment Armory rout us," I said as I scrummed Anne from the square.

In the street, she stopped to braid her hair, having left her hat pin in her adversary's rump and, as a consequence, her hat beneath the feet of the mob.

"Are you still hungry?" I asked, afraid of reprisals and wanting to hurry her along.

"I could eat a Chinaman raw!"

We walked east to Sixth Street, where Chinatown begins. Men in black quilted vests and pigtails eyed our white faces with a mixture of scorn, wariness, and something I couldn't decipher. It may have been their anger at having no women to marry after the Chinese Exclusion Act of 1882 confirmed them in a lonely state of chronic bachelordom.

The place where Anne and I went to eat noodles called itself the Gold Mountain, named for the temptation that had brought Chinese laborers from their homeland to toil, as coolies, for Leland Stanford's Central Pacific Railroad, begun at Sacramento and finished almost six years later at Promontory Summit, Utah. They mined a mountain of rock as they dug, dynamited, and died in the snowcapped Sierra Nevada. But they got no closer to their pipe dream than the final spike, called "golden," or the mining camps where they washed not precious ore in pans but the dirty clothes of the white ghosts who despised them. In time, the Chinese drifted east and settled like a yellow dust where cities dream in secret of strange races. There they washed clothes and cooked meals for those who believed that the Chinese were alien beings unlike themselves.

The Gold Mountain was not like the Oriental restaurants of New York, Chicago, or San Francisco, furnished in black teak and hand-carved screens, nor would we be served diamond-shaped or octagonal morsels robed in gay colors and arranged like confections. Our chop suey arrived on white plates scarred by knives.

"Anne, did you see anything out of the ordinary in the sky?" I wondered if I had shared in a communal delusion inspired by fervent speeches and songs and a shoal of gray clouds that had gathered in advance of an unsettled night.

"I saw the face of Abraham Lincoln," she replied, fumbling with her chopsticks.

"I saw him, too. Don't you think it strange?"

"What isn't strange these days, Ollie? Half the country tells lies, and the other half falls for them." Annoyed, she put down the chopsticks and took up a knife and fork. "What about Robert's friend? Is she willing to pose as Eve was before she ate the fatal fruit and caught the world's first cold?"

"She is. Do you have a nightdress, or whatever the article is called?"

"I borrowed one from John Wanamaker, although he doesn't know it. What about your costume?"

"The outfit worn by the Ottoman ambassador in the play by that name, which closed at the Walnut last week, came to me by mysterious means and will return by them, if my pledge is to be redeemed."

"What did you pledge?"

"Why *you,* my dear."

She scowled and chased a slippery bean sprout around her plate.

As we tended to our dinner, a brickbat shattered a window of the Gold Mountain. Two Chinese men ran in from the kitchen—one wiping his hands on his apron, the other brandishing a cleaver. They looked at the broken glass and then at us, who sat like a pair of petrified dragons.

Some boys put their heads in through the empty window frame, stuck out their tongues, and waggled their fingers from the ends of their noses. "Yellow monkeys!" they shouted before beating it for the river, in advance of a mob of imperially minded citizens running harum-scarum from the mounted soldiers dispatched by the armory. The riot in Franklin Square had spilled into the streets of Chinatown.

Race Street in an uproar, Anne and I hurried into the kitchen, where a man was eating dumplings. He looked at us over the rim of the bowl and jerked his billy-goat chin toward the alleyway. That look and toss of the head—replete with intelligence and contempt—shattered the mask he had been made to wear the moment he'd passed through the Golden Door.

In the yard, we struggled against the damp embrace of sheets strung on clotheslines. The gate squawked behind us as we ran through other yards crowded with drying clothes, barrels of rotting cabbage, chicken houses, galvanized tubs brimming with rainwater and dead leaves, and, here and there, sitting on a box, a Chinese man smoking an opium pipe, careless of all the world save that of his pipe dream. We came out of the alley into Arch Street. I was feeling put out and out of breath; Anne, however, was breathless with laughter.

I put on my best pout. "I don't see what's so funny."

"Don't be such a boiled shirt, Oliver! We've had an adventure!"

"Some adventure! My Florsheims are scuffed— and look at yourself! Your skirt hem is ripped, and your hair bedraggled. I'll take you home before they hang us from a lamppost."

"What a stick-in-the-mud you are! Go home to your smelly attic! I'm not finished taking in the sights."

"Stieglitz is showing his 'Japanese' pictures at the Quarles," I said, feeling that I might salvage something from the wreckage of the evening. "It's not far from here. Pearson saw them and said they're quite the thing. Of course, one takes what Pearson says with a grain of salt. But I think it's safe to say that Stieglitz's Pictorialism proves the camera is every bit as sensitive to tone and atmosphere as the brush."

"If that's the best you can do, I'll be on my way. And don't think you can put me off with the dime museum, either!"

"What do *you* suggest?"

"Janet and Marcie were all het up over the Carncross and Dixey's Minstrels at the Eleventh Street Opera House."

I despise Ethiopian delineators. Even now, nearly ten years later, I see my father sitting beside the Berliner Gramophone, a glass of beer and a plate of crackers at his elbow, listening to Billy Golden sing coon songs.

"Say, Anne, why don't we take a squint at Stuart? The papers are raving about him."

Everett Stuart, known as the "Male Patti" on music hall and minstrel stages, was the best female impersonator of the day. That night he would be performing at the Gaiety Theatre, near Franklin Square, after a grand European tour. To see him dressed in the latest Paris gown, his hair curled and brushed back onto his lovely neck, the convincing rotundity of his bosom can take a man's breath away. By such stratagems is desire's interest compounded and, at the same time, confounded, making sex a labyrinth where we poor devils go insane. I saved the program from that night:

"What say we take in the show?" She hesitated. "Everett has a fine soprano voice."

"Well, all right, then."

I took her arm and we walked into the night, as if it held a secret yet to be disclosed.

Sitting by the window overlooking Cherry Street, I heard "the long sobs of autumn's violins" rising from a page of Verlaine:

> *Les sanglots longs*
> *Des violons*
> *De l'automne*

Because of my father's enmity for the "garlic eaters" of Italy and France, I was made to study German during my time at Frankford High School, under "Bismarck" Schenk, in spite of my wish to learn the language of Baudelaire. (How I came to be called Oliver has never been explained, although of all the English whose names have come down to us in the history of that island nation, I've heard my father invoke, respectfully, that of Cromwell.) My knowledge of French I owe to an uncle of Albert Tremblay, a boyhood friend whom I pulled from Tookany Creek when his leg cramped after he'd eaten too many wieners cooked on a stick. Claude had worked on the Philadelphia wharf, translating bills of lading and cargo manifests into English, until a crate of Camembert disabled him. After school, I'd stop at Albert's house, where Claude was then living, and receive a lesson, after which I'd say, *"J'adore le chocolat"* and be given a piece of Bonnat. A friend of his on the pier kept Charles supplied with French confections and wines pilfered from the holds of arriving ships.

"Mr. Fischer."

For my seventeenth birthday, Claude gave me Rabelais's *The Horrible and Terrifying Deeds and Words of the Very Renowned Pantagruel King of the Dipsodes, Son of the Great Giant Gargantua*, in French.

I had gone no further in it than Claude's wish that I should have "many happy returns of the day," when my father snatched Claude's gift from my hands and pitched it through my bedroom window. I've not forgotten the self-satisfied look on Father's face, as if the book had landed in the birdbath's filthy water by any other means than chance.

"Mr. Fischer!"

I looked up and saw Thomas Eakins looming above me. "Hello, sir."

"You were lost in your book."

"I was. Sorry."

"Let me see."

I handed up my book to him. (He is a tall man.)

"Poèmes saturniens," he said in excellent French, having lived among them in Paris, where the garrets are lofty and the cellars deep.

He returned it without comment. "Still drawing necrotic livers at the Mütter?"

I replied with a charming smile that, in former days, had had the power to disarm my critics.

He smiled in return, but I knew he could see clear through me to my back collar button. "Care to show me what you're working on, Oliver?"

"I work at home," I replied too quickly. I didn't want him to see the risqué painting I'd just completed, in the naughty manner of Franz von Bayros, drying in my corner of the studio.

"I see. The muse is more apt to show herself in your garret."

"I did these last night!" I said abruptly, handing him my sketchbook.

He studied my caricatures of Everett Stewart in décolletage, F. F. Proctor, the juggler, and various persons sitting in front of the Gaiety's gaudy proscenium arch. Encouraged by the late hour, whiskey, and my desire for Anne, which had flamed as I walked her to her rooming house, I'd let my pencil have its way.

His lips pursed, Eakins said not a word as he examined several pages of drawings. The intensity of his gaze could have burned ants to death the way small boys do with a magnifying glass.

Nervously, I cleared my throat.

"Do you want to be Henri de Toulouse-Lautrec?" I squirmed in my chair as though a ferret were loose inside my coat. "Oliver, you can read Baudelaire and go to the Gaiety every night of the week, but it will never be the Moulin Rouge, Philadelphia will never be Paris, and you'll never be Toulouse-Lautrec or any other Frenchman. Nor should you wish to be. One of him is enough. One of Rembrandt is enough. One of any artist you care to name is quite enough if he's any good at all." He turned his back on me and walked away.

Embarrassed by the dressing down, I gathered my things and went out into Cherry Street.

"Ollie!" Pearson caught up to me. "I saw you

chinning with the old man. You looked like you'd stepped in horseshit."

"We were discussing Toulouse-Lautrec," I said drily.

"Oh, the little guy. What do you say we get lunch?"

We went to a lunchroom on Watts Street, a favorite of doctors and nurses at Hahnemann Medical College, as well as coppers from the Twentieth Precinct, who could never decide where to put their tall helmets and would usually leave them on their heads.

"Eakins wanted to know what I was painting," I said, picking at a chop.

Pearson had chosen fried scrapple, which always made him colicky.

"You're a blockhead for eating that when you know it doesn't agree with you."

"I like the stuff. What *are* you painting these days?"

"Not much."

"You'll have to show them something, or they'll throw you out like last year's calendar."

"I know!" I watched him shovel pig's offal done to a crisp into his bottomless pit, while I sketched him in caricature on the oilcloth with my fork.

"Aren't you eating?" he asked.

"I lost my appetite. So, Robert, what are *you* painting?"

"Bottles."

"Bottles?"

"Bottles from an old cistern in my aunt's yard. Last summer when I was putting in rosebushes for her, I poked my fork in the ground and heard a clink. My aunt Mary's an old scold, but she bakes an excellent rhubarb pie. Nothing like stewed rhubarb to keep the enema at bay. It used to be called a *clyster*—a word that always makes me think of the Irishman's answer to the Englishman's question, 'Where do the nuns live?'"

"What kind of bottles?" Talking to Robert could be like a game of hare and hounds.

"The sort patent medicines come in—syrups, elixirs, nostrums, cures, and remedies. I have a blue bottle that, once upon a time, was filled with Phillips' milk of magnesia. It's pretty when the light shines through." He stabbed a gray morsel with his fork. "I like painting bottles better than I do vases of flowers or plates of apples." He turned his head to regard a young nurse who had entered the lunchroom. "Gee rod, I'd like to have a go at her!" he said. "But I'm not good enough yet to paint people, with or without their clothes."

We left the lunchroom and walked down Broad Street in time to see a platoon of soldiers march into

City Hall courtyard. Their sky blue trousers encased by burnt sienna canvas leggings, their blouses of a darker blue crossed by white Sam Browne belts, their dun campaign hats fresh from the hatmaker's block—all were spanking new in the brilliant light of a late-summer afternoon. Prendergast would make a fine job of the scene, I thought, but I expect it will be someone like Bellows or Sloan who will paint them when they come shambling home.

"Will there be war, do you think?" asked Pearson as fifty pairs of polished army boots in lockstep echoed in the walled courtyard.

"We'll either fight the Spaniards or ourselves."

At the Broad and Market Street station, we took a westbound subway car toward the Schuylkill. Just before the river, the car burst into sunlight, which stung our eyes when the train passed onto the elevated tracks. We got off at the Forty-third Street stop, near the Provincial Hospital for the Insane, whose grounds only Fairmount Park surpasses. Not even the sprawl of Woodlands Cemetery, a city on a hill peopled with generations of dead Philadelphians, is larger than that parkland set aside for the refreshment of the mad.

"Strange, don't you think, that the insane and the dead have been given so many acres in which to stretch their legs, while the rest of us go about in crowds?"

"I never gave it a thought," said Pearson.

The asylum grounds are a favorite resort of the public, who, on Sundays in fine weather, escape the city's narrow built-up streets to stroll the lawns, which are as lovely as the pleasure garden of a khan. We roamed and talked about nothing more consequential than the Athletics' chances in the pennant race. Although I didn't give a hang for baseball, I spoke of the matter gravely, as befits one of the demos.

We walked into a grove of newly planted saplings, which brought to mind the soldiers who had been parading on Broad Street. They're green like these, I thought, as I felt the smooth skin of a linden tree. But the bark of Spanish howitzers will toughen the hides of the young men, except for those who die of them.

We sat on a bench and smoked like two souls in hell. He took out the drawing case that he carried in his coat pocket. I watched him sketch and admired the sureness of his hand as the charcoal lines grew into trees on the rough paper.

"You have talent, Robert." I wanted to be kind because, at that moment, I was afraid. I could not have said of what.

"Care to try your hand?"

I shook my head and smoked.

He put the little case aside.

On a branch of a copper beech, a bird announced its presence in the language of its species.

"Why don't you draw birds?" I asked.

"There's only one Audubon."

"Has no one else painted bottles?"

He shrugged, fell silent, then asked, "Will you enlist?"

Will I? I asked myself as I studied the tips of my shoes. It would be an adventure. I saw myself in uniform, saying good-bye to Anne. Who's a stick-in-the-mud now? Will you write to me, will you send me your picture and a lock of your hair?

"I guess I will," I replied, not at all sure that I would. "What about you, Robert?"

"For pineapples and Domino sugar? Hell no!"

"Let a pretty girl show you her dimples, and you're likely to do the damnedest things. Let her kiss you, and you'll jump off Billy Penn's hat!"

He went quiet again.

"You think the eyes of her, don't you, old man?" I did not have to say her name.

"Ollie, I do. But I haven't a chance with her. So there it is, and what the hell!"

"She's looking forward to Sunday. She's keen on swimming."

I remembered my first love, a pretty Sicilian named Natalia Mannino, fifteen years old, whose father owned a candy store next door to the grocery.

Do you know how to swim, Ollie? She had followed me into the grocer's and crept up behind me as I was picking through a basket of potatoes. Mother had sent me to buy two pounds of white Maines "without too *many eyes." I was curious about those eyes, which sprouted in McGuinn's cellar, where potatoes spent the winter in the company of turnips, parsnips, onions, and rutabagas. What did they see in the pitch-dark?*

"Of course!" I replied indignantly. Swimming across Tookany Creek was no less heroic for a boy than Leander's or Byron's crawl across the Hellespont.

"Then tomorrow bring your bathing suit, and we'll go to the asylum. Tomorrow's going to be a stinker!" She looked over the potatoes I had bagged and took one out. "Too many eyes," she said, and then she went back to her candy counter.

Whitey and I often followed the creek as far as the asylum near Adams Avenue, where the water was deep and shaded by willow and alder trees. We'd dry off in the sun beside the asylum wall and listen to the gibber and cries of the lunatics. I was deathly afraid of insanity. My father, who did not care for a gentle Jesus or a merciful God, declared it to be the result of low morals and broken taboos and liked to embarrass my mother and her card-party friends by talking about Mendel and his peas.

My thoughts returned to the lawn of the Provincial Hospital for the Insane. The sun in its slow decline had withdrawn its light from the roses that, not long before, had blazed in scarlet battalions. A troop of dirty geese walked into an enormous shadow cast by the main building and was seen by me no more.

"Say, Ollie, it's time we got out of here, before they count heads and find us missing."

We walked back the way we had come, climbed the stairs to the elevated platform, and waited for an eastbound train.

Neither of us felt like talking as the elevated train clattered toward the terminus. Sitting beside the car window, I enjoyed a God's-eye view of the streets below. Eyes shut and a hand resting on his chest, Pearson appeared to be struggling with some weighty matter. Indigestion was my guess. You'll be wanting a bicarb soon as we detrain, I told him—in my mind, which was, as always, floundering in William James's so-called stream of consciousness.

Once more, I fell back to the summer of 1892.

On the morning Natalia and I were to go swimming, it rained. I was relieved; I wasn't comfortable around girls I liked, nor am I now. Besides, Natalia might have laughed to see me in a bathing suit, which hung on my skinny frame. Not that I cared what a fifteen-year-old girl thought of me! I'd be better off forgetting her pretty face, dark eyes, and serious mouth, better off forgetting the way she had of standing, impudently, with one hand on her hip, the other in her lovely hair. So I told myself.

By afternoon, I'd thumbed through The Count of Monte Cristo *and glanced at colored maps of the Holy Land. I could go to Woolworth's and play the Try Your Luck machine, or to Whitey's house in Unionville and study his father's Chalmers Knitting Mill catalogue of women wearing camisoles and drawers. I didn't feel much like smoking cigarettes beneath the railroad bridge with Jack Braxton or swigging his old man's beer. My thoughts kept returning to Natalia. Was she waiting for me? I wondered. I should walk over to her house and pretend to be sorry about the rain.*

The car swayed, causing Pearson to fall against my shoulder. The minor disturbance was enough to jolt me into the present. With a toss of my head, I shook off memory as a dog does rain. I concentrated my attention on the fleeting world beneath me—lumberyard, livery stable, sash factory, steam laundry, telephone exchange, trolley barns of the Philadelphia Traction Company, a school, a slate-roofed church, the William Penn Hotel, Hamilton Trust, Eli Kindig's mule yard, St. James's Hall, the Ice Manufactory, the Chocolate Works, Philadelphia Novelty Iron Works, Quaker City Flour Mills, the immense Pennsylvania Cold Storage Company (what dreams wait there to be thawed?), George B. Newton's Coal Company, a bewildering musical score of railway tracks, coal barges wallowing like hippopotamuses and bellowing black smoke. On the east side of the river, at Twenty-third, the train plunged beneath Market Street, and darkness swallowed us.

As the train roared from the underground tunnel into the vault of the Broad Street subway station, I nudged Pearson from his own netherworld. He grunted his greetings from it, stretched his legs in the aisle, then followed me out the car door and onto the platform. The air was hot and stale and smelled of the underprivileged who linger at depots where luckier mortals with jack in their pockets might be persuaded to part with a nickel or two.

Together with a troop of poor devils, Pearson and I climbed out of the miniature hell that a subway station in the dog days resembles. Up above, the air was sweet, if only by comparison. The pavements were jammed with fashionable women carrying parcels or followed by flunkies bearing them like porters on safari. A band of would-be pickpockets from a nearby grammar school slipped cunningly through the moiling crowd. The newsboys were out in force, hawking the evening editions. Broad Street bustled with electric trolleys and horse-drawn conveyances of every sort. The side streets rang with bicycle bells, omnibus gongs, policemen's whistles, and the hoarse pitches of peanut vendors exhorting passersby to "Get 'em while they're hot." Western-facing windows were in flames, those opposite so many blank faces. On City Hall, Attic figures cut from stone standing beneath the architraves had backed up into shadows that would thicken into night. Soon the dinner hour would be rung, called Vespers by the Roman churches.

Pearson and I dithered on the pavement, while pigeons picked avidly at avian delicacies in the cracks. The uneasiness that, lately, I'd been prey to at this hour of the day discouraged me from spending another night alone in my attic.

"Say, Robert, why don't you show me your pictures?"

His pleased reaction was complicated by suspicion. Until that day, I hadn't shown much interest in his artistic pursuits. "Well, I don't know, Ollie . . ."

"Come on, old scrub! We'll stop and get a bottle of wine, a bag of baguettes, and a tin of pâté made from the exploded liver of a goose. My treat."

"It's my treat, Ollie. The *Bulletin* paid me for a pen-and-ink this morning. But I don't like your fancy grub."

"What would you like, then?"

"Brisket and potato salad, dark bread, and beer. Bottles and bottles of the stuff!"

"Any beer but Ortlieb's."

We clapped each other's back and went in search of a grocery store.

Pearson rented a third-floor room on Juniper Street, across from the Philadelphia *Bulletin* building. His room was much as mine would have been without a hookah, books and journals of decadent poetry intended to impress my visitors, and an extravagantly colored rag rug recently acquired from an ash heap. He busied himself at a scarred sideboard inherited from the room's previous tenant. I sat on a coal box.

His appetite amazed me. To please him, I ate with all the relish I could muster.

I did not know what to make of his pictures. Stolid and lumpish bottles sat on the canvas, with a narrow space between them that appeared to emit darkness or light. They did not fascinate so much as disquiet. I didn't like them.

"What do you think?"

"Are they symbols?"

"No, Oliver, they're bottles."

I fingered my ear, scratched my nose, shot my cuffs from my coat sleeves, waiting for my mouth to fill with words that would assemble into a compliment. None did.

"Empty glass bottles, Ollie." His feelings were hurt.

"Has Eakins seen them?"

"No one has seen them until now."

Tacked to a wall was a print of Albert Pinkham Ryder's *Dead Bird*. I exulted in its small, delicate pathos.

Pearson produced two bottles of beer. "You sure as hell know what to make of these, bub!"

We abandoned the coal boxes and sat on the floor. Robert's feathers, which I had ruffled, were soon smooth. He was a good fellow, not given to grudges, which were, he would have said, if the saying weren't a waste of breath, too damned heavy to bear.

Later that night, too out of sorts to light the gas, I sat in my dark attic room, stuffy and unromantic, for all I wished it were otherwise. Through the open window came the sound of a distant trolley car—its gong respectful of the late hour, the slur of its wheels against the rails like gravel softly raining into a pail. Pretend all you want that it's running down the boulevard de Clichy toward the Moulin Rouge, that outside the window is Paris; it is and always will be the sober city that buttons up for the night before night can be said to have started.

Across the street, Miss Hub's secretarial bureau lay shrouded in darkness, like the typewriters themselves inside their dustcovers, waiting for the endless, pointless clatter of the city's commercial life to begin anew. Night pressed against the roofs of buildings opposite my rooming house, draping their cornices with shadows that were darker than night. Röntgen's X-rays were everywhere present in the universe, just as Anton Mesmer's fluid had been a century before, and before it God. In less than nine hundred days, the nineteenth century will lie down in dust, where time writes its history. What waits behind the curtain of the twentieth century? What words? What stories of goodness or horror? Will the curtain ring up on the Gaiety Theatre stage or the cabinets of Dr. Mütter?

Closing the window and pulling down the shade, I lit a candle and began to draw bottles.

Only when I had finished, put down the stick, and wiped the charcoal from my fingertips did I realize how many I had drawn. There were pages of them, most smudged by my struggle to get one right. I remembered with what assurance Robert had captured their likeness. I glanced at the banjo clock on the wall that Franklin had given me, along with his injunction against looking at it, except in case of an assignation, saying, "It's rude to keep a young woman waiting."

Although the hour was going on three o'clock, I was not tired, or else I was in the throes of something that made weariness beside the point. I could not have said what the point of it, of any of it, was.

I started in again, this time with a pencil. Hardly aware of myself, I drew fanciful bottles, each enhanced by the addition of a nose, mouth, eyes, and ears. My hand moved rapidly across the paper as Robert's had done, only mine produced caricatures. When I'd finished, I had drawn a bottle instantly recognizable as President McKinley. Another was the spit of Charles Warwick, mayor of Philadelphia. In yet another, I had caught the exaggerated essence of Teddy Roosevelt right down to his horse teeth and pince-nez spectacles. I anthropomorphized a bulging demijohn as Grover Cleveland and a Kentucky whiskey bottle as the "Railsplitter." The business end of a brush sprouting from the neck of a bottle became the unruly mop atop Mark Twain. I gave my father's thin nose, hard mouth, and Prussian chin to a bottle of bitters. For the night's finale, I transubstantiated an empty bottle of clearest gin into God Almighty.

And then I rested.

At eight o'clock in the morning, my earthly father knocked.

Had my father not knocked at my attic door, little, if anything, of what was to follow would have occurred. His unannounced, unprecedented visit caused a stir in me that swelled into a running tide that swept me out to sea and, its molecules having spent themselves, deposited me on Cuba's shore—green and pleasant, except for a fusillade of Mauser bullets that had been waiting for me, as well as Robert Pearson and Stephen Crane.

"Father?" My tone was that of astonished inquiry. "What brings you here at this ungodly hour?" I think that I gaped at him. I know that he gaped at me, having answered his peremptory knock wearing a tatty blanket and my Persian slippers.

He looked at my slippers, at the garish rug behind me, and at my face, which would have struck him as belonging to some other man's dissipated son who had squandered the family fortune, sold off its heirlooms, and tarnished its name beyond the power of any patent polish to remove. He leaned toward me and sniffed my breath, cautiously, as one would a suspicious substance clotted at the bottom of a jar. Involuntarily, his head shot back, and his nose wrinkled in response to the obvious distaste of its owner. I'd have thought that a man who adores Stilton cheese would be inured.

"You've been drinking!"

"No, I haven't. I was chewing on a caraway seed."

"You don't fool me, Oliver. I know what tricks you loafers get up to."

"I'm not all that much of a loafer, Father. And it's damned *sans-gêne* of you to drop in unannounced."

"You're a spoiled idler, and I'm here, at this 'ungodly hour' when responsible men are already about their affairs, to put my foot down once and for all!"

He had put his foot down many times during my unhappy career as his son. I was used to it. So I waited without any high expectation of hearing something new.

"Put on some clothes, for God's sake!"

I went into the corner and dressed. I left the ascot and yellow socks for another day. I washed my face, brushed my hair, and bit into an apple to clean my teeth. Looking sideways at him—the safest vantage, in my experience—I saw him peering through his wire frames at my drawings.

"I detest caricatures!" he snarled. "They're potshots taken at good men by inferior ones. McKinley is a fine president. Mayor Warwick sits on the board of the Western Savings Bank." He'd have crossed himself if he hadn't despised Roman Catholics. "I grant you that Roosevelt is a muckraking prick." He pointed to my drawing of the gin bottle. "Who's this supposed to be?"

"God." I gave the word no special emphasis or inflection. Neither He nor Charles should have taken exception.

He turned to me, his specs glinting with animus. "God? What do you mean by 'God'?"

"Him." I pointed at the ceiling. "The Divine Being, who thunders in the organ loft and whispers in your ear when to buy low and sell high to plump up your portfolio."

His fist sent me flying. My father is a small man. Even in his derby, he stands level with my chin, which was bleeding from a cut incised by his Masonic ring. I washed my face and then, turning from the basin, flashed him an insolent grin.

Enraged, he tore the drawings to shreds. Leaning against the windowsill, I took a Turkish cigarette from the box and began to smoke. His face turned a shade of red that I could not have mixed with pigments. I'd need a drop or two of blood. Watching him grow apoplectic, I was in high hopes that he would drop dead on my carpet. But he only sat down heavily on a coal box.

I tossed the cigarette out the window. "What is it you came to say, Father?"

Sitting on the box, his derby askew, he reminded

me of the hatted dog soused to the ears, painted on Doolittle's barroom wall.

"Oliver, I have come to the conclusion that you are not cut out to be an artist. Those hateful caricatures only confirm my low estimation of your abilities. There's nothing shameful in attempting a profession and, having failed, finding another, more suitable. I gave you your head; I let you sow a young man's wild oats. But the time has come to take stock. You will finish out the term and then take a situation in the bank. It's an excellent one, and as your responsibilities grow, so will your wages—and with them, the opportunity to set up a household of your own. I look forward to seeing you married one day, so long as the girl is not a Catholic. I presume you take no notice of colored girls. The shock would kill your mother, and I, Oliver, would kill you."

He got up, straightened his hat and tie, brushed his trousers with his hands, polished his shoes on the backs of his trouser legs, and said, "You have until the end of term. Refuse and I will cut you off without a cent." He walked out the door like a villain in a melodrama.

It was then that I went off the rails.

On Sunday morning at eight, Robert, Anne, Sarah Jenkins (she who was to be photographed in the altogether), and I rendezvoused at the Philadelphia and Reading Railroad depot on Market Street. Harry Owens, bearing his box camera and tripod, joined our party at the junction of the Tacony and Kensington connecting line, which would carry us to its final stop near the pier where Pop Barrett docked the *Myrtle Jane*. In the car, we cut up as the Baldwin locomoted through the city's river wards: Northern Liberties, where, in 1682, William Penn had treated peaceably with Tamanend; Kensington, where sugar mills groaned for more Cuban cane; Richmond, where a gargantuan elevator fed grain to a famished Hamburg-bound ship; and Bridesburg, where the arsenal was minting bullets, each accompanied by the fond hope of lodging in a Spaniard's chest.

We left the train at Sanger Street and walked east to Point No Point. Seen from the south, it juts into the Delaware River; from the north, it doesn't appear to be there at all. (Much later, I would remember that geographical sleight-of-hand as an instance of a universe no less deceptive than a shell game or hand of three-card monte.) The *Myrtle Jane* lay just beyond the point, on Frankford Creek, where buttonwoods and willows shimmered in the August heat and our sutler, Michael Teplov, sat on a hamper, chewing his nails. He, together with our provisions, costumes, and theatrical props packed in a pair of wicker hampers, had arrived in Mikhail's horse-drawn delivery van.

"Hello, Michael!" I said as I walked out onto the pier, followed by Sarah, who was fixing her hair.

"Hello, Ollie!"

"Sarah Jenkins, be acquainted with Michael Teplov, the 'founder of our feast,' as Bob Cratchit said of Scrooge. Mr. T.—I hasten to add—is the furthest thing in the wide and weary world from that famous skinflint."

"Hello, Michael Teplov!" she said breezily.

I thought his heart would seize! He blushed and stammered, picturing her, I suppose, as she soon would be, unencumbered by everything except her roseate flesh.

She gently removed her hand from his.

"Well, let's get a gait on, gents!" she said in the brisk way of the red-haired tribe as she stepped aboard the *Myrtle Jane*.

Harry Owens followed, his tripod slung across his shoulder.

Michael and Robert stowed the two hampers in the cabin, while I installed the steam valve, without which the boat could not have budged.

"Where's your cane?" asked Anne.

The dandy wearing the tarboosh in Manet's *Luncheon* holds a mahogany crook in his left hand; the right points toward the naked woman, its index finger limp, while his eyes appear to be on the other man, whose glassy gaze is fixed on no one we can see.

"In the hamper, among the other props. After the

business with the sword stick, I couldn't trust myself to carry it on the train."

"For once, you showed some sense."

The picnickers seated themselves around the cabin table and began to prattle.

"How far to Croydon?" asked Sarah.

"Twelve miles," I replied.

"As the crow flies or the snail paces?" asked Robert to bedevil me.

I did not deign to answer him, knowing that the fish wins that doesn't take the bait.

"Anyone care for a sandwich?" asked Michael Teplov, opening a hamper.

"*Mais oui.*"

"Ass!" said Anne, who could always be counted on to put me in my place.

"Ass on rye for the lady!" I twitted.

She stuck out her tongue at me.

"Make that tongue!"

She wrinkled her freckled nose. "I'll take ham on rye."

Michael obliged her with the item wrapped in butcher paper.

"Make mine a chicken sandwich," said Robert, who was always hungry.

"Harry?"

"Nothing, thanks," he replied, pausing in his polishing of the camera lens. "The crumbs, you understand."

"Miss, ah, Jenkins?" Michael stuttered when he spoke her name. I pitied the poor fellow, who had clearly been undone by her abundant charms.

"I'll take a pickled egg," she said.

In his confusion, Michael's hand trembled, and the egg slipped off the spoon and rolled across the cabin floor. One would have thought it had teeth like a garden-variety mole the way Anne and Harry picked up their feet.

"Don't be upset," said Sarah, putting an arm around Michael's narrow shoulders, a kindly act that pumped every last drop of blood from his extremities and left him weak at the knees.

"How long till we get to Croydon?" he asked to cover his embarrassment.

"Two hours, maybe less." Exchanging my panama for one of Franklin's yachting caps, I wiped the forward-facing window with my sleeve and took the wheel.

"As long as that!"

"Take a look in the dunnage box," I said, jerking my thumb at the hinged crate squatting in the corner.

"Oh, I wouldn't if I were you!" said Anne. "That's where he keeps his creditors."

Robert pinched his nostrils shut. "The dead ones, by the stink."

"What you smell is wafting from a New Jersey pig farm across the river," I said as the boat left Frankford Creek and debouched onto the Delaware.

"Say, look here—musical instruments!" said Sarah, opening the dunnage box, where Pop kept squeeze boxes, cowbells, ukuleles, swanee whistles, toy trumpets, and drums with which his guests would concertize during river outings—the ladies dressed in white summer skirts and blouses, the men wearing collarless shirts, duck trousers, and newspapers folded into admirals' hats.

What a terrible racket we made! Any chance of harmony was ruined by Mikhail Teplov's wine, which was harsh and left our throats raw, as did our caterwauling. After half-a-dozen rounds of "Little Tommy Tinker," we ceased—first Michael, who was easily winded, then Anne, Sarah, and I, who had been ringing the boat's brazen bell. Robert, being Robert, went on awhile longer, until he, too, shut his gob. Conscious of his responsibility for the outcome of the project, Harry had abstained. In the ensuing silence, loud as any din, I could hear the engine clunk, as if in mockery of our musicale.

"Anyone for a game of hearts?" asked Robert when the silence had become too great for him to bear. (I couldn't make out which of the two young women was making him squirm.)

"Don't know it."

"Cinch?"

"That cowboy game, not likely!"

"Rummy?"

"I hate the game!"

"Poker," suggested Sarah, pulling a suitable face.

"You're hot stuff, Miss Jenkins!"

"I'll say!" agreed Michael, whose heart—that valentine—was in his mouth.

Having dealt, Robert fanned his cards in his big mitt, pushed back his straw boater, and squinted as the wind blew in from starboard, plucked his ace of clubs from his hand, and carried it out the portside window.

"What're the odds!" cried Harry, flabbergasted.

"A bad omen," said Anne gravely.

"Don't be cracked!" I said from the helm, turning the wheel to skirt a snag.

Robert tossed what was left of the deck through the window. "If there was a bad hand in those cards, it's gone."

Anne treated him to a smile.

I caught him stealing a look at her breasts, firm inside her shirtwaist.

Harry polished his camera lens.

Michael did likewise to his glasses, which were spotted with pickling and mustard.

I hummed "And Her Golden Hair Was Hanging Down Her Back" and imagined that I was the picture of savoir faire.

Robert rolled up his sleeve. "Have a go?" he asked Anne, offering to arm-wrestle. His motive was obvious to all.

"Fat chance of that!" she said, tossing her head. Anne was no fool!

She suggested that we play charades.

"I'd rather recite *Hiawatha*!" Robert replied peevishly.

(Oh, I could see right through him!)

"Or the multiplication tables," said Sarah, a supercilious remark that raised Anne's eyebrows.

A silence fraught with hostility enfolded the *Myrtle Jane*.

"Look there!" I shouted over the burble of the boat's teakettle engine. A dozen men, hatless and shirtless, their trouser legs rolled up, swung into view as the *Myrtle Jane* rounded a low headland. They were hauling a net from the river that, measured by the effort told on their faces and beefy forearms, was loaded with fish. They might have been the same men—or their sons—whom Eakins had painted in *Shad Fishing at Gloucester on the Delaware River*, a picture Franklin Barrett admired. They stopped a moment to ogle Sarah Jenkins, who threw back her head and laughed. They understood that her laugh was not unkind. They waved and blew her kisses.

We continued upriver at a leisurely pace. My passengers were quiet and content to gaze upon the passing scenery, as was I. I didn't care if we ever reached Croydon. What business had I with Manet and his picture? For a moment, I thought of throwing the hamper of costumes and props overboard. I could put in at the next cove. We could eat, drink, and play badminton. Anne and I could walk along the shore and into the trees. But the smart of my father's Masonic fist—fresh in flesh's memory—stung. How he would rage at this latest instance of my reckless-ness and disregard for his position at the bank should news of it ever reach his ears! (I wanted him to burn with shame, and at the same time, I was afraid that he would beat the living hell out of me.)

"It's raining!" shouted Anne, her voice raised above a mad clattering on the cabin roof.

"It can't be!" said Harry, throwing a towel over his precious Hawk-Eye camera. "There's not a cloud in the sky."

The rattling ceased, only to begin again. I saw a bright smutch on the New Jersey side of the river that proved to be a red shirt belonging to a minor hood-lum. "Over there! Those kids are throwing stones." They cocked their skinny arms and let fly fistfuls of gravel. "Duck!" I cried as a third fusillade showered down on the roof.

"Cut that out, you little shits!" bellowed Robert, tumbling out the cabin door onto the aft deck, fol-lowed by the rest of us.

I objected to the scatology on account of the ladies.

"Oliver, what would you like me to call them?"

"Try Roach Guards, " I replied to egg him on.

"I've always liked the sound of Plug Uglies," proposed Harry.

"My favorite is Dead Rabbits," opined Anne, always a good sport.

"Clear off out of here, you little pricks!" shouted Sarah, much to our amazement. "I know how to talk to the likes of them!" Her small hand on her hip, she was the very image of defiance.

"Ah, we blokies kin lick deh hull bunch of youse!" retorted the dirtiest urchin.

Michael Teplov produced a blunderbuss from the hamper of costumes and props. He had only to brandish the antique weapon to send the hooligans scrambling into the underbrush, where, I hoped, thorns waited to receive them. He turned to Sarah, and with a show of nerve quite out of character, he bowed. Had he been wearing one of those great feathered hats in vogue at the time of the cavaliers, he would have doffed it and swept the deck with its yellow cockade.

With the nonchalance of a funambulist crossing a high wire, she walked over to Michael and then— by God!—she bussed him.

"It's not a real blunderbuss," he said, astonished by the attention of the red-haired siren. "It's from a stage production of *Rip Van Winkle* at the Philadelphia Dramatic Society. My cousin played Rip. The reviews were mixed."

I would have reminded him that an antique

weapon had no place at a late nineteenth-century French picnic, when Robert shouted, "Hooray for Teppy!" Who was I to deny him his moment of glory? I joined the rest of the party in cheering him. That kiss and the acclaim may have been the triumphal moment in Teplov's life. The poor fellow died in September 1901 of typhus, in the contagious diseases hospital at Twenty-second Street and Lehigh Avenue.

Except for the appearance of a large bird that swooped down from the upper air, nothing else occurred to mar our stately progress toward Croydon. Its webbed feet made a little run along the foredeck before it tucked its wings demurely behind its sleek gray body.

"It's an albatross!" Dredging the Coleridge poem from the cellar of my fancy, I recited:

> 'God save thee, ancient Mariner!
> From the fiends, that plague thee
>   thus!—
> Why look'st thou so?'—With my
>   cross-bow
> I shot the Albatross.

"Don't be an idiot!" said Robert. "It's a seagull of the laughing sort." Indeed, the bird was laughing—at me, I could have sworn.

"Anyone care for a sandwich?" asked Michael, as

if he were Aladdin and existed only to satisfy our carnal appetites.

My green malachite ring caught the yellow sunlight as the *Myrtle Jane* came in sight of Croydon. This glorious summer afternoon, I thought to myself, is one of the promised days.

At one o'clock, I ran the *Myrtle Jane* up a quiet backwater in the midst of a grove of trees and tied up to a willow whose green whips hung low over the water. Robert and I manhandled the hamper of props and costumes ashore, while a smitten Michael Teplov danced attendance on Sarah Jenkins. Harry Owens carried his camera as if it were the skull bone of a saint.

We walked through a wood and entered the glade where we would stage our *tableau vivant*. The shadowed grass, the color of the air, the poplar and the hazel trees were like those Manet had painted in the suburbs of Paris. Robert and I went behind a tree to change into our costumes. Anne and Sarah hunted for a secluded spot, despite the fact that we would shortly see one in her chemise, the other in her skin. Referring to a postcard of Manet's picture, Michael set out on the grass a straw hat, a blue-dotted sateen dress, a flask intended for spirits of turpentine, and— trophy of my wrangle at the department store—the rattan basket. He scattered cherries and spread an azure cloth for Sarah to sit her bottom on. While Robert and I took our places, Anne hitched up her shimmy and waded through the shallow water, where little rivulets lasciviously lapped her knees.

Sarah was the last to join us. Modesty had not delayed her; a small green ceramic frog had been mislaid, then found—a detail that had escaped me. She set it in the lower left-hand corner of the mise-en-scène.

"*Charmeuse!* I forgot Manet's frog," I said, hoping that I'd smeared enough mucilage on my false whiskers to keep them from falling in my lap.

A bedazzled Michael Teplov gazed at Sarah as at a fire dancing in a Bessemer furnace.

Sarah Jenkins was the spit of Victorine-Louise Meurent, Manet's model for the nude in *Le Déjeuner sur l'herbe* and *Olympia*, painted that same year of 1863. The latter sent Paris into sniggers, fits, and splutters of an outrage even noisier than that produced by the *Luncheon*. His Olympia, a common name given to prostitutes in the demimonde of his day, lies on a divan, naked except for a muddied pink flower in her pinned-up hair, a thin black ribbon at her neck, and a plain gold bracelet on her wrist. She has on a slipper; its companion lies provocatively on the bed. Her face and her attitude are defiant. Most scandalous of all, Meurent looks her viewers in the face, daring them to protest. Even Charles Baudelaire had disapproved of her slender frame, declaring thin nudes to be more indecent than fat ones. Known by the artists who painted her as *la Crevette*, "the Shrimp," Meurent had a petite figure, rosy complexion, and Titian hair.

Harry fiddled with the camera, and with expressive gestures of his hand, he indicated the subtle rearrangement of his subjects—that is to say, us.

"Manet composed his picture on the Renaissance principle of the pyramid," he said. I waited for him to simper. Fortunately, he did not.

He took another look through the viewfinder, then another, and still one more. Only a man of stone would not have been enraptured by Miss Jenkins.

How rosy was her flesh, how charming the breast, how dainty the foot, which was within inches of committing an indecent act on my person. I twitched, as I had once seen a dead frog's leg do, induced by an electric current from a galvanic battery. (Am I any less sensitive than an amphibian in rigor mortis? By God, the ceramic frog might have hopped, had its eyes not been glazed!)

"Hurry up and take the damned thing!" I shouted, irritated by a drop of sweat coursing down my neck.

Harry's head jerked from the viewfinder. "The boat!" he bellowed as he strode toward the watery margin of the cove, mashing spilled cherries as he went.

Unfolding her graceful attitude, Anne let go of

the hem of her chemise. "What's wrong?" she asked, cross because she had broken her difficult pose.

"There ought to be a *rowboat* pulled up on the bank! And two oars! Look!" Exasperated, he held up the colored postcard, as though evidence in a murder trial.

"Oh, what does it matter?" asked Anne, annoyed as she picked river weed and muck from her leg.

"It's not at all like the painting."

"Semblance, Harry," I said soothingly. "We can't hope for more."

"Get on with it!" shouted Robert, sweating in his buttoned brown coat and collar. "What idiocy to dress like this in August!" He gazed at Sarah with unmistakable longing. Likely, it was not desire that he felt, but envy for her state of undress. She seemed so cool and self-possessed.

Frustrated beyond measure, I'd have stripped naked, too, if Sarah Jenkins had not cried out in pain. Enticed by the bleeding cherries, a scout sent out from a colony of wasps had stung her on the breast, mistaking the rose-colored nipple for a delectable morsel. She jumped up from the grass and, shedding the last vestige of her modesty, ran like hell into the trees. Robert and I went after her, followed by a perplexed Michael Teplov. Harry stayed behind to guard his sweet emulsions from aerial attack. Having fallen into the water, Anne dragged herself ashore and sat, sodden and sullen, on a log.

The woods were filled with shrieks. I felt apprehension for Sarah, bewilderment at the universe's contempt for the projects of our puny selves, and the strain of my overworked heart. The chase proved too much for Teplov's weak constitution. He put his arms around a tree and wheezed. Robert and I continued through the spruce grove, in hot pursuit of the runaway nude.

The woods thinned. The sky jumped up before me. The river dazzled and stung my eyes. And then I saw a host of angelic folk, dressed in shining raiment, standing on the shore as they beheld—in astonishment—Sarah, who was sitting in the shallows, her hand pressed to one red and swollen breast.

"Jumping Jesus! We've stumbled into a Baptist picnic!" exclaimed Robert.

She was stunned like a fish yanked from the water and hit on the head with an oar. Whether the cause of her incapacity lay with the wasp or the Baptists was anybody's guess.

"Sarah!" I cried, fearing for her sanity. A fantasist by nature, I pictured her confined in a madhouse, the glory of her radiant flesh dimmed. I saw her once lovely body recumbent beneath the saw of surgeon Gross, who would donate portions of her anatomy to the Mütter.

Like a man who had been temporarily rendered mute, the preacher worked his jaws until he was once more the instrument of the Lord, and in the words of the Son of Man, to be spoken at the end of days to

His servant John of Patmos, the preacher cried unto heaven, "'Behold, I will cast her into a bed . . .'"

"Why you old lecher!" shouted Robert, full of wrath.

"' . . . and them that commit adultery with her into great tribulation . . .'"

The congregants shouted, "Amen!" and turned their communal gaze skyward, as though waiting for the hand of God to hammer the naked harlot and her two procurers into the mud.

Sarah might have been painted by Dante Gabriel Rossetti before he sank into a chloral and whiskey haze—his Lady Lilith combing her red-gold hair. The pinkish flesh of her shoulder, throat, and breast were lovely, but beneath her skin was a corpselike blue.

Michael Teplov splashed through the shallows. Covering Sarah with his coat, he glared at God's elect wet with the water of salvation, and, with an arm around her slender waist, he led her to the shore.

Anne walked, dripping, from the trees. The congregation howled, as if her shimmy had been soaked by the hoses of the firemen of Gomorrah. A few women picked up stones. The men stood back, as most men do when women grow furious. Shielding Sarah with his body, Michael cried, "Stone me!"

Sarah fell into a swoon, while I took an interest in a butterfly that had landed on my shoe.

That swoon, that August afternoon, Anne's wet shimmy, the righteous women's stones . . . they seem to me now to have been the start of my remarkable undoing.

Having daubed Sarah's wounded breast with Croydon mud, Michael Teplov bolted, leaving her to the mercy of women whom not even Jesus could shame into putting down their stones. The butterfly went in search of a less turbulent atmosphere. Unnerved, Robert pulled a water lily to pieces, while hidden among the trees, Harry Owens memorialized the scene with his camera. In my mind's eye, I saw a platinum print exhibited at the Philadelphia Photographic Salons—THE MARTYRS OF CROYDON, 1897 engraved on its brass plate. When immersed in the developer bath, the negative proved to have been ruined by an excess of light. I leave the question of its source to photographers and theologians to debate.

"When sorrows come, they come not single spies, but in battalions," wrote the Bard of Avon. At Croydon, however, our sorrows arrived in a squad of four deputies, their baptismal gear dripping from their recent dunking. Scooping us up in nets such as dogcatchers use, they bound our wrists with whips of green willow.

And what of Michael Teplov? He had *not* turned tail and run, but had gone to get the blunderbuss. Though the deputies may have looked ridiculous in their wet white gowns, they were not fooled by a theatrical prop. One by one, we martyrs to the fine arts were introduced to the interior of a conveyance that, by its smell, served both the Croydon constabulary and its dog pound. The bleating of the Baptists grew fainter as the van headed for the jailhouse. The man at the wheel sang a variation on Paul Dresser's popular air:

> On the banks of the Wabash,
> My dear old mother drowned
> Her sorrows in a washtub of gin;
> The old darling went to Heaven
> with some vomit on her chin . . .

Sarah's head lay on brave Michael Teplov's lap, the rest of her hidden beneath a blanket that smelled of dog. Harry cursed the loss of his camera, which the constables had confiscated as "evidence of an unsavory enterprise" intended to profit by confounding men who purchase dirty postcards. The tripod had been dismembered in the scrummage. Robert was desperate for a cigarette, all of which were sodden.

I took Anne's hand in mine. With her other one, she slapped me. "Never speak to me again, you duff!"

We junketers, who two hours before had been merry, were plunged in gloom. Robert, Harry, Michael, and I were shown to a cell that, until the revival brought down the temperance ax, had been patronized by the town's most notable sots. All that remained of them was a complicated odor of urine, stale tobacco, vomit, lye soap, and carbolic. Anne and Sarah were put elsewhere, to await death by stoning or some other ghastly mode of execution practiced in the provinces.

"What a fiasco!" cried Robert, pulling at his beard. (Mine had been lost in the fracas.)

The sensation of standing in soaking socks may have been foremost in my mind, but I was truly sorry for the day's disaster. "It's all my doing."

"It's just as much mine," said Robert. "I knew you had a loose screw in your character."

A woman arrived bearing clean clothes and a clam pie for the men, and a raisin pie, smocks, and stockings for Anne and Sarah, who, in their cell, were no doubt huddling beneath scratchy blankets left from the Civil War. The town shunned the good woman as a freethinker, she told us. And in violation of federal regulations governing her office, the Croydon postmistress had let it be known that the pariah corresponded with a person in Paris, whom she addressed, on the envelope, as "Monsieur."

I prevailed upon her to wire Thomas Eakins:

ARRESTED BY CROYDON PENNA
CONSTABULARY FOR BLASPHEMY &
INDECENCY STOP WILL YOU VOUCH FOR
MY CHARACTER STOP = OLIVER FISCHER

I will not dwell on the terrors of that night, except to say that, stumbling from my cot to employ the slop bucket, I counted my toes, under the impression that a rat had been at them. We were roused at an ungodly hour by a trio of salvationists singing out of tune for our destruction, to the wheeze of an ancient harmonium. We answered them in strong language that sent them packing.

We broke our fast on gray lumpish gruel and washy coffee, after which we exercised in the prison yard, stung by cherry pits blown through straws by little terrorists whose passions had been inflamed by bubbling public sentiment in favor of hanging us. Through the palings of the fence, I saw Anne and Sarah being driven like a pair of geese by a scowling matron dressed in black.

"Do you think they'll put us to work?" asked Michael, who, as I've mentioned, was far from robust.

"First our characters will be examined and our souls checked for holes, as housewives do socks before getting out their darning eggs and needles."

"Tomorrow, smart aleck, we'll be made to dig real holes for a public privy!" Poor Robert had not slept well, and breakfast had been too scant for a man of his appetite.

"And on the following day, we'll be given brushes, buckets, and Bon Ami with which to clean bird shit from the monuments," I said, hoping to lighten their spirits.

"Then set to weeding the Baptist burying ground, for our sins." A witticism it may not have been, but Harry's remark was welcome, for he seldom made any at all.

"A gallows is more likely," snarled Robert, whose sullenness was beginning to annoy.

I began to dig through the plaster wall with my spoon. "Would you care to hear the story of the Count of Monte Cristo?"

"Save it for later, when we have our port and cigars."

"We ought to write our congressman!" said Harry, boiling over the confiscation of his property.

"Who is our congressman?" asked Robert, taking a sudden interest in politics.

"William Stone," replied Michael, whose father did business with the city's elite.

"I expect that he lives up to his name," said Robert, losing hope of ever leaving Croydon, which had yet to be incorporated into the benevolent city of Philadelphia and, as our treatment showed, followed the example of Christ militant instead of William Penn the wise and tolerant, who had welcomed the Mennonites and the Welsh to his sylvan paradise.

"Say, did the bell strike three just now?"

"I heard four."

"You're both cracked! I counted six clappers."

"You dreamed it."

"Maybe so."

Harry opined with a crack of his knuckles, a sound that brought to mind the knee-splitter and the rack, once in favor with Spanish inquisitors.

"Perhaps a chaplain will visit," said Michael, who was a staunch Catholic.

None did. Denied the comforts of the Savior, we sat and stewed, napped and fretted, and waited to see what would come next.

What came next—or rather, *who*—was Thomas Eakins. He had buttonholed the justice of the peace, who—after the artist's stature had been verified by the cultural editor of the *Croydon Bee*—had ordered our chains struck off. We four men were once again reunited with the ladies.

"Miss Jenkins, Miss Neel," said our deliverer, tipping his hat. "I trust you are unharmed. Art is not normally so harrowing. I've arranged for you to return to Philadelphia by train, along with Mr. Pearson, Mr. Teplov, and Mr. Owens. Mr. Fischer and I will be taking the boat."

Unable to meet his glowering gaze, I lowered mine. "How prettily the green bottle flies decorate it!" I said, regarding a road apple that, in the sun, was as golden as any that grew in the Garden of the Hesperides. One must have the hide of an elephant and an iron stomach to make remarks like Oscar Wilde, who also had wanted "to eat of the fruit of all the trees in the garden of the world."

Eakins and I collected the costume hamper from the scene of the spoiled luncheon. As we carried it through a pine grove to the river and the waiting *Myrtle Jane,* I caught sight of my false beard snagged on a branch. I wanted no part of it. It did not escape Eakins, whose gaze could penetrate the gloom of a surgery, to the putrid matter festering in a boy's leg.

"You'll be wanting to return your whiskers to whatever wardrobe you ransacked in the name of art. It *was* art that brought you here?"

"It was, sir. This was to be my term project."

"Tell me."

We put down the hamper. He sat on it and smoked a cigarette. It would have made a fine picture—the light blowing in the upper stories of the trees, the smoke stretching itself with feline languor into the blue-green air. I should have been a French Impressionist instead of an Asbury Park caricaturist and an artist manqué dressed in motley. A crow cawed in raucous derision.

I explained my conception, the orchestration of details, and the moments leading to its frustrated execution. "It was all the fault of a wasp!"

"Painting *en plein air* has its risks," he said wryly. "Just think if it had been a lightning bolt. That would have shaken your ideas up!"

"It wasn't meant to be a painting! A photograph was what I'd had in mind!"

He looked at me as he would have at a gnat that had landed on a wet canvas and stuck.

"I didn't mean to shout, Mr. Eakins. And I'm grateful for your getting us out of jail."

"What did you hope to accomplish by photographing the Manet?"

I realized that I had not the slightest idea.

"Had you been wearing modern clothes, say, or been sitting in the middle of a Fishtown ash heap, well, that might be a reason to stage such a thing. But what value is there in a clumsy reproduction of an original work, except as pastiche? I see the answer in your eyes. Did anyone ever tell you that you have rat's eyes? Too lazy to attempt a work of art of your own— however derivative it's bound to be—you hoped to stage a succès de scandale. Well, it *was* one in 1866 when I went to Paris to study with Gérôme. But even a French scandal will cool in thirty years."

Oh, he was hard on me!

"There are graver matters for the young artist to consider than a monkey on the Île de la Jatte or van Gogh's ear."

"Such as?" I asked irritably, tired of being lectured.

"Oliver, what do you know of ordinary men and women?"

I shrugged noncommittally.

"The content of their dreams would stump a congress of clairvoyants!"

What does that have to do with the price of butter? I asked him—in my mind, of course.

As we took up our burden once again, he said, although I had the impression that it was not to me he spoke, "I carried Walt Whitman's coffin to the cemetery. I made his death mask. I applied the wax to his cold face. He was my friend."

We continued on to the *Myrtle Jane* in silence, except for the noises of the natural world.

I was happy to be aboard, where I could busy myself with the boiler and see to other nautical duties. To take a boat—even one resembling a floating ice-cream parlor—down a fast-moving channel of turbid water, skirting shoals, snags, stumps, and trash is a grave matter, Mr. Eakins. Read Mark Twain's *Life on the Mississippi*, and you'll understand how harrowing river travel can be for the pilot, while his passengers sit and drink mint juleps.

"The Delaware is hardly the Mississippi River," said Eakins.

Had he read my thoughts? More likely, my inner voice had partly betrayed itself.

We putt-putted southerly, steam writhing from the stack.

"Whose boat is this?"

"My grandfather Barrett's."

"Ah, the painter! You'd do better to apprentice with him instead of saddling your father with debt.

But I guess you prefer to strut about the academy, whose studios, I'm told, you seldom bother to visit."

I said nothing in reply. I kept my eyes on the river.

Eakins took out his sketchbook and began to draw.

I imagined several plots in which I saved him from drowning, and several others in which I did not. I wished that the dirty roughnecks who had stoned us would lay down another barrage. But the Jersey side of the river was empty of delinquents. I saw two bums tipping back bottles on a bulkhead, but nothing else of the common man that Glackens, Luks, Shinn, and Sloan harped on. I peeked at Eakins to see if he noticed the derelicts, but his gaze was concentrated on an alder tree leaning over a cast-iron drainpipe. I spat, forgetting Pop's adage: "Never spit to windward." The nasty gob flew back into my face.

"Draw *that*, why don't you?" I shouted to Eakins above the engine's plunk, plunk, plunk. A dead cat was floating by in the current, kept afloat by its own internal combustion. "Is that real enough for you?"

"You don't have to draw a dead cat to be true to observable life," he replied calmly. "Nor do you have to invent it in Croydon. Take your box of colors downriver to Gloucester City and paint the shad fishermen putting out their nets. There you'll see life!"

Oh, how I burned! I would have rammed the boat against a bar had there been one handy.

"Do you know what I find most obnoxious about

your attempted pastiche?" I felt his eyes on the back of my neck like a chunk of ice. "That you would have reduced the exultant liberation of the human body to a snigger!"

Had I dared, I would have told him that I saw precious little exultation in Manet's picture. The figures on the grass seemed occupied with their own thoughts, which—I'd have put money on it—had nothing to do with one another, much less with the joy of sex.

By the last reach in the river before the mouth of Frankford Creek, my irritation had been replaced by dread. What punishment would Eakins mete out to me? What penance would I need to make? I stowed the yachting cap. I rolled down my sleeves and fastened my shirt's top button. Eyeing my face in the shaving mirror Franklin used when backing into a slip, I was shocked by my unkempt hair. Taking the wind into consideration, I spat on my hand and combed my fingers through it. You look bedraggled, Ollie, old stick! You look like what the cat dragged in and the woman of the house finished off with a shovel.

Nervously, I brought the *Myrtle Jane* to rest against the dock. Tripping over a cleat, I nearly fell into Frankford Creek but recovered my balance, if not my poise, before I could be baptized in its oily water. Industrial America erected its temples on rivers and their tributaries and made burnt offerings to progress of various odors—none so pleasant as frankincense or myrrh. I took the kettle off the stove, so to say, tied up the *Myrtle Jane*, and prepared to face a music such as Earth will make when the Almighty, with a sweep of His hand, flings it into outer darkness. To be plain, I waited for Eakins to skin me alive. His wrath, however, was forestalled by the appearance of my grandfather.

"Hello, Ollie! How was your outing?"

"Pop! What are you doing here?"

"I came by trolley to draw the river." He smiled at me as though the wild oats of youth were clinging to my clothes. "I see you made a night of it. Where's Anne?"

"Indisposed. She took the train home."

"She slipped through your fingers, then," he said sadly.

Eakins joined us on the dock. "And who might this gentleman be?"

"Mr. Thomas Eakins, this is my grandfather Franklin Barrett."

They shook hands not in the effete way of two swells met by chance at the Union Club, but as equals in the rough-and-tumble democracy sung by Whitman in his *Leaves*—that is to say, each tried to squeeze the other's hand blue.

"I'm glad to meet you, Mr. Eakins. I'm a great admirer of your work."

"As I am of yours, Mr. Barrett."

"You've seen something of mine?" Franklin's eyes lit up.

"A big painting of a jolly woman with a flower in her hair."

"Where was she hanging?"

"Over the bar at Kelsey's."

"There's a sad story there, Mr. Eakins."

"Call me Tom, and, if you'll allow me, I'll call you Franklin."

They sat on the dock, legs dangling over the water, in much the same attitude as the two bums I'd seen taking the air beside the river.

"The woman in the picture is dead. Her husband, a knob-headed Pole, was an oiler on a merchantman. 'Stosch,' he was called—short for Stanislaw. When his ship put in to the yard for repairs, he decided to drop in on the missus. But first he stopped at Kelsey's for a drink."

"I can picture the scene: the man standing at the bar, his large hands around the neck of the beer bottle—"

"It was rye whiskey, Tom."

"The drink of frontier America," said Eakins, watching the dusty toes of his shoes pass in and out of a slant of sunlight, which broke in pieces on the water. "I drank plenty when I was out in Dakota Territory in '87. You were saying?"

"Stosch tipped back his glass and saw, as the rye

slipped down his gullet, a woman who reminded him of his Stella."

"You caught her likeness, then."

"Dead-on. Stosch saw red, jumped clean over the bar, and shredded the picture with his folding knife."

"A sad end for a work of art."

"It was. Then he broke Kelsey's jaw, went home in a rage, and threw poor Stella out a second-story window."

"He defenestrated her."

"He did."

Eakins shouted over his shoulder at me, "There's real life for you right under your nose, you horse's ass—not some sophomoric parody of a French picnic that never happened!"

"What's the boy been up to, Tom?"

"Well, let me tell you." And so he told the tale of my downfall.

Now and again Pop would guffaw, gasp, or shout, "You don't say!" "I'll be damned!" "The cocky so-and-so!"

Franklin and Eakins gave me a look such as Brutus and Cassius did Caesar before they stabbed him. But the two artists—one great, the other middling—couldn't keep a straight face. "What're you going to do with him, Tom?" asked Franklin, all laughter spent.

Eakins turned serious. "I was prepared to throw him out on his ear, but having made your acquaintance, Franklin, I believe I'll give him a second chance."

"Don't go out on a limb on my account." Pop got up from the dock and wandered off to sketch the river. I had the feeling that he was giving Eakins a chance to light into me, or me the privacy in which to humble myself.

"Ollie, it's not your lack of originality that's at fault. We don't expect our young men and women to know what they want to say, much less how to say it."

"I don't have anything to say."

"The artist learns to speak through his pictures."

I considered pirating the *Myrtle Jane* and lighting out for Mexico. I would sit in the sun and make clay pots or, if she proved seaworthy, do as Gauguin did and make a run for Tahiti. What swell pictures I could paint, surrounded by such delicious fauna!

"You don't have to paint like John Sloan or Robert Henri. Factory workers rolling up their sleeves to scuffle in the yard, prostitutes, toughs, broken-down bums, and pugilists are not the only subjects for an artist. Paint a picnic, if you must, but make it modern—something you'd see on a Sunday in Fairmount Park and not in the Bois de Boulogne or the Tuileries."

"My grandfather paints sailboats, tulips, and naked taproom Delilahs!"

"To be an amateur and to know it is contentment. To be one and think you're something more is to be an affected, pompous snot." For a moment, I thought that he would punch me.

Walking to the end of the dock, Eakins squatted beside Franklin, who was translating the creek that his eyes saw to the creek that his hand laid down in pastels on a sheet of paper.

I stood behind the two men. How could Eakins be forgiving of Franklin's incompetence as a draftsman? On the following day, when I went to his office to receive my formal dressing-down, he said in answer to that question, "Franklin's work has the charm of naïveté, which is forgivable in those who paint for their own pleasure and that of their friends or to put bread on the table when nothing else will."

I guessed that Pop had mentioned the things he'd painted on old glass negatives and sold door-to-door after the panic of 1893, which, four years later, still pinched.

By the shore, the reeds stirred and quickened as the water rose and fell. I could feel them tremble each time a little wave washed through them.

"The play of light and shadow on that dilapidated boathouse—you caught it, Franklin," said Eakins approvingly.

"Get down your highest light, then your shadow, then work in between until you get them harmonious."

"I do the same."

A bird flew into the scene.

"My father and I had a shack in the southern

New Jersey marshes. We went there to hunt rail. Do you know the bird?"

"I do indeed," replied Franklin.

"Wonderful days! We'd cross the river by ferry to Camden, then take the Jersey Central Railroad to Bridgeton, county seat of Cumberland, and finish the trip on a spur to the village of Fairton on the Cohansey River. We hired our Negro neighbor to pole a johnboat through the tidal meadows fed by the Delaware Bay, flushing the small birds from the salt grass as we went. They grunt, you know, rails do. Did you ever hear one?"

"Not that I recall," replied Franklin, who had been listening intently to the other man.

"I don't know this part of the river."

"Not much sculling on the Delaware."

"The Schuylkill's the river for rowing!" said Eakins, closing his hands as if to feel the oars in his fists.

"That's so."

They went on like that until a great shadow swung across the water and the light went out of the creek like a rag wrung dry. We stood and watched it become a dead thing. Franklin closed his sketchbook.

"I'd like to have that picture, Franklin."

I nearly fell over.

"My pleasure, Tom." He tore a sheet from the book.

Eakins folded it as one might a manuscript page written by George Washington or the Venerable

Bede and put it in his coat pocket. "One night we should tour the 'galleries' to see your painted women."

They shook hands warmly.

"Say, Tom, why don't you have supper with us?"

"Another time. I have to get back to the city."

"What about you, Ollie? Supper? Your grandmother would be pleased."

To escape Eakins's slams on the long trip back to town, I went home with Pop.

In the morning, I went to see Eakins. He stood behind a drawing table that was gouged, fretted, and had a knocked-about look made worse by dried smears and puddles of paint. A quantity of Mars red put me in mind of butchery. I waited to be acknowledged, nervously biting my nails, a childish habit resurrected by dread.

"Stop that!"

I shoved my offending hands into my pockets. His teeth looked sharp, and the words in his downturned mouth could cut a peacock to shreds till nothing was left but the eyes on its tail and its simper.

He was tormenting an artist's manikin. The little wooden man looked in danger of being torn limb from articulated limb or having its white oak head yanked off.

"Miss Prudery can dabble in the guts of a dead

man filleted on the dissecting table, but all hell breaks loose if she's shown a male model's penis."

He had spoken to the little man, and I saw no reason to comment. My throat felt as if a slug or a toad was sitting on my epiglottis. I had to clear it or choke. I spat into my handkerchief.

Eakins's eyes blazed.

I waited for sparks to fly and land in the pencil shavings on the table. I shut my eyes and heard the screams of women running, panicked and naked, from the drawing-from-life classes. I heard the frantic gongs of the engines and saw two firemen named Ajax and Hector carry them from the conflagration and into the street, to the cheers of assembled gawkers. (My imagination is of the feverish sort.)

"Well, Fischer, what am I to do with you?"

I referred him to last night's mention of a second chance. Either I was speaking in a dead language or he'd forgotten the conversation. He fiddled with the damned manikin. Suddenly, he opened a drawer, tossed in the little fellow, and shut it with a bang that made me jump. "Do you deserve it? Director Morris thinks not."

"He knows?"

"News travels fast when public decency is outraged. A journalist from the *Inquirer* got on to Morris this morning and ruined his breakfast. He's fit to be tied. Is he right in wanting to kick you out?"

It was a heads-or-tails moment. Hazarding all, I replied, "Yes, sir, he is."

He rubbed his hands together like a spiteful witness at a hanging.

"I want you to conduct an experiment."

"What sort of experiment?" The word conjured up test tubes, retorts, and petri dishes put to nefarious purposes in the laboratory of Dr. Frankenstein.

"In misery."

"I don't follow."

He opened the desk drawer and took out a yellowed newspaper. I thought I could hear the little man's anguished cry before Eakins shut him up inside again. He pulled out a section of the paper and turned to the second page, which carried an article entitled "An Experiment in Misery," by Stephen Crane.

Eakins leaned back in his chair and worked his jaw. "Crane wasn't much older than you are now when I met him at the New York Art Students League. He was living hand to mouth in the league's old building on East Twenty-third Street, along with several young men who knew the difference between painting a picture and pulling a prank." He scowled at me. "Crane was, in fact, a starving artist driven to a life of ruinous destitution because of a necessity that few who do not burn can understand. It destroyed his health; I expect he will flame out before much longer."

"Mr. Eakins, what do you want me to do?"

"You should be able to answer that after you've read the story."

I put it in my bag, beside my drawing things.

"Your grandfather is not a serious painter, nor does he see the world as a cadaver spread on the dissecting table, waiting for the knife. He paints a world that has never and nowhere been. I tried as much when I painted *The Swimming Hole*, which the public naturally misunderstood as something Greek. Walt Whitman tried in *Leaves of Grass*."

I started to speak, but he waved me away as one would a fly from a jam pot. "The world has a heavy hand, Oliver. Don't be such a fool as to think that it will spare a bug like you. Now get out!"

I peeked into the life class and was satisfied to see that Sarah's swelling had gone down. Then I waited for Robert, who, at that hour, was in the lecture hall, listening to Thomas Anshutz rail against the Pre-Raphaelites, trompe l'oeil, and William Morris's Arts and Crafts movement.

When the lecture had finished, we sat on a park bench beneath a genial sun, where misery surely could not flourish, though maggots might.

"What's that?" asked Robert.

"Eakins pulled it from the *New York Press*."

"April 22, 1894. Say, this old rag should have been martyred to cigarette wrappers years ago!"

"He told me to read this piece." I pointed to "An

Experiment in Misery." Leaning our heads together, we read Crane's preface:

Two men stood regarding a tramp.

"I wonder how he feels?" said one, reflectively. "I suppose he is homeless, friendless, and has, at the most, only a few cents in his pocket. And if this is so, I wonder how he feels?"

The other, being the elder, spoke with an air of authoritative wisdom. "You can tell nothing of it unless you are in that condition yourself. It is idle to speculate about it from this distance."

"I suppose so," said the younger man, and then he added as from an inspiration: "I think I'll try it. Rags and tatters, you know, a couple of dimes, and hungry, too, if possible. Perhaps I could discover his point of view or something near it."

"Sounds like one of your crackbrained ideas," said Robert, spitting a lunger on the grass.

"Eakins wants me to do the same. He was grouchy as hell."

"You know, he's in hot water with Morris and the board."

"Because of me?"

Robert scuffed up some dust. "Paula Meyers

asked him how the male pelvis works, and he showed her his."

"Oh, murder!"

"When he got hauled up before the board to explain himself, he said that 'the beauty of a body in motion can't be taught by looking at a corpse.'"

"Double murder!"

"Their blue noses have been out of joint ever since he ordered the male models to take off their loincloths."

We watched a pair of sparrows beat their wings in the dust.

"I'm not sure I know where the poor live," I said, turning my head, as if I might see them lurking just beyond my peripheral vision.

"Alban will know."

I looked up at the statue of Billy Penn, lording it over the city. Smart alecks like to show him to the girls. They point out his raised right hand. Stiff and admonishing, it seems to urge us to slow our pace as we travel along God's path. Viewed from another angle, the hand becomes Penn's bronze willy, ready to sow seeds of brotherly love. Perspective is the great thing in art, as it is in politics. The Chinese see a rabbit in the moon; we see a man.

Flimflam

A newspaper is a market
Where wisdom sells its freedom
And melons are crowned by the crowd.

—STEPHEN CRANE

Philadelphia

The atheist and Marxist of our clique, Alban Weisz painted dismal allegories of corruption and oppression. For motifs, he favored neoclassical banks like my father's, squatting on the back of the People, crucifixions and martyrdoms in modern dress, octopi strangling ragged women and children, and—something of an idée fixe—Kansas farmers skewered on pitchforks, gory scenes evoking Vlad the Impaler. If it hadn't been for Eakins, Alban would have painted his pictures in the home for Philadelphia's wayward sons.

"Where's Alb likely to be at this time of day?" I asked Robert.

"At his uncles' store on Kelley Street, building a float for Saturday's Anti-Imperialist League parade."

Kurtág brothers' store was within spitting distance of the mint, several marbled halls of finance, and churches praying for the rich who tithe their way into paradise and from whom all blessings flow, although not into the pockets of the poor. At certain hours of the day, the shadow of the Keystone

Bank engulfed the furniture store on which it had foreclosed. The signboard had been removed, and the windows whitewashed to conceal the interior from curious eyes. Robert knocked at the front door.

"Hello, Robert!" said his paint-bespattered friend.

"Hello, Alb! Are you sharpening the guillotine?"

"The better to cut off your prick."

The two young men gave each other a comradely embrace.

"Come in."

"You know *this* enemy of the people," said Robert, shaking an accusatory finger at me. "Off with his head!"

"Ollie," said Alban—somewhat coolly, I thought.

Before I could say a word, he turned and shouted at a young woman who was slapping black paint onto an enormous boot. Six other artist manqué types were applying paints of garish hues to a behemoth that rose up to the skylight. The floor where Biedermeier chairs had once sat like prosperous burghers admiring themselves in the wax and varnish was beyond saving by mere mop and broom.

Alban caught me frowning. "My uncles don't give a bloody shit if we turn the place into a shambles."

"How in hell will you get it out of here?" exclaimed Robert, his head thrown back to take in the gigantic uncle of us all.

"In the dead of night, as befits our sinister

purpose, and in pieces. My uncles will take them over to the brickworks in the van. It belongs to them till the end of the month. We'll put Humpty Dumpty back together again in the yard."

He showed us a sketch of Uncle Sam. Constructed of wood, plaster, lath, a stump-pulling chain, and odds and ends collected from the city's dumping grounds, he would stand twenty feet tall, from his Congress gaiters to the top of his white beaver hat. Alban pointed to its wide blue band of stars, as well as the old geezer's red-and-white-striped trousers, blue swallow-tailed coat, gold vest, wing collar, and loose red bow tie. The expansionist Yankee's right foot rested on the neck of a Cuban peasant, a dusky babe at her breast. He held a chain fastened to an iron collar around the throat of a Cuban cane cutter. The embossment on the collar proclaimed its owner: THE AMERICAN SUGAR REFINING COMPANY.

"Can I count on you lunkheads to march with us?"

"Absolutely!" said Robert.

"For sure!" I enthused.

"That's white of you!"

"Say, Alb, did you ever read this story by Stephen Crane? Show him, Ollie."

He sat on a broken-backed chair, Robert and I on a threadbare Empire couch—all that remained after the inventory had been seized.

"I heard it read during the Pullman Strike. Gee,

that Crane can write! Did I ever tell you I shook Eugene V. Debs's hand?"

"What's it about?" I asked, hoping to get the gist and skip the rest.

"A man gets himself up as a Bowery bum. It was Crane himself, taking a turn in the gutter for one of his articles. He's got on a shabby suit, an old derby with a torn brim, broken shoes, and a dirty coat. To see him, you'd take him for another down-and-outer tramping the streets on a cold, drizzly night. He shuffles down to Park Row and sits on a bench surrounded by other sorry cases. They get rousted by the cops and slump off to Chatham Park. 'An Experiment in Misery,' see?"

"What else?"

"He falls in with an honest-to-God tramp. They put together their pennies for a two-cent beer and a bowl of soup, about as nourishing as green scum on a rain barrel. Night's coming, so the guy shows Crane where they can flop for four cents apiece, together with a hundred other stinking, snoring bums packed like fish on slabs of ice. It's that cold, see. In the morning, they have a two-cent roll and a penny bowl of coffee."

"That's it?" I ask, somewhat disappointed.

"Stephen Crane, Hamlin Garland's another— they've got what William Dean Howells calls 'proportion,' which is what most people lack who've got their noses stuck up their asses. Give it here."

I handed him the newspaper. He turned to the end of the story and read in the voice of moral authority he sometimes assumed: "'And in the background a multitude of buildings, of pitiless hues and sternly high, were to him emblematic of a nation forcing its regal head into the clouds, throwing no downward glances; in the sublimity of its aspirations ignoring the wretches who may flounder at its feet. . . .'

"Here's the crux of the matter, Ollie: 'He confessed himself an outcast, and his eyes from under the lowered rim of his hat began to glance guiltily, wearing the criminal expression that comes with certain convictions.'"

Alban gave me back the paper. "What's it to you?"

"Something for Eakins."

"I guess he raised all kinds of hell with you two over Sunday's agony."

"You heard about it?" asked Robert.

"Who hasn't? Fischer, you're a nasty old lobcock!"

"Where would Crane go if he wanted to take in the lower depths of the Quaker City?" asked Robert.

"Mifflin Street down by the river, maybe. The Southwark neighborhood."

"Alban, how many stars on the hatband?" asked a girl, teetering at the top of a ladder.

"Three." He turned abruptly to a young man standing on a chair, a housepainter's brush dripping American vermilion. "Holy shit, Stowman! Look what you did to Uncle Sam's pants!"

"We'll see you at the brickworks on Saturday at seven," said Robert, starting for the door.

"Righto!" Alban strode to the counterfeit giant and started in on his gold buttons. As we headed for the door, he shouted, "Down with despots! Up with lobcocks!"

On a bench behind City Hall, Robert and I sat and contemplated pigeons wrangling over scraps. Where is the peaceable kingdom William Penn dreamed of, when the lion shall lie down with the lamb?

"You're on your own, Ollie. One pig's breakfast is all I can swallow in a single summer."

"Crane went on his own hook, and so will I."

We watched the pigeons pecking one another.

"What happens if some big brute thinks it great sport to bust your head?"

"I'll bequeath it to the Mütter."

I was not so full of mustard as I let on to be. But at the time, I had a compass (I wouldn't have called it a moral one) that pointed the way forward: If my father wouldn't approve, I did it. To be a son is, oftentimes, to act out of spite and stupidity toward one's progenitor. One doesn't have to be Kronos to hate his pater.

"You'll need a costume," said Robert, following

a pause in the conversation in which he gave up any hope of dissuading me.

"I'll find some old rags in a bin somewhere."

"My aunt is wardrobe mistress at the Walnut Street Theatre. She'll hook you up with some duds that won't give you scabies."

At the theater, Robert introduced me to a woman ironing Romeo's tights.

"Oliver Fischer, meet my aunt Lucille. My friend Ollie is in dire need of a favor." He summarized my plight, his hands sawing the air, contrary to Hamlet's advice to the players. "I told him you might fix him up with some rags and tatters."

Lucille ruminated awhile, chewing a cud of Frank Fleer's bubble gum. "I have a suit of clothes that belonged to Edwin Booth when he owned the theater back in the seventies." She found it at the bottom of a hamper of cast-off and mismatched apparel. "I've been saving it to patch torn coats and pants. Booth was about your size. Try them on. Here, take this, too." She handed me a frayed and yellowed shirt lacking a collar button.

I went behind a screen and dressed. "It stinks of camphor flakes."

"All to the good," she said.

I showed myself.

Robert and Lucille conferred. She tugged down the coattails. She put a few stitches in a shoulder seam that was ready to give way. She buttoned the coat, then undid the button beneath my chin so that the shabby shirt would show to best advantage. Still not satisfied, she bit off a button and replaced it with a safety pin. She pumiced the elbows to make them shine and found, in the apparently inexhaustible hamper, an ancient top hat such as cabbies used to wear. "What do you think, Robbie?"

He made a face. "He looks like a lunkhead in that hat."

She took an old slouch hat spotted with grease and rain and stuck it on my head.

"That's the ticket! How about it, Ollie?"

I stepped in front of a pier glass and studied the effect.

"He looks a treat!" said Lucille.

"What about a pair of shoes?" asked Robert.

"None to spare."

"That's all right," I said. "I'll smear a little mud on mine."

I went behind the screen and got into my own clothes while Lucille wrapped up my costume in brown paper and string. Robert and I left the theater for the larger playhouse of the streets.

Swinging their truncheons, two policemen stood in the shadow cast by City Hall, which took the shine from their badges and copper buttons.

"Say, bum, where're you off to?"

Glad to have them confirm the strength of the theatrical illusion in which I had cloaked myself, I replied, "To take in the sights on Mifflin Street, Officers."

I smiled at the towering pair. Their tall leather helmets increased their visibility and self-importance, not to say, menace. No longer dangling, their sticks bristled dangerously.

"What for?"

"To improve my mind."

The good condition of my teeth and the nicety of my grammar caused the pair to take a giant step backward. They glanced at me and then at each other before closing in on me again. I felt their big boots pressing on my toes. I feared for my corn. I could smell the beer and pork pie they'd had for lunch.

"How may I be of service, Officers?" I asked with the urbanity of a swindler and the solicitude of a priest. The two minced and smirked like the smart alecks Kolb and Dill on the stage of the Trocadero. Try as I might to keep my nerve, the blood in my banging heart gushed upward, putting color in my cheeks.

"Would you look at him blush! Ain't he sweet?"

Just then a police sergeant climbed down from a horse-drawn Black Maria. "What in the hell are you two idiots doing?"

Instantly, the lowly plods lay off the pantomime

and stood at attention. "Just having some sport with this vag'," one cop replied. The other cop nodded so emphatically that his helmet flew from his head and bounded into the street like a melon jumping from a grocer's wagon.

"You're not here to enjoy yourselves! Get him in the van."

They shoved me inside and slammed the door. When I started to object, the sergeant beat the barred window with his stick. "That's enough out of you!"

I began to sweat and feared that panic would undermine my bowels. Until then, I'd been the merest sketch of a man, waiting for experience to enhance it. My doubts had not been so keen as Thomas's nor my sorrows so oppressive as young Werther's; they had been proportionate to a sheltered life, when a toothache seemed monstrous.

The heavy door swung open. For a moment, I thought they meant to let me go, with a caution, perhaps, or a kick in the ass. "Now listen, you bums . . ." said the sergeant. Unnoticed by me, five other men were sitting in the deep shadows at the rear of the van. "This here being a democracy, you get to choose. What'll it be? Madhouse or poorhouse. The jailhouse is full at the present time. Make up your minds!" He slammed the van door and left the tiny republic to decide its fate.

The five initiates argued the relative merits of both houses, mainly the beds, the bill of fare, the ferocity of the vermin, and the scenery on view through the windows. One praised the asylum's stew meat. In rebuttal, another cited its bedbugs and spoke warmly of the poorhouse. A third, who had been a recent guest of that venerable institution, recalled that the stink from a nearby tannery had been almost past enduring. The fourth and most ragged of the caucus spoke disdainfully of the asylum for its neglect of elementary standards of hygiene. Sitting aloof, the fifth man refused to commit himself.

I began to retch in the unwholesome air of the "meat wagon," as Robert called it.

"Don't spill your guts in here!"

The sergeant opened the door. How fresh was the air that poured into that dark and fetid box! How invigorating! Had I the skill, I'd have penned a sonnet on it in my sketchbook. "Well, gents, what's it to be?"

"You be spokesman," said the worst-dressed fellow of the company, who, now and then, coughed as one does in the preliminary stages of consumption.

"Let's put it to a vote," I said, taking no pride in my preeminence.

"The asylum."

"Poorhouse."

"Asylum. The cemetery behind the poorhouse is a depressing sight."

"Poorhouse."

The quiet fellow acquiesced.

"The deciding vote is yours," said the sergeant, an able parliamentarian despite his rough manner.

"Poorhouse," I said emphatically.

"The people have spoken!" He slammed the heavy iron door with enough force to ruffle my mustache.

I closed my eyes and, lulled by the swaying of the van on its leaf springs, dropped off to sleep.

I was floating down Broad Street not on Alban's pageant wagon bearing the American colossus but on Cleopatra's painted barge, on the river Nile, as witnessed by Mark Antony:

> *The barge she sat in, like a burnished throne,*
> *Burned on the water: the poop was beaten gold;*
> *Purple the sails, and so perfumèd that*
> *The winds were lovesick with them . . .*

Instead of "Egypt," the Shrimp sat beside me, both of us without our clothes. Instead of "pretty dimpled boys, like smiling Cupids," black boys dressed in spotless livery stood in the gutters of the flooded street, holding lanterns and singing, "I'm going down to the river of Jordan."

Even after one of the vagrants with whom I was to lodge had roughly shaken me awake, I was reluctant to leave the dream behind me. *I smelled the "strange invisible perfume" and saw Thomas Eakins ply an oar and Franklin Barrett, his yachting cap pulled down over his ears, ply the other as the royal barge made its stately progress to the poorhouse.*

We climbed down from the van into Meadow

Avenue, where Blockley Almshouse stands on the western side of the Schuylkill River, which separates the destitute, the bedeviled, and the dead from the strongholds of capitalism in the city proper. The castaway who had complained of the proximity of the poorhouse to the cemetery was right: They are the last stops on the way to a lying-in without end. When the front gate had groaned open to receive us, a woman laid waste by Bright's disease was being carried out the back.

North of the poorhouse, the University of Pennsylvania shone like John Winthrop's "city upon a hill." The college was founded by Benjamin Franklin, who had emigrated from Boston in 1723. His capital consisting of "three puffy rolls," Ben was no better equipped than Crane's man in "An Experiment in Misery." With neither a destination nor a friend, he met a Quaker by chance in Chestnut Street who took him to the Crooked Billet, where he could get a cheap supper and a bed. The poor are always with us, sayeth the Lord. They are seen to best advantage at a distance, sayeth the righteous, or in the pages of Jacob Riis's photographic essay *How the Other Half Lives*.

The stink of unwashed men was almost masked by the stinging odor of carbolic soap, varmint powders, and a smell that put me in mind of a burning match, which instantly incited a craving for a cigarette. Applying to my fellow inmates, we discovered that there was nary a crumb of tobacco among us, with the exception of a few golden flakes stuck like lint in the pocket seam of Joe S—. Joe was the fellow in the van who had stood aloof from our debate on the relative merits of the city's so-called charitable institutions. He was a kindly soul, notwithstanding his stammer, and shared his tobacco crumbs with us.

We were ushered—or rather, shoved—into a gray room containing half a dozen cast-iron bathtubs filled, nearly to sloshing, with hot gray water. The windows, placed high up on the wall, were dripping with steam. Leaving our clothes in the anteroom, where we'd been dowsed with flea powder, we got into the tubs and allowed ourselves the luxury of being scrubbed, head to toe, by a pair of fat fellows looking like my idea of eunuchs, wielding long-handled brushes. They applied themselves to their work until our skins reeked of phenol and shrieked—unheard by human ears—like boiled lobsters. Finished, we were handed towels. They were frayed and gray. Returning to the anteroom, we found, waiting for us, gray trousers, gray shirts, and gray underclothes. The color of arsenic was the theme and uniform hue of Blockley Almshouse.

"Excuse me," I said to an orderly. "Where are my clothes?"

"In the incinerator."

"Good God, that suit belonged to Edwin Booth!"

"Hard luck to him."

"Where're my things?" asked another of the well-scrubbed fraternity.

"You had no things."

"I ought to have had something!" said the inmate, suspicions raised and feelings hurt.

The orderly wearily shook his head. I supposed that the palaver was old hat. He handed a mouth organ to another of the fallen. It made a sour wheeze through reeds doubtless rusted by his spit.

A broken tobacco pipe went to a short man, who shined it on the side of his nose.

The despot of the bath gave me back my pencil and sketchbook. Chance or divine ill will had provided an assortment of character types such as I would have sketched on Mifflin Street, in my pursuit of abject misery. "Where's the money that was in my pocket?" I asked. Lacking Crane's courage to attempt the experiment with a "couple of dimes," I'd sallied forth with two dollars in quarters wrapped in a handkerchief.

"Weren't none."

"I had them when I took off my clothes!" I shouted.

The man gave me the hairy back of his hand. I had fallen into the mill of justice and was being coarsely ground. He laughed and pulled me after him into a workshop. Hammers and saws in hand, my new friends were making birdhouses. I was turned over to a burly fellow wearing a leather apron, who showed me to an empty workbench. After that, we were shown—or rather, pushed—into the refectory, as the dining hall was called. We ate gray soup flavored with pieces of stringy meat and lumps of uncertain origin. The bread may not have been weeviled, such as is fed to mutinous sailors locked in the forecastle, but it was stale. The consumptive of our coterie, who'd had some education before falling on hard times, called it "toothsome." He had only one of them, standing solitary in a ruined gum, which reminded me of a tombstone.

Dinner at an end, I thought I'd stroll the poorhouse grounds and get some fresh air into my spongy gray lungs. I would make do without a cigarette. Let that be my sacrifice to the art that Eakins espouses! The door was locked. Turning to an attendant, I asked, politely, that it be opened. He gave me a smack in the face.

We were herded into a common room and there encouraged, with the stick that beat the time, to sing patriotic songs then in favor with lovers of Cuban sugar and Hawaiian pineapples. I recall being impressed by a fervent refrain that voiced, undisguised and unabashed, America's desire to become a world power:

> Ten thousand miles from tip to tip
> Uncle Sam will bestride the Orient;
> From Puerto Rico to the Philippines,
> The plucky eagle will shit on the pleasant

Isles of Hawaii, Guam, and Wake—
Then sell the guano at a profit.

We were rewarded with tea and Maryland beat biscuits, which, instead of leavening, are coaxed into rising by axes.

The musical evening having concluded, a spinsterish, sallow-faced fellow packed up his melodeon and left. Until bedtime, we could do as we pleased within the almshouse walls, rules, and regulations. Proponents of hygiene and Malthus's principle of population, the authorities forbade the intermingling of the sexes. Willy-nilly intermingling, as everyone knows, is at the root of poverty, crime, and madness. (The same can be said for certain acts of Congress.)

I took up my book and sharpened the pencil point between my teeth. My pocketknife had been confiscated before I had been helped, with a kick in the ass, into the Black Maria. Well, Ollie, old friend, you did not have to go in search of the poor—your corn nagging at each step—the poor have been brought to you, a wonder on par with that of Muhammad and the mountain. I began to sketch the men around me. From envy and spitefulness to gentleness and good humor, they displayed, unself-consciously, the human qualities that artists' models are paid to emulate. I captured A cheating at cards, and B covetously glancing at C's wedding ring. What sorrow of forsakenness did it signify? Grimacing, D plunged a finger in his ear, as if bees resided in its hive. With a face empty of all emotion, E twisted a dead tooth in his gum, while F fingered a wen. G blew his nose on his sleeve. H sat apart and silently wept. Most poignant of all, a man—only a few years my senior—stood at a window and looked out across the unlighted poorhouse lawn at the blazing windows of the university.

"What a spectacle!" he cried, as though the gas and electric lights blooming in the citadel of learning were a thousand flaming girandoles.

"What do you see?" I asked, as one would a spiritualist at a séance.

After a lengthy silence, he spoke, "I see myself as I was only a year ago."

"You were a student there?"

"Of music, yes." He spoke quietly, somewhat distantly, like someone in a trance.

"What happened?"

"The music of the spheres turned sour because of a hostile astronomical conjunction."

I took a step back from the window, thinking that he'd been brought to the almshouse by mistake and that he belonged in the asylum. I started to walk away, when he grabbed me by my arm. "Let me borrow your pencil and paper a moment."

I gave them to him and watched, amazed, as he sketched . . . a kind of music, I suppose, such as might be heard at the twilight of the gods, called *Götterdämmerung* by Wagner.

After my rehabilitation, I saw the thing again, in a newspaper story about a young musician who hanged himself in the Blockley Almshouse lumber room—tired, I shouldn't wonder, of making houses for birds he would never hear sing.

I went upstairs and sat on the edge of my cot. I looked at the drawings, none of which was an exaggeration of the original, because the poor are their own caricatures. A man with a running sore, a child with rickets, a woman with a shriveled breast are rarely seen amid the well nourished. A man who drags one leg behind him after a railway accident, a child who lost her toes to tenement rats, a woman whose jaw has been eaten away while working in a match factory or has gone blind from her husband's venereal disease—poverty has made them less than human in the eyes of those who shun them. They're the unlucky ones, we tell ourselves as we sit beneath the trees, watching smoke from our cigarettes writhe among the breathless leaves, on an ordinary summer's night.

Stephen Crane, your so-called experiment in misery was no more than a walking tour of the lower depths. Such men as those that lay groaning in their cots cannot wash their hands of it so easily.

I woke to find myself in a room packed with sleeping men. Stephen Crane described the scene thus:

> The youth sat on his cot and peered about him. There was a gas-jet in a distant part of the room that burned a small flickering orange-hued flame. It caused vast masses of tumbled shadows in all parts of the place, save where, immediately about it, there was a little grey haze. As the young man's eyes became used to the darkness he could see upon the cots that thickly littered the floor the forms of men sprawled out, lying in death-like silence or heaving and snoring with tremendous effort, like stabbed fish.

When I bent down to get the chamber pot, I saw that my sketchbook was gone. I'd left it underneath my shoes. Angry, I would have searched every man and cot, but desperate men with nothing to lose should never be underestimated or roughly awakened from their dreams.

Three years before, on the knife edge of the depression, such men had marched in Jacob Coxey's army, from Ohio to Washington, demanding that they be put to work building bridges, roads, canals, and aqueducts. On the green mowed lawn of the Capitol Building, Coxey and his lieutenants were arrested for walking on the grass. The Army of the Commonwealth in Christ, as it was called, disbanded and went home, its soldiers footsore, broken, and still poor.

No sooner had I washed my face and combed my fingers through my hair than I knocked on the superintendent's door.

"What do you want?" he asked brusquely.

"Mr. Armitage, last night someone stole my sketchbook."

"This sketchbook, Mr. Fischer?" It was underneath the morning's *Public Ledger* on his desk.

"Why, yes. Where did you find it?"

"Mr. Greeley found it under your cot."

"Why didn't he leave it there?"

"He thought you had stolen it."

"It was stolen from *me*! By Mr. Greeley!"

"What's a vag doing with such an expensive item?"

"I'm an artist. Look, don't you recognize the inmates? I drew them last night."

"They all look the same to me." He folded his hands on a drawing of a man gazing at his palms, as if to see his future there. "Can you prove it's yours?"

I could not think how.

Armitage slid the book and pencil across the desk. "Draw me if you can."

Damn it, my hand began to shake!

"I thought so!" he jeered, taking back the book. "You're a thief, Fischer, if that's really your name."

"I'm a student at the Pennsylvania Academy of the Fine Arts!" I shouted. "My teacher is Thomas Eakins!"

"Eakins is notorious and no better than a pornographer who lets young men and women cavort in the nude! You both belong in Eastern State Penitentiary. I'd like to see you talk to the warden the way you talk to me! You'd be spitting teeth, mister."

"Let me send Mr. Eakins a telegram!"

"A character reference from that degenerate won't do you a bit of good."

"My father, then. He's comptroller of the Western Savings Bank."

His eyes narrowed as his suspicions grew. "What's a banker's son doing on the bum?"

As I told my story, his eyes were fixed on a glitter of light playing on a paper knife. I wondered if he was even listening. Having finished my tale, I coughed to get his attention.

"How do you intend to pay for a telegram?"

My pocket having been picked, I was stumped. "You can have the sketchbook. I paid ten dollars for it."

"Do I look like a fence, a mover, a receiver of stolen goods?" He made a face signifying indignation. He looked at me ferociously until his stomach growled and the mood in the room became slightly comical.

"Do you happen to be a Mason, Mr. Armitage?" If a human voice can be said to sidle, mine did.

"I am not!"

"My father earns a thousand a year." (I lied; my father keeps his earnings as secret as the Masonic rites.)

"As much as that?" By the gleam in his eye, I knew that I'd become a person of interest.

"Last week he ordered a Duryea Motor Wagon from Springfield, Illinois." (Another lie—well, call it a story in search of a happy ending.)

Armitage handed me a scrap of paper and a pencil.

IN BLOCKLEY ALMSHOUSE, W PHILADELPHIA
STOP MISUNDERSTANDING STOP
PLEASE CLAIM ME = OLIVER

"Thank you. Now may I please have my drawings back?"

He ripped them from the book before putting it in a drawer. The cover was crocodile and clearly valuable, the drawings plainly not. "While you're waiting for an answer, why don't you make a birdhouse, Mr. Fischer?"

I had time to make one before my father wired back:

PUT OUT THE RUBBISH STOP MY CHECK FOR
$20 TO FOLLOW =
CHARLES FISCHER, COMPTROLLER

I left Blockley without a backward glance, as Oliver Twist had done before me when he escaped Mudfog workhouse. Eager to show Eakins my new drawings, I hurried to the academy.

"Mr. Eakins, what're you doing?"

"Fischer, will you never see things as they are? I'm packing. My career as a pedagogue has come to an end, at least in the City of Brotherly Love. My anatomical demonstration of my pelvis has caused an uproar. A tempest in a teapot—but that's Philadelphia for you. I have been asked to resign for the good of the academy and the tender feelings of its students. Why, it seems that I scandalized the great surgeon Dr. Gross, who ought to have seen enough naked bodies not to be shocked by the removal of a loincloth for an anatomy lesson!"

"I'm sorry, sir."

"What say you, Mr. Fischer? Have I done harm to your character? Have I misbehaved?"

"No."

"Look on the bright side, Oliver; you'll have one less monkey on your back." His anger subsided; his manner toward me softened. "I was guilty of any number of stupidities when I was your age." He regarded the little wooden man a moment before giving me a final word of advice: "I once told you to read Stephen Crane. Now I would ask that you read Walt Whitman, whom I knew and admire."

I set my poorhouse sketches on the desk that was no longer his.

"Oliver, these are good. They show the promise of an eye that sees, attached, by the fine wire of sympathy, to a soul that feels. Keep it up, and you'll become a worthwhile human being. The art will take care of itself."

I'd had no moment of awakening, no epiphany, and one may scoff at such a change in a single night. I had, then, to convince myself that it was possible and hope that it would stick.

Eakins closed his hand over the little wooden man, as if he meant to crush him. "I want an art of weight and solid forms." He released his grip on the manikin and laid it almost tenderly in a box. He fixed me with a gaze that had looked upon the works of the great Velázquez in the Prado. "Let no one say that life was wasted on you, Ollie."

I wanted to hear more, but there was no time. We shook hands and parted.

YOUR IMMEDIATE PRESENCE REQUIRED
STOP EXPECT YOU AT 8:30 = C L F

My father's telegrams are always more than informative; they convey a personality. Reading the cable that had been slipped underneath the door to my attic room was enough to make me shiver.

By virtue of his character, position, and lodge affiliations, Charles L. Fischer requires no man's intercession with his God and is contemptuous of men in Geneva gowns. Nonetheless, he reads the Bible and has, over the years, committed certain passages to memory that will support his prejudices. He is argumentative at home and likes to goad me into debating a vexed issue of the day or even a point as trivial as the proper way to pare an apple or thread a bloodworm onto a hook, although he hates fishing and has never gone near "Big Deepy," where I once spent happy hours casting worms or bread upon the muddy water, hoping to land a brown trout but managing only sunnies.

Pigeon racing, not fishing, is his passion. He keeps them in a two-story loft in the yard. I hated them and it, which I was made to clean each Saturday, shoveling the noxious slurry into burlap bags. The dung is put on the flower beds, the smell lingering in the yard and wafting, in summer, though open windows. Neighboring housewives complain bitterly that they cannot hang their laundry up to dry because of bird droppings, raddled with the half-digested fruit of our wild cherry trees.

"Do they expect me to put a nappy on a bird's ass?" he would shout through the pickets of the garden fence, behind which I would hide among the climbing lima beans. "Birds shit where they like. The neighbors' sheets and pillowcases have nothing to do with me."

My mother, Tillie, a sweet-tempered, soft-spoken woman, went about the house as though afraid to disturb the dust (as if dust were allowed on her husband's premises!), which, along with my sister, Dot, she harried with cloth and rag, brush and broom, and the first electric sweeper on North Third Street. Apparently, housekeeping is beneficial exercise for housebound wives with rheumatic hearts.

As I rode the car up Third, I thought once more of Natalia Mannino. Through the store window, after spending the pocket money that would allow me to enter that child's paradise, I used to watch her weigh and bag sweets. Even now, I pause outside a confectioner's to look at the colorful array, under glass, like jewels—better than jewels, which don't smell of peppermint, licorice, rose, clove, butterscotch, cinnamon, lemon, wintergreen, horehound, lavender, vanilla, birch, orange, and sugarplum. How could I escape boyish love in so heady an atmosphere? She was pretty besides—her eyes almost black like her hair; her nose thin and nicely drawn by the pantograph that copies the ideal.

One morning at the breakfast table, Charles laid down the spoon with which he had just beheaded his soft-boiled egg and waited for Mother and Dot to finish buttering their toast. "Oliver, I have something to say to you."

"Yes, Father?"

"Last night, I saw you holding hands with a colored girl."

I sat like a citizen of Gomorrah petrifying under Father's strangely excited gaze, while my mother and sister lowered theirs to their plates.

"I don't know any colored girls," I said, my voice near to breaking.

"Are you contradicting me?" He took the same authoritative tone with me that he used to deny an applicant a bank loan for lack of collateral and character.

Gone red in the face, I pushed back my chair and stood, an untouched napkin tucked into my knickerbockers.

"Sit!" my father commanded, and I complied like a dog trained in obedience.

"Charles . . ." said Matilda cautiously.

"Quiet, Tillie!"

Rebuked, she sat and trembled lightly inside her gingham dress.

"You're upsetting Mother!" cried Dot, who is four years older than I am, but no less terrified of our familial Bismarck.

"It's your brother who has upset her. Your brother goes with Negresses!"

A silence, such as followed the Angel of Death in Egypt, passed through the house.

"I—do—not!" I said, breathing through my nose, which whistled twice derisively.

Charles jumped up and slapped my face. Mother gasped. Dot began to sob. The clock resumed its stifled ticking as the Angel left through the kitchen door.

"Dorothy, take your mother to her room."

I listened to Mother's footsteps dragging up the stairs and my sister's tripping after them. On the white linen tablecloth, the bread knife winked in a sudden slant of morning light. I saw my hand pick it up and run it through my father's chest. I smiled at the thought.

"Don't you dare smile!"

"She's Italian—Sicilian; she's Mr. Mannino's daughter."

"Italians are another of the colored races." Swarthy types are no better than Negroes in my father's book. (It is an old book; the outer edges of its pages are browning, which, I've been told, is the result of burning slowly in the atmosphere.) For my benefit, he would illustrate how readily the "darkies" could adulterate the white race, by stirring a pinch of cocoa in a glass of milk. "Does Mr. Mannino's daughter have a name?"

"Natalia."

"A perfectly good dago name. And I suppose you think it's all right to be seen holding the hand of a darky in a public street?"

"I don't see anything wrong in it," I said doggedly. "She's a nice girl; she's—"

"A person you'll never see again. And if I catch the two of you together, I'll pack you off to Aunt Stella's, where you can pray and learn to knit mufflers for the Seamen's Institute. Do you understand me, boy?"

"Yes, sir."

"Finish your breakfast."

"I'm not hungry."

"Don't be sullen, Oliver. Eat your egg. A chicken laid it just for you."

I ate the egg and did my best not to give Father further cause to come at me. I strained to hear upstairs, in my mother's room, but the door had been shut on the family drama below. It was always thus, but I never blamed Mother, whose heart was fragile as a china cup. Dot, I knew, would have already given her a dozen drops of aromatic spirits of ammonia for her sick headache.

Charles demolished his egg. In his mind, the incident was closed. He seemed to have forgotten his harsh words and, turning from the financial section to the baseball results, talked about the Philadelphia A's. "Worse than St.

*Louis!" He was indifferent to the game itself but kept up
with the statistics. Wins and losses were nothing but credits and debits; a score sheet was a page in a ledger. "Eddie
Boyle's record is abysmal. I doubt Connie Mack will carry
him on the roster next year. What do you think?"*

*"I don't think so, either." The words were like marbles
in my mouth. (I can imagine them sitting in a little box
in the Chevalier Jackson Foreign Body Collection, after I
choked to death on them.)*

"Who's your favorite pitcher?"

"Davey Dunkle."

*"Quite right, too. Last summer's no-hitter against
Cleveland was a beaut." Charles would sometimes fall
into the vernacular to make himself agreeable to me.*

*"A walk shy of a perfect game," I said, the sting of my
resentment fading with the imprint of his hand on my
cheek.*

Fifty-five thirty-one North Third Street—
address of the house that I was as eager to put behind
me as Stephen Crane was New York City. But that
night I went there at my father's behest, as obedient
as Isaac had been when he followed Abraham into
the mountains of Moriah.

The gate to the front yard creaked. The sound
reminded me of Edgar Poe's raven quoting "Never-
more." I tiptoed up the steps, wishing, for once, to
take Charles by surprise. But the porch light went
on before I'd gotten halfway to the door. I imagined
him waiting, his ear cocked, so that he could watch

me, through the slightly parted curtain, flinch when he switched on the light. Even then he would open the door only a crack, as though I were a salesman for a burial society or an evangelist handing out tracts.

"Good evening, Father."

He let me inside.

"I've sent your mother and Dot upstairs. I have something to say to you."

My face went hot. I tasted pennies in my mouth. I felt my legs wanting to give way.

He led me into the shed behind the kitchen, where the boiler and laundry tubs stood. It was the place where I had received punishment. The shed had only a single chair, on which he would sit and polish his shoes. He seemed to dare me to take it. He opened a drawer in the dry sink and took out a folded newspaper.

"Ah! What have we here?" He pretended to read an item on the front page of what I would shortly learn was the *Croydon Bee*, mailed to him by a lodge brother. Now and then, he would glance sharply at me in amazement and, finally, in horror. "A naked harlot polluted the holy water of baptism, splashing about as if at a Roman bath, at the instigation of a degenerate calling himself Oliver Fischer. Yes, Oliver, it's true! You're sure to be as shocked as I was when I read it. The question is what shall we do to rid your name and mine of this shame?" The paper rattled and snapped as he shook it in a show of righteous fury. "After due consideration, I intend to hire a detective to hunt down this impostor. Put your mind at ease, Oliver. I'll have this son of a bitch found, punished, and, if he has any assets at all, ruined beyond all hope of redemption."

His little eyes glittered. He was beside himself with anger, which he tamped down like a hot ember risen in a pipe bowl.

"What do you say, Oliver? Shall I take charge of the matter?"

"What do you want, Father?" I asked coldly.

"To exonerate you! It appears to be my lot in life to clean the mud you seem determined to leave on the family name. Why, just yesterday, I had to ask Mr. Slocum if he would not mind waiting while I got my son out of the poorhouse—and that, only three days after he spent a night in jail!"

I opened the door to the yard and walked through it, swearing that I would never return to that house. I pitied my sister, who, I sensed, would never leave it, except through death's door, which, for a previous generation, had meant the parlor door, through which corpses passed. I felt my father's eyes on me as I looked up to see if she was at her window, peeking through the cretonne curtain. Her room was dark. He shouted neither "Come back" nor "Good-bye."

On the evening of the Anti-Imperialist League parade, Robert and I arrived at the brickyard as darkness was rolling over the river wards to the east, on its way to the engulfment of the city. Turbulent and prophetic, it brought to mind the black smoke that rose from the burning of Moab, as reported in the Book of Numbers, which Charles would read to us in the parlor for the good of our souls. Uncle Sam had been hoisted onto the back of a wagon, one high-buttoned shoe on the neck of an abject Cuban peasant modeled in plaster of Paris. A team of horses stood in the yard, their long necks bent, as in prayer, their hard-bitten mouths eating straw. The wagon may not have been the bronze chariot of the Apocalypse, but the horses were red.

Alban pumped our hands. "Thanks for coming! How does the stiff look?" He cracked his neck as if in sympathy, then shouted to a man tugging at a rope. "Careful you don't pull Uncle's head off!"

Equipped with an applewood pipe, dungarees, and hobnailed boots, Alban struck me as an idealized portrait of a workingman. I smiled sympathetically at the affectation, having, until my recent escapade, posed as a dandy and an aesthete.

He fished up his watch from a pocket. "At half past eight, we'll head down Sixteenth Street to the Friends Burial Ground. That way, we'll skirt the police station. We'll take Cherry Street to Broad, then head south till we get to Walnut."

"We'll go right by the academy!" I was in enough hot water without being seen parading with a gang of unpatriotic anti-McKinley anarchists by Morris and the board.

"We'll let the dried-up old shits know we're not having it!" shouted Alban, his large mouth practically frothing.

Starting from the Odd Fellows Temple, we would haul our colossus past the hallowed grounds of capitalism: the Fidelity Mutual Life Insurance Company, the Third National Bank, the Girard Trust Company, the United States Mint, the Masonic Temple, the Philadelphia Land Title Company, and the Union League. Our parade would be viewed by church and state as a desecration of all that is holy. We would march onward to Washington Square, where Andrew Carnegie and Samuel Clemens waited to address anti-imperialist sympathizers and entreat President McKinley to keep America's hands off the rich green fields of Cuban sugarcane.

At a signal from Alban, a teamster laid the leather reins lightly on the horses' backs. Uncle Sam lurched onto Sixteenth Street and began to float toward the city's imperial heart. Would it prove to be made of stone, or could we soften it by appealing to Christian principles?

Night had transformed the academy's pile of brick, sandstone, pink granite, and purple terra-cotta into a coal black butte. It had charred the Odd

Fellows Temple and pierced the thick walls of the mint, nor had the money-changing dens been spared Christ Militant's scything shadow. Only the Union Club showed signs of life, its opulent rooms made bright by electric chandeliers. Men in evening clothes stood easily behind the open sashes, their faces gilded by cigar light. They took no more interest in us than in a gnat before they swatted it. Onward we went, disturbing the peace with our iron-shod horses, hard on the asphalt of the streets.

Washington Square was jammed with hundreds of men and women milling on the grass like pigeons hunting for bread. Jeering, they made way for Uncle Sam. The light of their torches painted him in the rich hues of which fire is constituted. (How beautiful is the house that burns!) Dressed in a rumpled coat of white linen, Samuel Clemens and a tweed-suited Andrew Carnegie stood beside each other in a band shell where, on the previous evening, Herbert L. Clarke had played "Bride of the Waves," the brass of his cornet flaring in the dying summer light.

"Welcome, friends of Washington, Jefferson, Monroe, and Lincoln!" bawled Clemens, his voice graveled by too many cigars.

"Welcome to all who've come to protest against America's colonial ambition!" cried the aging Scotsman, who sounded like a man with a cold in his chest.

His droll mouth, buffed cheeks, merry eyes, and beard brought to mind Clement Moore's Saint

Nicholas "opening his sack." Carnegie's sack held not toys and apples, but dollars in their hundreds of millions. Having come to fear a last judgment by the flinty God of the Scots, he had turned to philanthropy, believing that "the man who dies thus rich dies disgraced." The son of a former master weaver in Dunfermline, Scotland, who was broken by the new steam looms of the industrial age, Andrew climbed from an immigrant bobbin boy in Allegheny City, Pennsylvania, to the highest rung of wealth and power. That night, in Washington Square, he had come to rail against war with Spain, while he was losing the war to divest himself of a fortune greater than that of Croesus. The crowd cheered him, as if he were indeed Saint Nicholas, forgetting that, in 1892, he had refused to bargain with workers at his Homestead steel mill in Pennsylvania. For five months, they suffered from hunger and sickness, which came to an end when his associate, the despicable Frick, hired an army of three hundred Pinkerton cops equipped with Winchester rifles to settle the strike in the company's favor. From Charles, I'd heard the biographies of the great men of industry and finance; their stories had been my *Treasure Island* and *Tales From Shakespeare,* by Charles Lamb.

Carnegie spoke with the exemplary canniness of his race: "Americans, hear me well as I put to you the greatest question of the age. Is the Republic to remain one homogeneous whole, one united people, or to become a scattered and disjointed aggregate of alien races?"

"No!" replied the crowd, which was not homogeneous, except as an anti-imperialist bent made it so. A part of it was made up of nativists, xenophobes, and run-of-the-mill gawkers; another feared for the integrity of the nation's institutions should America begin to covet and steal.

"I say that imperialism is tantamount to watering single-malt scotch whiskey with soda water. It is an adulteration!" He opened his checkbook and took out a pen. "I'll write a check for twenty million dollars and send it to President McKinley, on condition that America give up its colonialist designs on Cuba and the Philippines."

Carnegie sagged beneath a storm of approval that broke over the heads of the dignitaries. The photographers took their shots, and the correspondents scribbled on their cuffs.

"And now Samuel Clemens will lead us in prayer."

Clemens bowed his shaggy head and fervently intoned, "O Lord our Father, our young patriots, idols of our hearts, go forth to battle—be Thou near them! With them—in spirit—we also go forth from the sweet peace of our beloved firesides to smite the foe. O Lord our God, help us to tear their soldiers to bloody shreds with our shells . . . help us to drown the thunder of the guns with the shrieks of their wounded, writhing in pain . . . help us to wring the hearts of their unoffending widows with unavailing grief . . . "

Stunned by his bloodthirsty appeal to the Deity, I missed the savage irony of his "War Prayer." Carnegie went weak at the knees and, finding no chair on which to collapse, slumped onto the wagon bed. Under the impression that Clemens had spoken in favor of war, the anti-imperialists would have drawn and quartered him had an American warship not steamed into Washington Square.

"Holy smokes, we're under attack!" cried a man dressed for the occasion in the costume of a professional mourner. A black funeral wreath bearing the words THE DEATH OF DEMOCRACY lettered in calligraphy fell from his gloved hands.

"Down with the imperialists!" shouted a woman dressed as a pineapple. She carried a sign that read HANDS OFF!!!

"Up the rebels!" shouted her companion, waving a machete.

Stirred to the roots of my soul, I wished I had brought rotten fruit to throw at the warship.

The Hibernian Society of Philadelphia had built the U.S.S. *Patrick Henry* inside the old lead works at Fifth and St. James Streets and christened her with Irish whiskey. Wood, iron, lath, tin, and plaster of Paris combined in a miniature dreadnought thirty feet long and half again as high from her bottom to her stacks, which billowed real smoke produced by an ingenious steam boiler and bellows inside her tin-sheathed hull. King Alfonso XIII of Spain dangled from a mast. (I thought that an eleven-year-old boy ought not to be abused even in effigy.) A mob of jingoists and war hawks—each one a David with a sling full of stones—followed in the ship's wake. (A correspondent for the *Philadelphier Sonntags-Blatt* described the crowd, in idiomatic German, as "het up and out for *Blut*.")

To leave no room for doubt of his anti-imperialist stance, Clemens threw down his cigar and burst into song:

> McKinley and American Sugar Co.
> Want a war, "a splendid little war!"
> Not a big one, just a little one—
> Only ninety miles from our shore.
> It's okay to step on Spaniards' toes
> And kick them from our hemisphere;
> But never should we take their place—
> Such a disgrace, no small one, either,
> To put Cuba's heroes in their place,
> As the British did the Sepoys!
> It's time to march against imperialists
> And cheer for heroes of every race!

Despite his voice, which would be scandalous in any opera house east of the Mississippi River, we cheered his rendition of the league's anthem, which the newspapers characterized in their morning editions as "the outrageous uproar of wild-eyed anarchists intent on provoking Philadelphia patriots." The *Inquirer* correspondent wrote in greasy cadences, "Incensed by the mob's disrespect for liberty and the heroic spirit shown by our young nation during a perishing Pennsylvania winter at Valley Forge, the good citizens of our great city sang in the dulcet notes of native hearts John Philip Sousa's 'The Stars and Stripes Forever'":

> Let martial note in triumph float
> And liberty extend its mighty hand;
> A flag appears 'mid thunderous cheers,
> The banner of the Western land.
> The emblem of the brave and true
> Its folds protect no tyrant crew;
> The red and white and starry blue
> Is freedom's shield and home.

Martial songs and partisan harangues were soon supplanted by obscenities that incited both sides to violence. The Hibernians and their roughneck accomplices made short work of the pacifists, but not before we set fire to the *Patrick Henry*. When her boiler exploded, splinters, nails, and screws rained down like shrapnel, injuring more than a hundred brawlers—a woman gravely and a man at the cost of an eyetooth. The explosion catapulted young Alfonso's head into the General George McCall Public School yard, where, on the following day, boys played kickball with it until only a painted sneer remained.

Uncle Sam went up in flames.

"Cheese it! Everything's dumped!" cried Alban in the colorful idiom of the streets.

Engine Company 32 was the first to turn out. Soon the fire club from Second and Quarry arrived and set its Macomber pumper next to its rival's apparatus, which, to the trained eye of an artist, resembled a brewery kettle mounted on rubber tires. Those stouthearted fellows showed signs of having poured too many growlers in honor of the fire gods before the gongs had begun to clamor. Overcome with emotion, the men joined in a nonpartisan canticle to arson. (Firemen, like small boys, love a blaze.)

> Twinkle, twinkle, little star,
> Come and set the world on fire;
> Up above the clouds so high,
> Like an ember in the sky,
> Twinkle, twinkle, little star,
> Come and set the world on fire.

All of a sudden, the wind changed, and the rubber-coated Goliaths who had had the upper hand were thrown back by the flames. What had begun as a modest incineration soon turned into a self-important conflagration that engulfed two houses and threatened my sire's bank.

"Let it burn! Let the money, deeds, bonds, and certificates of ownership go up in smoke!" I would have taken off my hat and whooped to see my father's house of worship smolder, if not for the fear of being mistaken for a pyromaniac.

Two hysterical women came between the feuding firemen. "Our houses are burning!"

The firemen continued their stolid hosing of the neoclassical hulk.

"Go ndéanfaidh an diabhal cipín dod' dhá chois!" cried one of the pair as she piteously wrung her hands.

"Dó agus bascadh ort!" cursed the second woman, pulling at her hair.

A Gaelic-speaking resident of the neighborhood kindly translated the first oath as "May the Devil make splinters of your legs!" and the second, "May you burn and be severely injured!" a potent imprecation when firemen are concerned.

Reminded of their duty, they turned their hoses on the flames and might have saved the houses had it not been for the watchman of the Western Savings Bank, who insisted that they be left to complete the natural process of combustion.

"What do a few sticks of furniture matter compared to the contents of a bank? Behind these granite walls, the city's lifeblood is at risk. Are your shoulders broad enough to carry the weight of responsibility for the financial panic that will follow should this building burn to the ground?" The man possessed the native eloquence that is sometimes found in the most unlikely of orators, even those who have taken the pledge and renounced strong drink, which loosens the tongue and sets fire to the brain.

The firemen aimed their hoses at the bank, which was saved in its marble and mahogany entirety. On the following week, Charles awarded a gold watch to the watchman, inscribed TO A GOOD AND FAITHFUL SERVANT.

By that time, Black Marias from surrounding stations had arrived to put down the violent challenge to the rule of law—nine tenths of which is enacted to safeguard the possessions of the rich. The Irish cops took a dim view of the anti-imperialists who had disturbed the peace of the city and destroyed private property, although precious little of it belonged to them, their kith, or kin. For the third time that week, I was manhandled into the back of a van, along with Andrew Carnegie wrapped in a tartan shawl, and Sam Clemens, his scraggly mustache scorched to the roots.

"Well, young man, what's *your* name and game?" asked Clemens, whom the world knows as Mark Twain.

"Oliver Fischer, and I'm an artist."

"You don't say?"

"More of a caricaturist, to be honest."

"Times being what they are, a man can't rightly tell where life leaves off and hyperbole begins," he said in that broad way of speaking he has. He related a droll anecdote concerning a drunk who went out to the barn and tried to milk his ass.

"How are you, Andrew? Up to snuff?"

Carnegie replied with a snuffle and a snore.

"Poor old fellow's played out. Well, Oliver, this rumpus is worth a tall tale for me and a blistering cartoon for you."

"Say, Mr. Clemens—"

"Hell's bells, Oliver, when two fellows are arrested for riot and arson, they're entitled to call each other by their Christian names, even if one of them is a god-damned heathen!" He gave me a wink, and I could not help but laugh to see his singed mustache. "So what were you about to say? A juicy morsel of gossip, I hope, to pass the time. Gossip is only a story in the raw."

"Last Sunday, when I was going up the Delaware on my grandfather's boat, I saw Jim and Huckleberry Finn floating down on a raft."

"Those two fellas sure do get around!" said Sam. "I've seen them on the Danube, the Humber, the Orange, and the Ottawa, not to mention the Coral Sea and the Pacific off Fiji. I can't rightly explain the phenomenon, Oliver. But as long as they keep going, I'll stay a jump ahead of my creditors. Paige's infernal typesetting machine has picked my pockets and wrung my wallet dry."

Clemens, Carnegie, and I were taken to municipal court, where Robert and Alban were already cooling their heels. A magistrate wearing tomato catsup on his vest had been summoned to lower the boom on the chief instigators of the mayhem, who had conspired to burn down the United States Mint and destroy the banking system, without which America could not become master of its hemisphere.

"I've got you three pyromaniacs down for parading without a permit, unlawful assembly, and destruction of private property," said the judge, who, by the sour look on his face, had been awakened from a sweet dream of Charles Darwin on the rack, recanting his monkey business. "The worst offense anyone can commit against a judge is to cause him to be shaken out of bed by a knock at his door to attend to a pack of agitators. Now let me tell you what's in store. . . ."

The droning of his voice grew muffled, like the protests of a hornet caught inside a bottle of cherry pop. My eyes glazed over and closed for a moment; then they opened on a page of that year's calendar, August 21, 1897—a gift of the Crossoup Steam Marble Works of Philadelphia, decorated with a hand-colored lithograph of a burnished headstone topped by a fat pink cherub.

"These three boys had nothing to do with it!" growled Clemens, his dander up. "If you believe those coppers who hide their jug heads inside their helmets, then you've got no more sense than a dung beetle!"

"You just won ninety days' room and board paid

for by the City of Brotherly Love. So when you get up on your lecture platform, you can tell the world that the Honorable William J. O'Donnell treated you squarely. Yes, Mr. Samuel Clemens, I know who you are. What's more, I don't give a hang if you can play a pennywhistle with your ass! That said, I will prove my fair-mindedness by giving you your choice of public accommodations. What'll it be, Clemens? The Provincial Hospital for the Insane or Walnut Street Prison?"

"I'll put my head in a noose if you let these young fellows go."

Robert, Alban, and I gave Clemens a look of adoration, like that which Tom Sawyer bestowed on Becky Thatcher when her skirt flew up while she jumped rope double Dutch.

"Your head is already in the noose, Clemens, and I've reserved three beds for these fine young men in the 'County Hotel,' which is what my guests call Moyamensing Prison—weevils, lice, and other vermin on the house!"

"Hang you for an old jackass!" snarled Clemens, his ferocity undermined by the state of his mustache. "I'm so steamed up, I could tear your shell off and eat you raw!"

"I wouldn't waste my piss on you if your pants were on fire!" screeched his honor.

That last remark set off Clemens like a Chinese rocket. He dumped the contents of a brass spittoon on

O'Donnell's derby, which the judge had not bothered to remove from his head, our presence undeserving of respect. (The hat may have been a democratic form of the black silk napkin English judges set atop their wigs before they commend the souls of murderers to God's mercy.) By the spittle, gobs, and chaws welling in the upturned brim, I guessed that the spittoon had not been emptied for a while. As O'Donnell spluttered, I remembered the Baptists coming up for air after they'd been dunked. The irate magistrate gave his hat a shake, but it was plainly ruined.

"You'll spend the rest of your life in Eastern State Prison, where solitary confinement is the rule, and there ain't no exception for smart alecks and wisecrackers!"

"Shut up and sit down!" said Carnegie, who had not spoken since our arrival. So quiet had he been, snug in an old shawl and his head sunk on his breast, that I thought he was asleep.

O'Donnell looked incredulously at the Scotsman, and then he spat. His spittle landed on the floor, where, the spittoon having been decommissioned, the black charwoman could wipe it up in the morning. "You must be a lunatic to talk to me that way!"

Carnegie raised his bushy eyebrows, which formed two quizzical arches above his blue eyes. "I want you to apologize to my friends. If you don't, Mr.

O'Donnell, there'll be hell to pay. And I doubt you've taken enough bribes to foot the bill."

"Andrew can afford to buy an acre in hell just to roast his enemies," whispered Clemens.

"You *must* be insane, old man!" screamed the judge. His red-veined eyes reminded me of aggies.

That such a public figure should have gone unrecognized passed all understanding. Then again, Wild Bill Hickok stripped of his buckskins would have been mistaken for any other old codger telling tall tales of his glorious youthful self.

Clemens rubbed his hands gleefully. "I feel like a ten-year-old who's just stuck a stick of dynamite underneath Muff Potter's outhouse!" In the ruckus, his remark went unnoticed by all except me.

"If you apologize this instant and send my friends home in a cab, I'll forget all about this unpleasant business. If you persist in making a jackass of yourself . . ."

Clemens poked me in the ribs. "Oh, this is rich!"

Carnegie stood, and although he is a short man, the voice that issued from his mouth would have brought Goliath to his knees. "You'll nawt be asked to judge so much as a dog show, *ya mawkit jobbie!*"

"I wish a stenographer were here to take this down. What a yarn it would make!" said our greatest living comic author. (She would have made haggis of the Scottish curse.)

The judge paled, but *still* he did not recognize his

by then dangerous opponent. "You are either mad or a dope fiend. I—"

Carnegie put up a hand to silence him. "Even in your peculiar view of the law, you must admit that I have a right to counsel."

The judge nodded warily.

"Will you send a telegram to mine? I assure you, the city will be adequately reimbursed. I might commission a bronze statue of you in memory of this night. What a boon to the municipal pigeons that would be!"

Unsure of his ground, the judged agreed.

"If you'll kindly wire Theodore Roosevelt at Sagamore Hill, in Oyster Bay, and say that Andrew Carnegie has need of him, I—and he—will be much obliged."

O'Donnell turned the color of poorhouse mush. In his eyes, I saw the struggle between skepticism and fear. Fear won, as it usually does. He dried the sweat from his brow with his necktie, judiciously cleared his throat, and mumbled to the effect that he hadn't recognized Mr. Carnegie.

"I'll bet my auntie's nightgown that the boob still doesn't," said Clemens.

"I apologize, Mr. Carnegie, and I hope—"

"Beg their pardon, too."

"I beg your pardon, Mr. Clemens, and yours, young men. I was misinformed." His voice was that of a man who mistook a glass of vinegar for whiskey.

"I will take steps to— I promise that I will deal severely with your traducers!" His panic-stricken eyes turned on the law books piled on his desk, as if they had failed him.

"Naturally, *none* of my friends assaulted by the mob or harassed by the constables will be charged," said Carnegie. "They're guilty of nothing but zeal and high spirits."

"Everyone is free to go!" He ripped up the charge sheets on the desk. "Mr. Worthington!" he croaked in a voice suitable to his shaken dignity.

A clerk of the court put his head through the door. Behind his flunky's mask, I could see his facial muscles struggling to suppress a grin.

"Go find a cab to take Mr. Carnegie and Mr. Clemens to their hotel."

"And Mr. Weisz, Mr. Pearson, and Mr. Fischer?" asked Carnegie.

"And a cab to take them home, Worthington. At once!"

"Not a cab," said Carnegie, his eyes bright with mischief. "A Black Maria." He turned to us. "Unless you would rather not." Robert, Alban, and I could scarcely get our mouths to work. "Naturally, you'll be shown every courtesy. And if you should want to stop to eat, the driver will see to it. Just let me know if anyone refuses to serve you, and tomorrow I'll buy the building and evict the wretch."

The judge would have collapsed had he not already been slumped in his chair.

Since that night, I've often wondered whether he believed that the man he nearly sent to the penitentiary was Andrew Carnegie or else a plausible megalomaniac, with equally plausible friends. A deluded man is as dangerous as a powerful one.

We had been delivered from high-handed punishment inflicted by the so-called Honorable William J. O'Donnell but not that meted out by Morris and the board. A reporter for the *Philadelphia Inquirer* had witnessed the battle of Uncle Sam versus the dreadnought. Unable to find either Clemens or Carnegie, he collared a Hibernian for comment, who got him soused. So persuasive an account of the cause and conduct of the fray did the Irishman give that his version made it into print without regard for truth. When not committing outrages against Protestant churches and shopgirls, he was a porter at the Pennsylvania Academy and thus could point the finger at Robert, Alban, and me.

The "Triumvirate of Terrorists," as we had been dubbed, was summoned by Director Morris on Monday morning and expelled from the academy as "undesirables." Moreover, I was singled out as "incorrigible, uneducable, and untalented." No letters of recommendations would be written, nor could we claim to be alumni of the academy.

"Well, friends, we've been shown the door," said Alban.

We were sitting on a bench in Washington Square like three pensioners, except that we had no pensions and, to the pigeon's indignation, no bread crumbs to scatter. They pecked at the toes of our shoes till we had two choices: forfeit our places or kick them in their feathered asses. We chose the latter. We were sunk in gloom, though the day was bright as ormolu. The leaves shone against the dark trunks of the walnut trees; the grass was Verona green, save where it was black from the fire. Hands in pockets, we kicked at char and intaglioed our sole prints into mud that had begun to harden into adobe. Robert found a singed lapel pin signifying membership in the Ancient Order of Hibernians. I found a battered cigar case. The cigar, miraculously unharmed, had been rolled in Havana. I smoked it. Henceforth, my hell would be fumigated by two-cent stogies.

"If I can only find a flask of gin!" said Robert. He did not. He did, however, discover a shoe underneath an iron boilerplate. "Where, I wonder, is its fellow?"

"Whither the feet they shod?" I asked. I was in a frame of mind suitable to reflection. I sat on a wagon axle. The tires had melted into a black rubbery ooze, as though intending to return to the Amazon and begin their lives anew as sap. "All things change. The universe is in constant flux. Thus said Heraclitus."

"The universe gives me the bloody flux!" growled Alban. "I'll tell you what, boys: I'm taking a train to Frisco. I'll grow a pigtail, powder my face with saffron, wear a quilted jacket, and agitate like all hell against the Chinese Exclusion Act. I'll show the Celestials how to make bombs out of wok oil and ginger jars. What about you, Robert? Want to join me?"

"Chop suey gives me the pip. No, I'm staying put. Smith at *The Press* likes my stuff. Say, Ollie, how about you and me put our coal boxes together and start a family?"

"I'll think about it."

"Well, you no-good lobcocks, I'm lighting out for the territories. Mark my words, you'll be hearing great things about me. I'm going to make a big noise and a big stink in this world. If I can't change it, I'll blow it up."

That was the last we saw or heard of Alban Weisz, erstwhile artist, committed anarchist. Neither a whiff of wok oil nor a rumor of war between the races ever reached my nose or ears.

"I think I'll go see Smith," said Robert, cleaning his shoes with spit and his handkerchief. "And mind what I said about shoving in together." He started off, then stopped. "It's time you either kick or kiss your old man's ass, Oliver." And off he went to take his chance.

Is it time to renounce ambition, if that is what has got me in this mess? Or is it obstinacy and the wish to annoy my father? I'm not an artist. I feel no gnawing in my gut, no grief or pain that can be lessened only with paints or clay. I've known misery like a child with a paper cut crying to a man with a bullet in his chest. So what now? "Do an honest job of work"—that's what Eakins would tell me—"and stop clowning." What work when men and women by the hundreds of thousands are without it? It's too late to set up on the boardwalk with easel and crayons. Maybe Ortlieb would hire me to shovel hops, or Burk to shovel guts and gore. Or I could rub neat's-foot oil into leather gloves for Connie Mack's baseball club. Pipe dreams! You know what you must do, Oliver, like it or not, unless you fancy being shot by Spaniards.

I saw my father before he noticed me. His head was bowed to a ledger, his thinning gray hair precisely combed; his sleeve protectors were unspotted, as though serving only an ornamental function. The black hair growing on the backs of his fingers never failed to surprise me by its luxuriance. His mustache, strictly trimmed, might have been an index to his mind's severity. I rapped on the open door to his office. His head shot up and swiveled toward the disturbance in that marble memorial to the industry and single-mindedness of men like him. His face paled. I thought I saw a momentary shiver pass through his body. Maybe not. Many times we see what we wish, not what we ought to expect. He glared, while I looked penitent. What did *I* expect? That he'd embrace the prodigal and order a fatted calf to be butchered and barbecued on the lobby floor?

"How are you, Father?" I asked, knowing the first move was mine to make.

"As you can see, busy. Have you come to open an account?"

I've come to beg, you shit! Can't you see even that far into your own flesh and blood?

"Our rates are highly competitive," he said, as if I were a stranger facing him across the desk, at which he had not invited me to sit. As an afterthought, he added, "We never gamble or take risks." That remark, I knew, was meant for me. He had wiped his hands of his only son the moment he left the back shed without a backward glance.

I said what I had come to say: "You once offered me a job. I'd like to be considered for it."

In its inhuman squawk, his chair expressed his ill will. He did not need to say more. But he could not stop himself from racking me. "Have you any experience working in a bank? Have you ever so much as been inside one until now?"

He did not expect a reply.

"Do you have a head for figures?" He leaned forward and leered. "I'm not referring to a woman's shape that recently you may have seen on shameless display. I have an idea what you idlers get up to! Do you see that young man over there—the one wearing the green eyeshade?"

"Yes."

"Wonderful hand! The hand of an artist. He's my new assistant. He came to me highly recommended by C. C. Harrison and Company. Every day he shows me his worth, and every evening I thank God for leading him to the Western Savings Bank. He will go far. Maybe one day, he will sit where I'm sitting now. Now as I understand it, you wish to take his place. You came here expecting me to sack him. What reason can I give him? That I found someone better qualified? Are you better qualified? Or that I found somebody with more zeal? Are you more zealous than he is?"

"No."

"Jobs are hard to come by in this depression. Business has been slow to revive since the panic. Was it your idea in coming to see me that I should put that young man out on the street? Why, he has a wife and child! Do you have a wife, a child, or any other person who depends on you for sustenance?"

"No," I replied, speaking to the floor, on which my downcast gaze hid its shame from the lowercase almighty.

"Well, then, you see how things stand. There's no place for you here—that is, unless you would care for the position of janitor, which happens to be open. Have you had any experience in sweeping floors and scrubbing toilet bowls?"

I saw how things stood. I turned and headed for the door. I hadn't far to go, no more than thirty paces. The hair on my neck stood up; my neck prickled; my spine felt like a swag of chain. He may not have had his eyes on me. More likely, he'd turned his back on his wayward son. But how my backbone burned!

Pink and naked as a boiled shrimp, Sarah Jenkins recited the Parable of the Fishes to an assembly of hungry men. My sister, Dorothy, sat in a tiny chair on the stage, knitting her a sweater. "What luxury!" I said, for a reason known only to sleepers.

"Ollie."

Here is a scene Eakins would relish.

"Oliver!"

"Ah, Robert, old slug! Take my seat while I go to the kitchen and check on the soup."

"Wake up, Ollie!"

The soup had boiled away till nothing was left but bones. "Bones!"

"Hully chee, Fischer! Wake up!"

"What's all the noise about?"

"You're off your head, chub!"

"I was dreaming of the Shrimp."

"I beg your pardon for the *interruptus*."

I smelled liquor on his breath. "You've been on a bender."

"Smith treated me to a swell feed!"

"Who did?"

"Harry Smith, Talcott William's right-hand man at *The Press*. Dust off the sand, man! Gee, I wish you'd been there! Beefsteak this thick!" He measured two inches of air between his thumb and forefinger or, in the argot of the printing trade, twenty-eight picas. That evening, Smith had hired him as an illustrator, and then, the dinner hour having chimed, he stood him to a meal at Parkinson's Restaurant on Chestnut Street. As Robert described the *table d'hôte* down to the last peanut, I grew hungry, not having eaten so much (or so little) as a crumb since breakfast. I took a mental inventory of my larder and found there a tin of oyster crackers, a pot of mustard, and a dried and salted hunk of sturgeon. I licked my chops and made an uncouth noise.

"What's wrong, Ollie? Jealous?"

"I'm feeling peckish."

"Puckish, you say?"

"No, goddamn it! Famished!"

"And here I am going on and on about my sumptuous steak dinner. Did I mention we had wine? I don't know one from another, but it was delicious. I'd have smacked my lips if I hadn't known better. Wine, and then an apple tart, and—if you can believe it—an after-dinner drink. I didn't know there was such a thing as an after-dinner drink. Among ladies and gentlemen of my acquaintance, we drink the same thing before, during, and after—and not wine so much as beer, ale, porter, stout, or, in a pinch, water."

I was ready to kick him out the door and down the stairs. "Shut up, will you, Pearson! I tell you, I'm starving!"

"As hungry as that?" He stepped into the hallway and returned immediately with a broad smile and a cardboard box, which he put on the table and invited me to inspect. "Never let it be said that Robert J. Pearson neglected a friend."

"*J* for *jackass*."

"Eat up, old juke." He had packed the box with a half of a roast chicken, a green salad, a loaf of crusty bread, and a growler of cider.

"I'll remember you in my dreams!" I said as I dismembered the chicken.

"No, thanks! I've been in one or two of your dreams. Awful places illumined by Tiffany lamps, papered in an Art Nouveau pattern, and scented with Moroccan hashish and Roman incense. You've got grease in your mustache."

Like any man of the people, I wiped my mouth on the back of my sleeve.

"A toast: To 'buckets of spondulicks,' as my old

man says, who hasn't a penny pot to piss in." He pulled cider straight from the bottle down his pulsing throat. Fascinated by the bobbing of his Adam's apple, I congratulated him on his luck.

"My luck is yours, Ollie!"

"How's that?"

"You, too, are to doodle for *The Press.*"

Putting a bone aside, I rid my mouth of grease with a long swig of cider, which was hard. "*Me,* you say? On the square?"

Robert beamed like Santa Claus caught in the parlor with the mistress of the house. "Our problems are solved for the foreseeable future."

Only an ingrate would have said that it was the *unforeseeable* that scared the living daylights out of me. "How did it come to pass?" I asked, using a biblical turn of phrase in recognition of a miraculous turn of events.

"I borrowed your poorhouse drawings and showed them to Smith. He was impressed, so much so that he's offering you a salaried position. You start on Wednesday. You'll be in no fit state to make a dazzling first impression tomorrow. I predict that you'll be sick as a dog in the morning. Now if you'll excuse me, Mr. Fischer, it's time for me to retire to my chamber. I beg you not to send your incubus to spoil my sweet dreams."

That night I dreamed that I crept downstairs into the yard and set my father's pigeon loft alight with

*kerosene. Once more in my room, I watched through the
window as he raged against the flames in German such
as Bismarck would have used against the French before
he beat them in the Siege of Metz. The fire roared high
into the dark; the wood beams of the loft snapped and
crackled as they charred. I could hear the popping of dry
feed corn. I saw birds fly like torches flung into a black
sky wreathed in smoke, only to fall—the fires in their
small breasts put out.*

*Next morning, Charles went through the smok-
ing rubble with a stick. He selected four small birds that
looked as if they had just been taken from the roasting
pan. These he ordered Mother to warm up and set out on
the table for lunch.*

*"Eat!" he said in the imperative mood he employed
even in the dreams of his children.*

*I struggled to get a bird down. Mother refused to eat
her portion and was sent from the table. Dot was sick in
her napkin.*

*He glared at me and asked, "What do you have to say
for yourself?"*

I stood on a chair and began to sing:

> *There was a man from Germ'ny,*
> *Who trapped a rat in his heinie;*
> *He cooked it in a pot of vinegar*
> *And ate it with a bunch of sprouts!*
> *Vinegar, vinegar, who likes vinegar?*
> *Herrs and fraus and little krauts!*

Before 1882, *The Press* had been the same as any other city rag whose publishers, like men with weak hearts, kept a nervous eye on their circulations. After 1882, its rotary presses steamed and thumped like the vents of hell. A story published in its pages that would have made Poe's heart beat wildly (had it not already stopped its useful work forevermore) drew readers as rotten meat does flies. Several students of anatomy were caught red-handed disinterring bodies at Lebanon Cemetery. (From buried corpse to a cadaver on a dissecting table at Jefferson Medical College was a bare twelve miles; the distance, as might be measured by moral philosophers, is a mystery tantamount to the Resurrection.) The story brought notoriety to the medical college and celebrity to *The Press*. Thereafter, much-improved circulation made the hearts of all concerned beat faster.

I was sufficiently humbled by events in my own history to knock timidly on the pebbled-glass office door marked HARRY T. SMITH, EDITOR IN CHIEF.

"Come in!" His words were garbled by a wet stogie clamped between his teeth. "Well?"

"Mr. Smith, my name's Oliver Fischer. Robert Pearson said that you might have a job for me."

He looked up from a layout he was slashing with a crayon.

"I studied under Thomas Eakins."

"Not the best reference, I'd have said."

That took the wind out of my puffed-up sail!

"If you want the job, it's yours."

"Yes."

"Well, speak up!"

"I want the job, sir!"

"Okay, then. And get your foot off my spittoon!"

In my nervousness, I'd been stepping on the tail of a brass turtle, whose shell rose and fell with a clatter. "I'm sorry, Mr. Smith—or should I call you 'Editor Smith,' or 'Chief'?"

He threw his wet cigar out the window. It might as well have been Ollie Fischer he had defenestrated into Chestnut Street. "Go see Slater in advertising. He'll tell you what to do."

"Advertising?"

"See Slater." He took another stogie from his vest and began to slash the front-page makeup with it. "Damn it all—get the hell out of here!"

I knocked at the advertising manager's door. I would soon learn that such niceties were unnecessary in the newspaper business, where people rushed about as though their hair were on fire. "Mr. Slater, I'm Fischer. Mr. Smith sent me."

Slater—his given name is Arnold—swiveled in his chair and eyed me up and down from beneath a green eyeshade. "You the new man?"

"Yes, sir."

He opened his desk drawer and took out a cloth-bound pocket-sized book. "Got a pencil?"

I looked at the desks and easels against the walls, all equipped with pencils, crayons, sticks of charcoal and pastels, bottles of India ink, pens, and brushes of varied bristle count. The question seemed superfluous in view of such abundance. Nonetheless, I showed him my pencil.

"Go see the firms listed under 'August First' and hit them up for payment. Most are cheap so-and-sos and will palm you off with something on account. Try to get the whole nut. Argue, but don't get nasty."

Was this to be my job? Debt collector. Accounts receivable clerk. Footpad and cutpurse. I considered telling Smith to go play marbles with somebody else. "Mr. Slater, I was hired as an illustrator."

"I know nothing about that."

I was in a corner. Marx and Engels were glaring at me. "To work, you bloody donkey!" My father stood with them—what an unlikely and unholy trinity!—smirking at me, tearing my birth certificate and baptismal record to shreds, obliterating my name from the family Bible with a red crayon, indicating loss. I dared not bite the hand that was prepared to feed me. I dared not cut off my nose to spite my face or my prick to spite my future progeny. The man sitting before me, as if in judgment, was all that stood between me and an experiment in misery that was certain to end badly.

"I'll do my best, Mr. Slater." I pocketed the small book (a breviary containing profane prayers offered up by every sort of enterprise, from stables to saloons, stationers to cemeteries), and went out into the madly turning street.

What *now*, Ollie? *This* now, Ollie.

I plunged into the city. By the end of that day, I would see it not as a pattern of shapes and colors, but as my father did: streets, lanes, and alleys overlaid by a Cartesian grid marked with debits and credits. And I was to be its dun.

First on the list of August debtors was Green's Hotel, a Victorian heap on Seventh Street, between Ranstead and Chestnut. The shade of Ollie past arose as I walked through the doorway and made for the front desk. I felt all the self-importance of an agent of the revenue or of a ducal envoy arrived to collect the yearly tithe from a reluctant tributary.

A middle-aged woman whose face showed the strain of competing smiles and frowns conveyed both expressions as I drew up to her desk, my little gray book in hand. "May I help you?" she asked.

"I've come from *The Press* about your advertising bill."

She kept her composure admirably. "You'll have to see Mr. Trench about that. He's not in today. Please try again, and thank you for your visit."

I had no better luck that morning with three other firms, all bent on stiffing Mr. Slater.

Hunger sharp and funds scant, I drank a sherry with an egg in it at a nearby lunchroom, where beefsteak loomed on the bill of fare like an unattainable desire. I reviewed my situation and discovered damned few reasons to be glad.

I was feeling less like a papal envoy and more like a beggar as I entered the office of Hastings Gold Leaf Manufacturers. Hastings had retired to Elmira after selling the business to John Taws, who had been his foreman. (I credit this piece of intelligence to a drummer exiting the front door after failing to sell a novel wire paper fastener manufactured by E.H. Hotchkiss Company, which today goes by the name *stapler*.) Taws was at his desk, doing the arithmetic of profit and loss. Red ink was much in evidence—not Persian, Venetian, Tuscan, or Mars—just ordinary red, the color of a hemorrhage.

"Good afternoon, Mr. Taws. My name is Oliver Fischer, from *The Press*. I'm here to collect your August payment for . . ." I ran a finger down a column in my sacred codex. "A two-column twenty-eight-agate advertisement. At three dollars the column inch, that's twelve dollars and sixty-five cents."

Taws scratched his head. "It didn't shake much business out of the trees, Mr. Fischer." I had no argument to make. "Still, I expect it's not *The Press*'s fault. Business has been off ever since the panic. It's hard to convince a proprietor to gold-leaf a sign to the gents when he can hardly pay the brewer." He smiled. "It's no fault of yours, young man." Having lately been a general-purpose scapegoat, his remark took me by surprise. "Would it be okay if I were to pay half today and the balance on the last of the month?"

"I'm sure it would be, Mr. Taws."

He opened a cash drawer and, wetting his thumb, counted out the greenbacks and then made a small heap of coins. I marked my book and wrote him a receipt.

"Next month, maybe your advertising boys can make me a smaller ad."

"I'm sure they can."

We shook hands like two heads of state concluding a treaty satisfactory to both sides. He poured each of us three fingers of Kentucky bourbon. We drank it off and then had another two fingers' worth.

I held up my empty glass, expecting to ratify our transaction with an integer of bourbon, on the three-two-one principle, but I had mistaken him for a postprandial sot.

"Can't get muzzy-headed, Mr. Fischer! We both have work to do this afternoon."

He caught up with me as I was walking down the street. "Something for you, Ollie." He gave me a leather pencil case decorated with an imperfect flourish of gold. "They don't always turn out, you know," he said in an embarrassed way. "You might find a use for it, regardless."

I entered the lying-in hospital at Eleventh and

Cherry Streets—blown off course by five fingers of whiskey.

"May I help you?" asked a woman, striking for a complete lack of anything notable.

"I've come about your August ad in *The Press*."

"Step this way."

She led me into the office of Matron McClellan, whose uncle had been the Civil War general George B. McClellan, known as "Young Napoléon" in recognition of his short stature and habit of posing with his right hand inside his tunic. His niece was cut from the same stiff cloth.

"Mr. Fischer, our hospital does not advertise. There's no need, nor would we wish to be seen in company with electric corsets, liver pills, homeopathic remedies, or cures for halitosis."

I rubbed my eyes, squinted at the page, and realized I'd come to the wrong place. "Sorry, my mistake. I meant to stop at the butcher's next door." I dropped the book, and, while attempting to retrieve it, I got entangled in her skirts. "Beg pardon, matron."

"You must be drunk!" She leaned forward and ordered me to breathe out. I withheld my breath, under the impression that it was mine alone. "Breathe!" she commanded. I exhaled; she recoiled. "You *have* been drinking!"

I smiled sheepishly.

"Leave at once, or I'll shout for a policeman!"

I flew from her office and out onto the street,

where I knocked down a mother-to-be, her blessed condition revealed by the absence of a corset. "I beg your pardon, madam!" I sprinted down Eleventh and disappeared into Apple Tree Street, where I stopped, drew breath, and felt sorry for myself. I stood on the verge of being done with dunning. Instead, I'd rusticate with the Barretts. What a lark it would be to guzzle beer and gorge on ham hocks underneath the pergola, along with Pop, his fellow eccentrics, and the redbone coonhound! Burk might give me a job in his abattoir. I can swing a sledgehammer as well as the next man. I felt my biceps. Maybe not so well as he. I felt them again. Maybe not at all. You're a scrawny dub, Ollie. You had better stick to dunning, at least till your shoes wear out and your arches fall. As to your spirits, they count for not at all, my good fellow.

That afternoon, I stopped at the Fiske Rubber Company, the Adelphi Theatre, the Hotel Hanover, and a sewing machine outfit in the Sibley Building. I had only to say "I'm here about your August bill" to be shown the door.

At six o'clock, I dragged myself up the stairs and into the advertising department. The artists were putting away their things, grumbling or laughing, according to their personalities. I approached Slater's desk with the confidence of one who has gone out into the world and come back beaten to a pulp. I turned over the receivables book, along with Mr.

Taws's contribution to the firm's solvency. As I turned to leave for the day, he asked, "Will I see you in the morning?"

On the next morning, at eight o'clock sharp, I cruised into Slater's office, my suit brushed and my shoes shined with Erdal polish. My freshly shaved mug stung with wintergreen. Slater was looking at a drawing of the Universal Food Chopper, which the illustrator had garlanded with a cabbage head, a string of onions, a bunch of carrots, an apple, a coconut, a fish, even a lobster. Chickens, turkeys, and ducks strutted two by two around the patented appliance.

"I don't know, Walker . . ." said Slater, pulling his lower lip like a drawer where he kept his thoughts. "It's kind of vague."

"What's vague about it?" the illustrator shot back.

"Ask yourself, Walker: Will the sucker get what all this flora and fauna's supposed to signify? You've got to make it obvious to the frau skimming pages in search of ladies' hats."

The artist snuffled in concession, then quickly sketched a pig, its head inside the item's churning maw, while a second pinkish fellow, its trotters on a ladder, waited with a smile to be ground into hamburger.

"Oink!" said Slater approvingly.

"Oink, oink!" said the illustrator, happy to have made the pig fly, so to speak.

"Sorry about yesterday, Fischer," said Slater, returning to his desk.

"Yesterday?"

"I took you for another guy hired to beat the pavement."

To this stunner, I said not a word, having learned that one should think before one speaks. (Whether Slater *had* mistaken me or tested me, my character and resolve, I never did work out.)

"It's up to you whether you want to continue as our sidewalk agent or trade your ledger and pencil stub for a taboret." He pointed to an unused artist's table in the corner.

And so it was that I became emperor of the inkwell and glue pot, at a corner desk in the advertising department of *The Press*, a job I would keep until I was packed off to the Caribbean to illustrate the American invasion of Cuba.

Slater put a wire armature shaped like a torso and fitted with a lady's brassiere on my table. "Draw this, Fischer."

"From what angle?"

"To best effect."

I said to myself, "Now I call that an oracular pronouncement!"

Waiting for an inspiration, I mulled and cogitated. I cracked my knuckles and dusted my shoes.

I went to the gents and splashed water on my face. I muddled and stewed and considered throwing in my eyeshade and paper cuffs. Erato, the muse responsible for the production of love poetry, had forsaken me for another scribbler. (Although callow, I knew that the muse Polymnia, invoked by geometers, would be useless in the case of a woman's undergarment.)

And then Iris walked out of the golden light of morning falling through the sash. She, too, was an illustrator in the ad department. Unlike me, she knew what she was about, having settled into her taboret six months prior to my arrival. She was kind, as well as comely.

"I suggest this vantage," she said, rotating the garment so that the thrusting bust was seen in three-quarter view. "Voilà! The Classique, manufactured in Paris, France. This lovely article is available in coquille, wool, satin, and brocade. Should madam need a boost, we at *The Press* recommend Dr. Scott's Electric High-Bust Corset, elegant in shape and finish, cut to the latest French pattern, and warranted against accidental electrocution. Mr. Fischer, you're blushing!"

Her burlesque had been innocent of all that insinuates and leers.

Slater spoke to me just once that first day, to ask what I thought of John Taws. "Did he give you one of his three-finger, two-finger Kentucky libations?" I nodded. "He's a card! And you're not the first footpad to take a nap after a nip at Hastings Gold Leaf Manufacturers!"

At six o'clock, we stowed our things and hung up our smocks. Slater's rolltop clattered down its rails and came to an emphatic stop, releasing the pent-up energies of his minions, who stampeded out the door.

"Can I buy you dinner?" I asked Iris, whose last name is Coates. She was, I plainly saw, more worldly than I, whose boyish face had bloomed when she mentioned the high-bust corset.

"Ask me some other night, Mr. Fischer."

On the way out to the street, I stopped at Smith's office. "I'd like a word with you, sir."

"What's on your mind?"

"I thought I was hired to illustrate the news or editorials—at the very least a feuilleton."

He glanced at me, as one would a simpleton, then, looking down at his desk, ran a stubby finger over the silhouette of the Classique that I'd drawn. "You should be glad Slater didn't give you a coal scuttle to illustrate." He heaved himself up in his chair and shouted, "Plenty of dubs would love to be drawing brassieres!"

"I know it, and I thank you again for giving me the chance."

"Thank that young friend of yours . . . Pearson. He could just as well have kept mum about you and eliminated a possible rival. Newspapermen and women are cutthroats when it comes to their careers. Remember that."

Mumbling platitudes, I backed out of his office like a courtier leaving a king's privy. Hands in pockets, a fag between his lips, Robert was waiting at the corner. "Ollie, old scout! How's life in the mule yard?"

"Swell!" I said, thinking of Iris. "Say, I looked for you at lunch."

"I was in court!" He was excited, I envious. "It's another 'Trial of the Century!' as the headline boys crow, even when the victim is a mutt accidentally killed by a boy throwing rocks at rats. Look here." He took a pencil sketch from his pocket.

"Pearson, you're a lucky son of a gun, to be drawing the news!"

"Maybe." He looked into the sky above the statue of William Penn, where, at that hour, a strangely beautiful, though unsettling, violet hue preceded the slow arrival of the summer night.

"No maybe about it." His mood having darkened, my voice had been less assured.

"I wonder how I'll do when I'm sent to draw the aftermath of a train wreck."

My life became like any other lived snug between the poles of euphoria and despair. I looked upon the world as people do who stand apart from it. From late August 1897 until February 15, 1898, the day the *Maine* blew up in Havana Harbor, I was as complacent a young man as any other with a job and a friend to share a room furnished in deal instead of coal boxes. My clothes and hat would not have seemed out of place at Delmonico's. I loved a woman who did not find my awkward groping grotesque.

In November of that year 1897, I drew my first lampoon of American presumption and hypocrisy. I had just finished illustrating the Goodell Company mechanical apple peeler. It was still on the modeling stand. My hand (it seemed autonomous) pinned a clean sheet to the board and began a second sketch of the contraption. In place of the peeled Newtown Pippin that I had drawn for the advertisement, I substituted Earth, poles pierced by the machine's opposing spits. Instead of an unspooling apple paring, I drew the western hemisphere skinned of the Caribbean, on whose shaving I drew Cuba and Puerto Rico. I drew three smaller peels, tagged PHILIPPINES, GUAM, and HAWAIIAN ISLANDS. At the top of the sheet, I hand-lettered the caption RIPE FOR THE PICKIN'.

"That's out-of-sight, Ollie!" I turned from the board and saw Iris, amused and nodding approval. "Here's to America the Gluttonous!" she said, lifting a glass of turpentine in which a paint brush steeped. Later, she composed a parody of Katharine Lee Bates's patriotic hymn to Kansas wheat, the view from Pike's Peak, and the "White City" of the Chicago Exposition:

> O beautiful for halcyon skies,
> For amber waves of gain . . .

That evening, Iris let me walk her to the hotel on Filbert Street, near the Reading depot, where she shared two rooms with a girl who worked at Wanamaker's department store. I was certain that she would be Anne, an irony arranged by the universe to spite me. I was spared, however; her name was Constance. Pretty and vivacious, she served "an ornamental function behind a perfume counter," as Iris unkindly put it. (I never saw her. Male visitors to the "ladies only" Excelsior were barred by a woman resembling Mary Surratt, hanged for her part in the plot to assassinate Lincoln.) That night, Iris let me kiss her. Her lips were dry; mine, I feared, too wet. My hands, which were cold, I kept in my pockets.

"Will we be lovers?" I asked shyly.

"What do *you* think, Ollie?" Not knowing what to think, I studied the expression on a face such as the priestess at Delphi would have shown to petitioners of the god Apollo. I felt feverish, and it was not the impending war that made me feel that way.

Two days before Christmas, my sister Dorothy came to visit. Her excitement boiled over like chocolate in a saucepan, before she could finish taking off her winter things.

"Ollie, I'm glad to see you! I don't have to be home till tomorrow afternoon. Father thinks I'm stopping at Aunt Stella's, while I buy Mother a Christmas present. What do you think of a beaded purse or a silk scarf with a Japanese teahouse on it? She admires Mrs. Willard's so. I wonder if they're dear. The sweet old girl deserves something nice for putting up with Stone Face. Sometimes I want to kick and scream the house down! If only she weren't ill, I'd leave in a snap! You bet I would! Mother asked if she and I mightn't go to the Christmas Eve service tomorrow and sing carols, like we used to do. The old crab said, 'Midnight is no time for women to be out in the streets.' He's impossible!" She put her coat and hat back on. "Get your skates on, Ollie, and show me the sights!" She stopped abruptly at the door. "Unless you have other plans?"

"I'm yours to command."

She clapped her hands like a schoolgirl contemplating a treat.

We went out into the cold, clear air of late December and walked arm in arm to Gimbel Brothers at Tenth and Market Streets. I watched, happily, as she searched the aisles for Mother's Christmas gift. Finding no Japanese habutai scarves silk-screened with a teahouse, she settled on one from China showing a pagoda. While she waited to have it wrapped, I bought her one adorned with a golden phoenix and tucked it into my pocket.

"Ollie, might we have something hot to drink upstairs?"

"That's nowhere posh enough for us!" I told her, leading her outside, into the nippy afternoon air.

"Are we as grand as all that, Mr. Fischer?"

"I'll say!"

I took her to Sandor's Café, across from the Mercantile Library, on Ludlow Street, the closest Philadelphia comes to bohemia. Not having been in Prague, Berlin, or Paris, I couldn't say what cosmopolites would make of it. Dot was ecstatic. She may

have been twenty-five, but her world was as circum-
scribed as that of a domestic, which she was and is
likely to remain.

"Brother, this *is* grand!" she said as she sipped
her chocolate in between nibbles of rock cake.
"There's nothing like it in dreary old Olney, unless
you count Michael's Oyster House or Hennessey's
saloon, which has—you may recall—a ladies'
entrance. Once I stuck my head in the door and
yelled that Carrie Nation was coming with her ax.
She wasn't, you know!"

I laughed to see her girlish happiness. "Aren't you
too old for high jinks?"

"Oh, it was years ago, and I did it on a dare." The
light went out of her eyes as she pensively stirred her
chocolate. "Hetty Keller passed, did you hear, Ollie?
Of scarlet fever."

"I'm sorry to hear it." Remembering the scarf
in my pocket, I told her to close her eyes. "Tight.
Tighter!"

She did, and the concentrated effort pulled her
frown up into a smile.

"An early Christmas present, dear Dot. I'm sorry
I didn't get it wrapped."

"Why, it's lovely, Ollie! Thank you!" She leaned
across the table and kissed my cheek. And then, as if
releasing the exotic bird from captivity, she shook out
the scarf so that it floated above her head before flut-
tering around her narrow shoulders. I've seldom seen

a more graceful motion. "Won't Mother and I look a treat this Easter?"

I wondered if King Charles would allow them to wear their "chink" scarves out of the house. Asiatics were disease- and vice-ridden aliens, and he voted for the Republican candidate who shouted loudest in favor of their exclusion. I'll never forget the one occasion when Dot had opposed him. He'd been raging against a Chinaman who'd had the nerve to speak to him on the street.

"What did he want?" asked Mother.

"Who the hell knows? He sounded like a turkey with too much corn in its crop."

Dot was scared right down to the toes of her lace-ups. Her legs shook as she got up from the table where we were eating our Sunday dinner. In a voice that escaped her like a growl, she berated him for his un-Christian attitude. She'd been to church and taken Communion. The dining room fell silent. I could hear the chandelier's crystal pendants tremble. Her anger spent, she sang in a small, weak tremolo:

> *Jesus loves the little children*
> *All the children of the world*
> *Red, brown, yellow*
> *Black and white*
> *They are precious in His sight.*
> *Jesus loves the little children*
> *Of the world.*

One might think that Charles had witnessed the revolt of the Haitian slaves. His stern jaw dropped; his mouth fell open. I had an unappetizing view of mashed potatoes and peas waiting to be swallowed. Mother turned white as a sickroom sheet. When Dot had finished and the echo of the doggerel's last line had been absorbed by the maroon-striped wallpaper above the varnished wainscoting, he threw his fork at his only begotten daughter. It nicked her cheek. For a terrifying minute in which Mother fainted and a nervous giggle escaped my lips, I thought that the fork had drawn blood, but it was merely gravy. He wet his palm with water from the pitcher and sprinkled Mother, a gesture lacking only an aspergillum. She opened her eyes and, much fuddled, asked if we were ready for our cherry tart. Dot took her upstairs to her room. Left with no audience, save me, to listen to him pontificate, he said, "Such bunk may be all right in Sunday school, but it has nothing to do with the world we live in. You may leave the table, Oliver."

"But what about the cherry tart?" I asked. I was only a boy of eight or nine. His eyes seemed to burst into flame. I expect that his eyeglasses had caught a beam of afternoon light coming in at the dining room window. I stood, and my chair rocked violently, driven by the engine of my nervousness. I walked backward from the room, transfixed by his burning stare.

Dot was going on about her plans for Easter: "Mother will sew me a new dress, and we both shall have new shoes and hats and gloves—well, maybe not shoes; last year's will do in a pinch. Oh, but they mustn't pinch! And we'll have to see about our hats. Mother may be able to perk up our old ones. But we really must have new gloves—lemon-colored for me, fawn for her. I must remember to clean the marcasite, and—there's so much to do! Easter comes late this year, so I can uncover the bulbs. How lovely if the tulips show! Did I tell you, Ollie? Father said I can invite Flora to dinner after church, unless Mother has a headache. Oh, but she mustn't! Maybe you can be there, too, Ollie. That would be nice! I'll make a chocolate egg for the prodigal."

I watched her animated face and hands and felt sadness, knowing that she was likely to end up like Emily Dickinson: a ghost in her father's house, making grape jelly, boiling rhubarb for his bowels, and gossiping with the neighbors across the privet hedge.

"Close your eyes, Ollie." I cocked my head like a parrot. "Close them. Tight. Tighter!" She placed a slim package in my hand. "Merry Christmas, brother! I was going to give it to you tomorrow before I leave, but I'm such a flibbertigibbet, I may forget." It had a pleasing weight on my palm. "Open it, silly!"

It was one of the new mechanical pencils with a twist-feed mechanism. It would have been expensive. Dot had no employment outside the hairpin fence. She cleaned and dusted the house, tended the garden, canned and jarred, and, ever since Mother became "frail," did much of the cooking and baking. On

Friday night, Boss Charles would present her with an "emolument." It was not generous. A woman without a job or nest egg is housebound. Her only escape is into marriage, but Dot's father—I will not call him mine!—discouraged suitors.

"Ollie, draw me!" she cried, her eyes bright as buttons. "Please do!"

I smoothed the back side of the Christmas paper, gave the mechanical pencil's barrel a twist, and started to draw her face. I realized, as I drew, that hers was not a pretty one, but her good humor and good heart always made it appear so to me. I drew her as she appeared at that moment: a girl filled to the brim with gaiety, mischief, and a pinch of treachery in having lied to her father.

"Finished."

She eyed the drawing shrewdly. "That's all well and good, Ollie, but I want you to sketch me the way you used to." She was referring to the caricatures I would make of her, which always left her howling in indignation and delight. But I hadn't the heart to distort the dear face. The bell above the door to the street jumped brightly, announcing the entrance of each new customer. The odors of citron, vanilla, coffee, warm bread, and cake arrived each time the kitchen door swung open. It was ordinary and wonderful. Before that afternoon, I would have captured Dot's quirks in quick, careless strokes, and since there would have been no deliberation on my part, the result would not have hurt. But I was keenly aware of her as she sat across the table, and worried that a caricature would be unkind. "Give me the funny face you used to!"

I sighed. Dear Dot, you really are plain, and I would not hurt your feelings for the world. Hoping that she would be satisfied, I drew her hat, a gift from Grandmother Barrett and, for Dot, uncharacteristically à la mode. According to the gospel of *Woman's World*, required reading for those in the advertising trade, "Fashionable hats all resemble walking gardens." Instead of the faux flowers piled on top of my sister's toque, I drew a luxuriant garden, my sister looking small and lost among the sunflowers.

January brought snow; the streets were clogged with gray drifts spotted yellow. Iris and I drew coffee mills, coal scuttles, Persian lamb muffs, felt slippers, ladies' ventilating boots in serge or cloth with waterproof lasting, improved hot-water bottles, warming pans warranted not to set fire to the bed, syrups for croup, catarrh, and colic, guaranteed remedies for lumbago and pertussis. I illustrated an advertisement for the Magic Washer, a laundry soap manufactured by the George Dixon Company of Illinois. Dressed in red-and-white-striped trousers, blue cutaway coat, opera hat, and Congress gaiters, Uncle Sam kicks a coolie off a cliff above the ocean, his braided hair as if electrified. The copy manages to promote both the powder's miraculous whitening agency and the company's patriotic hatred of the race: LEAVE NO YELLOW IN YOUR CLOTHES and, on the bottom of the package, THE CHINESE MUST GO!

Armed with pencils, pastels, and charcoal sticks, we so-called artists fought winter's grinding war against our species, while the news of the day seeped into our castle of flimflam and hokum like icy drafts. It arrived in front-page headlines and indignant asides that grew ever bolder and louder as squibs grew into diatribes. The temperature of the nation's war fever could be told by the number of exclamation marks:

200,000 SPANISH TROOPS ARRIVE IN OUR HEMISPHERE TO QUELL CUBAN RIOTING!

ooooo

WIDESPREAD DESTRUCTION OF CUBA'S SUGARCANE!!

SEVERE SHORTAGE AGGRAVATES ECONOMIC DEPRESSION IN U.S.

ooooo

GREAT HEAVY COLUMNS OF SMOKE SIGHTED ABOVE BLAZING FIELDS OF SUGARCANE

Often after we had put away our drawing things for the night, Iris and I would walk the streets as much to see the angry crowds as to satisfy a mutual wish to postpone our parting. She didn't hide her feelings.

That first kiss in November was followed by others in doorways, alleys, a storage closet in *The Press* building and on its roof, and, once, in the Hanover Street Burying Ground, where her father lay "plotting his revenge on the living." Our shared animus toward our fathers—hers dead, mine ossified—appeared to excite her. She kissed me with a wildness I have not known since that night among the granite tombs. Her tongue rooted in my mouth, startling me, who had never imagined that use for the muscular organ. I put my hands into her coat and felt her breasts like two small birds waiting to be let out.

Afterward, we went to the Bijou Theatre to see the Lumière brothers' moving pictures, shown between the variety acts. Neither of us was in the mood for the patter and pratfalls of the comics, the bravado of knife throwers, the juggling of dinner plates and chairs, or the antics of a trained seal that balanced a ball on its nose. Had a magician caused an elephant to disappear, we would have been left unmoved. Something was happening on *our* side of the footlights. Sex was in the air most certainly, but also a nervousness that had nothing to do with the electrification of the senses. I know now that the impending war with Spain had raised the general temperature. Iris's and mine would have been tending toward a crisis, immersed as we were in current events, which spilled from *The Press*'s serious departments into frivolous ones concerned with fancy-dress balls, reviews of the latest romantic and gothic novels, glove etiquette for ladies and gentlemen, and advertising. (Obituaries occupy an ambiguous place in newspapers, being of the utmost seriousness for a few readers and objects of mild curiosity for the rest.)

After the footlights were extinguished, Iris and I sat spellbound in the dark as men and women in Lyon made of lights and shadows captured by Auguste and Louis Lumière appeared before our eyes in a theater in Philadelphia. That afternoon we had seen their like leaving the Cornelius Building. In the morning, we could watch a train arrive at the Reading Railroad depot that would look hardly more substantial than that in *L'Arrivée d'un train en gare de la Ciotat*. In the summer, we could go to Asbury Park, where I'd drawn caricatures of boardwalk strollers, and see costumed bathers playing in the surf identical to those in *Baignade en mer*. The brothers had outdone artifice; they had created its opposite. Fifty-six feet of film cranked by hand through their cinematograph surpassed all previous spectacles. Nothing in any book by Verlaine or Jules Verne could astonish like those translucent parings startled into existence by light. The Lumières had skinned the apple to its essence, which was not—strange paradox—its juice or fragrance, but its surface, that tender place of contact and encounter.

"I felt as if I could get out of my seat and walk home with those French girls," said Iris in the hushed tone that people use in church or at funerals. The moving pictures had left us reverent and nostalgic for a world slipping from our grasp—and also afraid that we would never possess it truly.

"The war will change everything," she said, biting her lip.

Uncertain if the change would be for better or worse, I said nothing.

We walked to my rooming house in a silence complicated by desire. Robert Pearson was in the state capital at Harrisburg, sketching the honorable members of the Pennsylvania General Assembly as they debated the removal of the dishonorable member for Bucks County who had been caught in flagrante delicto with a girl who roasted peanuts and cashews at Woolworth's.

"Don't be nervous!" she said as I fumbled at the buttons of her blouse. "Here, let me."

I laughed to see myself in the mirror. Is there a more ridiculous sight than a man without his clothes? And then I remembered something Eakins had said aboard the *Myrtle Jane*: "Beauty is to be found in the living animal form."

> One, two,
> Buckle my shoe;
> Three, four,
> Knock at the door;

Five, six,
Pick up sticks;
Seven, eight,
Lay them straight:
Nine, ten,
A big fat hen;
Eleven, twelve,
Dig and delve . . .

"*Now,* Ollie, we are lovers."

The room was cold. We dressed hurriedly. I walked Iris to her hotel. My lips chapped, I kissed her cheek, and walked back the way I had come.

I gazed at my unmade bed and shivered for a reason having nothing to do with the cold. No other bed unmade by love would ever move me so poignantly.

THOUSANDS OF CUBANS
ARE SICK AND DYING!

DISEASE AND STARVATION RAMPANT!!

As the northern hemisphere pitched headlong toward the depths of winter, and the United States toward war with Spain, newsboys could not keep papers on the street. Morning, afternoon, and evening editions, and extras run off at all hours, carried the cri de coeur of the Cuban people and, after the sinking of the United States warship *Maine*, of our own enraged citizenry. In New York City, William Hearst's *Evening Journal* would print as many as forty editions in a single day—broadsheets, most of them, a few pages of newsprint, maps, smudgy halftone photographs, sketches of battlefields, and cartoons ridiculing Spanish greed, cowardice, and atrocities.

As early as 1896, Republicans had been up in arms over the Reconcentration Policy of Valeriano Weyler, the "Butcher," as he was called in the American press.

GOVERNOR GENERAL VALERIANO WEYLER ORDERS CUBAN CIVILIANS INTO MILITARY GARRISON TOWNS

The Cuban *reconcentrados* had been confined in towns garrisoned by Spanish soldiers. They died by the thousands of starvation, cholera, typhus, dysentery, and nameless fevers. The death of so many men, women, and children inflamed American sentiment against the tyrants in Madrid.

The Press fattened like a goose fed grain through a funnel as entrepreneurs took note of its expanding circulation. Confectioners, wine merchants, restaurateurs, variety theaters—every kind of commercial enterprise dreamed of a legion of customers eager for treats in the grim days ahead. In the advertising department, we drew Singer sewing machines, Berliner gramophones, Beecham's Pills ("Wise Folks Take Them"), Grape-Nuts ("For Wherever Brains and Brawn Are Essential"), and a hundred other marvels that promised to save us from the pain of piles, blisters, chilblains, dyspepsia, and lumbago. (Suffering caused by war was elegized as ennobling, as long as it was not ours.)

The popular stage actor Wilton Lackaye took a moment from performing Svengali to pen a ditty critical of the journalistic profession:

> But since our statesmen have agreed
>   Old Glory to protect,
> No tasteless huckster now the flag
>   to odium may subject;
> We want a law enacted with
>   specific intent
> To trepan a sense of shame into
>   the advertising "gent"!

On a Sunday evening toward the end of January, Iris took me to meet her aunt Jessie, who rented a "Father, Son, and Holy Ghost" in Kensington, near the Delaware Rolling Mill. Three poorly heated rooms were stacked like blocks of ice, one atop another. Iris and I entered by the kitchen door and climbed a winding stairs to a sitting room on the second floor. The stairs continued on to the sole bedroom at the top floor. "Trinity houses," like the Mütter Museum, are peculiar to Philadelphia.

"Ollie, this is my aunt Jessie Mullins."

"Make yourselves comfortable," she said. "How is your mother, dear?"

"At death's door, so she says."

"My sister is always at death's door! You tell the old soak she's too woolly-headed to find it."

Jessie Mullins took in manuscripts the way other women do washing. She had learned to typewrite at the Philadelphia Normal School and was employed by one of the many secretarial bureaus in the city. Her invalid husband was confined to the bedroom. I would not have known he was in the house had it not been for his chronic cough.

"How's Uncle John?" asked Iris.

"He has his good days and bad days."

Jessie struck me as one of those people who get by and get by until the day comes when they fall sick, drop dead, or find themselves on the sidewalk, along with their meager belongings. Or like the cheerful Wilkins Micawber in *David Copperfield*, they are transported—not by joy—to a penal colony. (Few of those cheated of their small dreams and modest hopes have the nerve to toss a bomb into a plutocrat's parlor.) "Go up and see him, Iris. He'll be glad for the sight of you."

While the two women were upstairs, I walked around the room, which was not large, and looked at pictures hanging on the wall of people who, by the old-fashioned cut of their clothes, would have been dead, and at the books on the shelf, mostly dictionaries, grammar manuals, and street directories—the accoutrements of a secretary or an office clerk. The tatty couch and armchair, the scarred table, the threadbare carpet, the mismatched cups, saucers, and plates in the sideboard spoke of a family at the end of its slender means. John Mullins had been employed by one of the textile mills along the Delaware until he came down with weaver's cough, a quaint name for a lung disease common to workers in the woolens trade. No longer able to earn his nine dollars a week, he was let go, another quaint expression, meaning "Go home and hang yourself."

Beside a Hammond typewriter, a stack of pages lay beneath a cold flatiron. Hearing the voices of the women upstairs—one cheerful, the other solicitous—followed by John Mullins's choked words and croupy cough, I satisfied my curiosity concerning their contents. On a page picked at random, I read Chicago anarchist Louis Lingg's last words before his death sentence was pronounced for the murder of a Chicago policeman during the Haymarket Massacre in May 1886:

> I repeat that I am the enemy of the "order" of today, and I repeat that, with all my powers, so long as breath remains in me, I shall combat it. I declare again, frankly and openly, that I am in favor of using force. I have told Captain Schaack, and I stand by it, "If you cannonade us, we shall dynamite

you." You laugh! Perhaps you think, "You'll throw no more bombs"; but let me assure you . . .

I heard footsteps on the stairs and turned to see the Mullins cat, its pads thumping heavily on the maple treads. I picked up the thread of the martyr's last words to those who were about to crucify him:

> . . . that I die happy on the gallows, so confident am I that the hundreds and thousands to whom I have spoken will remember my words; and when you shall have hanged us, then—mark my words— they will do the bomb-throwing! In this hope do I say to you: I despise you. I despise your order, your laws, your force-propped authority. Hang me for it!

I had reached the final exclamation mark just as Jessie's shoes came into view as she descended the stairs. I anchored the typed pages with the flatiron before she could catch me snooping.

"Ollie, would you like something to drink? Beer is in the kitchen shed—or maybe you'd like some of John's Irish. It's no use to the poor man now. I've been saving it for his wake."

Although I'd have liked whiskey, I might have made a poor impression on Iris to ask for it under the circumstances. "Beer will be fine," I said, wondering what kind of face I should be wearing—brave like Jessie's or rueful like Iris's.

The soon-to-be-widowed Mrs. Mullins went downstairs to the kitchen shed. I could hear the faint jangle of beer bottles, "the music of the spheres," Robert called it. I glanced nervously at Iris, afraid that she knew, by the mysterious intuition that makes every woman a psychic, that I'd been poking my nose into her aunt's business. But when our eyes met, she smiled. I sighed in return. I suppose she took it for the sigh of a lovesick beau, since I was often one in her presence. Mrs. Mullins returned with three bottles held between her fingers by their necks. They brought to mind that of Louis Lingg, broken by Death's strong hands.

While I opened them, Iris brought three tankards from the cupboard. To toast the dying man's health seemed the wrong thing to do, so I mumbled an all-purpose "God bless this house," an infelicity that uncorked Jessie's anger. No longer Micawberish, she raged against an unjust universe, as Melville's Ahab had done his whale. "If wishes were horses, beggars would ride!"

"Forgive me, Mrs. Mullins," I stammered, glancing at Iris, who was preoccupied with a loose thread on her sleeve.

"Young man, don't allow yourself to be sucked into the maelstrom! You'll see: Before long, McKinley will call for volunteers." (A month after she uttered her prophecy, he did so, if reluctantly. Before long, 125,000 men had enlisted in Secretary of State Hay's "splendid little war.") "If you must fight, fight big business—the behemoths and piranhas that crush and nibble us to death. Go bayonet Arthur Boggs, who turned out my husband after twelve years of good and faithful servitude. If you want to do something useful, burn down the Frankford Woolens Mill, preferably with the old miser inside, counting his profits! I'll give you carfare and a bottle of kerosene. I'll gladly go with you and light the match!"

Clearing my throat of what felt like wool ticking, I assured her that I would not enlist in the army, navy, or, recalling Croydon, the Baptist Missionary Society.

"Don't mention those do-gooding good-for-nothings in my house! What do the godly do when men, women, and children suffer for want of bread and the common necessities of life? I despise the lot of them!" She jumped up from the couch, flew across the room, and took out a manuscript from a drawer. "Let's hear what the Reverend W. Bishop Johnson, D.D., had to say at the National Baptist Convention." Jessie thumbed through its pages till she came to the odious passage. She tore into it as a butcher's dog would a bloody piece of meat:

> In this country the torch put to the factories that have discharged hands for good or bad reasons; obstructions on the rail-tracks,

in front of midnight express trains, because
the offenders do not like the president of
the company; strikes on shipboard the hour
they were going to sail, or in printing offices
the hour the paper was to go to press, or in
the mines the day the coal was to be delivered, or on house scaffoldings so the builder
fails in keeping his contract—all these are
only a hard blow on the head of American
labor, and cripple its arms, and lame its feet,
and pierce its heart. Traps sprung suddenly
upon employers and violence never took
one knot out of the knuckles of toil, or put
one farthing of wages into a callous palm.
Barbarism will never cure the wrongs of
civilization. Mark that.

"Mark that, indeed!" She glared at me as if I were an
apostle and apologist of capitalism.

"Did you hear that, Oliver?" Eyes popping in
indignation, Jessie repeated the remark by the stiff-
necked Reverend Johnson, in a voice pitched to the
heavens, as if to bend God's ear: "'In this country the
torch put to the factories that have discharged hands
for good or bad reasons . . .' The Frankford Woolens
Mill discharged my husband for *breathing*! For twelve
years, sixty hours a week, he carelessly breathed the
air inside the mill. But the torch has yet to be put to
the factory."

If only Eakins had been there to see me in the

company of an anarchist, my sleeves rolled up and my hand thrust into life's entrails, so to speak!

"It falls to you, Oliver Fischer, to call down His Almighty wrath on Arthur Boggs of the Knights of Pythias and the First Church of Profit!"

The spring of action having suddenly relaxed, she collapsed in a heap of mended clothes and darned stockings.

"Mrs. Mullins!" I pillowed her head on a souvenir of the 1893 convention of the National American Woman Suffrage Association, while Iris dredged up from the bottom of her reticule a vial of Crown Lavender Smelling Salts ("It clears the brain, steadies the nerves, and counteracts faintness and weariness"), which she had sketched and then purloined that afternoon. Pulling the glass stopper, she stung her aunt back into consciousness.

Jessie waved away the bottle. I would not have been surprised if she'd commanded me to replace the sal volatile with kerosene and make an inferno of the Frankford Woolens Mill, but she asked only for a drink of water. "I'm sorry, Iris, and you, young man. I . . ." Whatever she had intended to say to explain or mitigate her outburst fell into an ellipsis, the graveyard of the unspoken.

"Are you all right?" asked Iris. Jessie nodded. "I'll make up the couch for you." The bed upstairs was taken by a man in the process of casting off his mortal coil.

"I must finish typing the speech for the labor lyceum meeting."

"You can finish it tomorrow, Aunt Jessie." Iris looked anxiously at me. "Ollie, I think I ought to stay."

"I think you had better do so."

She helped Jessie onto the couch, unbuttoned her collar, loosened her dress, and took off her shoes and stockings.

"Don't let them sucker you into the fight, Oliver. If the imperialists try to drag you into their war, bite the bastards. And if you end up in Cuba, hide behind the nearest tree."

BLOODTHIRSTY SPANIARDS BLOW UP UNITED STATES MAN-OF-WAR MAINE IN HAVANA HARBOR!!!

○○○○○

Destroyed By A Torpedo!

○○○○○

Many Seamen Killed— War Will Probably Be Declared

February 15 EXTRA!

CRISIS IS AT HAND!
CABINET IN SESSION.
GROWING BELIEF IN
SPANISH TREACHERY!!

After February 15, 1898, the day the *Maine* struck a torpedo mine and sank in Havana Harbor, anti-imperialist voices grew weaker. Henceforth, Uncle Sam would be pictured as a benevolent giant, one hobnailed boot in Cuba, the other on the throat of the queen regent of Spain. Dealers in cotton waste and scrap iron looked forward to immensely profitable contracts with armament manufacturers, shipbuilders, and makers of shoddy. Although I hadn't seen Henry Burk since the August afternoon when Anne and I visited his estate, doubtless he was tinning meat for the army and navy to last them till doomsday. With no scraps to spare for the alligators, I wondered how long before they, too, would be skinned, stewed, and canned.

The public had a keen appetite for news, never mind how it was spiced or slanted. So *The Press* didn't depend on Gold Dust washing powder, Sapolio soap, and O-Cedar mop polish to keep its rotary presses going. Now and then, when the grind of turning out ads would slow, I'd amuse myself by scribbling cartoons.

Remembering the Universal Food Chopper, I drew a picture of Spanish soldiers standing on a plank, waiting their turn to jump into a meat grinder. Secretary of State Hay is turning the crank, while Uncle Sam takes his ease on a chaise longue, his spangled vest unbuttoned and his teeth clenched on a cigar rolled in Havana.

Lampoons, I found, came easily to me, so like in attitude and line are they to caricatures. My favorite was inspired by John Stanley's stirring lyric:

> I want to be a soldier,
> I want to use a gun;
> I want to slaughter Spaniards
> From dawn to set of sun.
> I want to smite them downward—
> To smite them hip and thigh—
> And never leave off smiting
> Till they all smitten lie!

I sketched a freckle-faced boy of six standing on a beach, beside a slapdash sign WELCOME TO CUBA. The waves, in triplets, splash the bottom of his rolled-up overalls. From out of the ocean sprawling behind him, Uncle Sam rises like a colossus, an American dreadnought tucked under each muscular arm. Aiming a popgun at a Spanish soldier pleading for his life, the boy intones, "I want to be a soldier, I want to use a gun; I want to slaughter Spaniards from dawn to set of sun."

One morning, Harry Smith sent for me. "Slater showed me your stuff, Fischer."

"My sketch of Ma Hankin's Improved Washing Board?"

"Your lampoons, you fool!"

I waited to be reprimanded for doodling on company time.

He swatted at a glowing shred of tobacco that had landed on his vest. "There's a desk in the editorial department with your name on it."

My enthusiasm was less than he'd expected.

"If you don't want it, I'll give it to somebody who does!"

"I'm happy where I am."

"Here's the thing, Fischer: You can be happy where you are for another week or two, and then be unhappy when I let you go. In case you haven't noticed, advertisers have been quitting us right and left. They don't need to advertise saucepans to housewives when they've got fat army contracts to make shrapnel." My dithering made him angry. "What'll it be, Fischer? The desk or the block?" He chopped his palm with the blade of his hand, a pantomime that brought to mind the beheading of a royalist or a chicken.

That night, Iris and I stopped for dinner at Horn and Hardart on Chestnut Street. I slid a dollar bill into the cashier's cage, and the nickel thrower shot twenty coins across the marble counter. We had only to put a coin into a slot and lift the window of our choice to satisfy our hunger. If only the universe were arranged on a similar principle! With its potted palms, gilt inlays, coffered ceiling, and stained-glass windows framed by Gothic arches, the Automat is more than a cheap eatery. It's a church where cabbies and clerks, drummers and shopgirls can sup in a communion of people whose lives are too small to have accomplished much in the way of sin or saintliness.

"Mr. Slater gave me my notice this afternoon," said Iris after a long pause, during which I had sketched her portrait in my mind, taking in her high forehead, heart-shaped chin, and auburn hair tucked up in a bun on top of her head. The stray ends of her hair gleamed like copper in the electric candle lamps.

I put down my fork and looked at the features of that pleasant face, which had organized themselves into an enigmatic expression, partly pensive, partly frowning, and partly angry. I had hoped that Slater would ask her to stay. I wondered if she knew I wouldn't be leaving. He may have mentioned it, or someone else may have. Secrets are hard to keep among those who work for newspapers, whose existence depends on disclosing them to the largest-possible public.

"It's a mug's game, Ollie, so don't beat yourself up."

She knew, then, that I hadn't been axed.

"What will you do?" I asked, my gaze fixed on the tomato soup dripping from her spoon.

"I'm thinking of moving to Chicago."

"Chicago . . ." I couldn't picture her in that city of stockyards, slaughterhouses, and pits where futures in wheat are wagered.

"My uncle owns a mail-order catalogue firm in Oak Park. He has a place for me in the art department."

"I wish . . ."

"If wishes were horses, beggars would ride," she said, and smiled.

As can happen to those who are intent on some small yet absorbing drama peculiar to themselves, Iris and I had been unaware of the Automat beyond our lacquered table. When we attended to our plates again, the world flooded back, carrying the clatter of tableware, clink of glasses, scrape of chairs, scratch of nickels shot across counters, snatches of conversation in many registers and in several languages. A voice made husky by cigars barked, "Remember the *Maine*! To hell with Spain!" A woman was singing in praise of Admiral Dewey, whose Asiatic Squadron was in Hong Kong, preparing to attack the Philippines by order of Assistant Secretary of the Navy Roosevelt— the same Roosevelt who, as New York City police commissioner, had turned on Stephen Crane, whose story would soon get tangled with my own.

He's a honey, a lulu,
And a fighter, too;
A hummer, a stunner,
And the truest blue.
He is handy, and a dandy . . .

April 21 EXTRA!

WAR IS DECLARED. AMERICA VS SPAIN! UNITED STATES NAVY WARSHIPS BLOCKADE CUBA

April 23 EXTRA!

SPAIN DECLARES WAR ON THE UNITED STATES!! SPAIN FIRES HER FIRST GUN

ooooo

How Moro Castle Sent 10 Projectiles Toward Our Fleet
VESSELS WERE MILES AWAY

May 1 EXTRA!

DEWEY SMASHES SPAIN'S FLEET!!!

ooooo

**Great Naval Battle Between Asiatic Squadron
and Spanish Warships off Manila**

○○○○○

VENGEANCE FOR THE MAINE!!!

May 8 EXTRA!

**TORPEDO BOAT U.S.S. WINSLOW
AND GUNBOAT U.S.S. MACHIAS
BLOCKADE CÁRDENAS**

May 11 EXTRA!

**AMERICAN SQUADRON
ENGAGES SPANISH GUNBOATS
IN THE BATTLE OF CÁRDENAS!**

May 12 EXTRA!

**U.S. NAVY WARSHIPS
BOMBARD SPANISH FORTIFICATIONS
AT SAN JUAN PORTO RICO!!**

I sat with a plate of mackerel and potato salad balanced on one knee, a glass of beer between my shoes, and a condoling expression on my face, which I sent out generally into the crowded parlor of the Mullins's Father, Son, and Holy Ghost house. Although there'd been a funeral and a burial earlier in the day, John Mullins had spoken from beyond the grave in his last will and testament, forbidding priests, nuns, and readings from Holy Scripture. Instead, a big man with large hands and a monumental head that might have been chiseled from a block of granite had stood among the mourners gathered around a hole in the unhallowed ground of a municipal cemetery and read from Henry George's book *Progress and Poverty*. The selection of texts did nothing to console the women who, being Irish, keened, while their taciturn husbands tugged their collars in embarrassment.

Save for Iris and her widowed aunt, I didn't know a soul—blessed or blasted—at the martyr's wake. The two women were fussing in the Father's precinct; I was feeling awkward in the Son's; a cohort of men had trooped upstairs to the Holy Ghost's realm to drink the health of the socialist brotherhood.

The bells of St. Mary's had tolled ten when I found Iris alone in the kitchen shed.

"I leave for Chicago tomorrow," she said, her sleeves rolled up and her arms in the sink.

"And Jessie?"

"She's going to stay with Cousin Hettie in Syracuse."

"Well," I said after a silence in which my eyes had rested on a plaster of Paris Statue of Liberty, its hollow torch packed with safety matches. "I'm sorry."

"Cheer up, Ollie! You and I were only names on a dance card."

"More than that, I think."

Her smile was of the inscrutable kind. "I'll send you my address when I'm settled."

I see myself, now, as I was at that moment, a turtle with its shell pried off.

The night was warm as I walked to the train stop—a spring night, but the songs in the air were not in praise of spring or love.

> Our boys in blue have gone to thrash
> the boasting Spanish Nation,
> Whose tyranny o'er Cuba disgraces all
> creation.
> Their medicine is shot and shell; the
> Spaniards now are quaking,
> For there is quite a difference before
> and after taking.
> This fact was quickly proved them by
> Dewey at Manila—
> The Spanish can't lick Uncle Sam, for
> he takes Hood's Sarsaparilla.

It is a mug's game, after all.

Robert and I turned to illustrating stories of Spanish outrages and defeats. News of the naval battles at Manila and Cárdenas buried domestic incidents like the Wilmington insurrection in North Carolina, when two thousand white supremacists overthrew the Fusionist government of lawfully elected white and black representatives. The rioters killed Negroes by the hundreds and wrecked their newspaper and businesses.

The central telegraph offices in New York City clattered with dispatches cabled from Jacksonville, Port Tampa, and Key West, their hotel bars packed with journalists sent to report on the arrival of the American troops destined for Cuba. Before war was declared, freebooting correspondents known as "filibusters" had been put ashore on the island by chartered steamers that ran the Coast Guard blockade enforcing America's neutrality. Bound for Cienfuegos on the last day of 1896, a cargo of Remington rifles, cartridges, black powder, and machetes in her hold, the steamer *Commodore* sank in the cold Atlantic, twelve miles off the Florida coast.

Her captain, cook, an oiler, and an able seaman named Stephen Crane spent thirty hours on the "grave-edge" of existence in a ten-foot boat. It rose, plunged, and wallowed in a heaving sea of slates, but would not—no matter how desperately the men rowed and bailed, cursed and prayed—be coaxed to make landfall. The sea raced and raged throughout the long day and night. Black waves lashed the hull while Crane and the oiler took turns at the oars.

The captain, whose arm was broken, steered. The cook bailed. Their feet were freezing in the icy water at the bottom of the boat. Afraid to be swept out onto the open sea, the four men staked everything on what would have seemed no better than a chip upon the water and pulled for shore. The boat capsized in a thundering avalanche of water. Crane lost his money belt. Oiler Billy Higgins, whose great arms had been their stay against drowning, lost his wager with the surf when his head was hit by the wave-maddened dinghy.

Crane never made himself out to be a hero. But after Captain Murphy had had his say, the press took him up just as readily as, three months before, they had torn him down. Crane would later tell me, "The papers know how to sling mud, rake muck, and praise a fellow's sand—the same fellow, mind you. They can wreck a person in one edition and rehabilitate him in the next. Best to stay clear of scribblers."

One morning in early June, Smith sent for me. Standing by his desk, I watched his hand jog across a galley page as he hummed a militant tune of the day. Expecting the worst, I stood neither at ease nor at attention, but in a manner often seen where men gather at a soup kitchen door.

He looked up at me, glowered, and then turned over a sheet of paper inked with a bloated Uncle Sam sitting at a table set with three plates labeled CUBA, PHILIPPINES, and GUAM. "What's for dessert?" asks the voracious uncle. As if in reply, I had drawn a black-suited waiter with the face of McKinley, holding a slice of pineapple on a dessert plate marked HAWAII.

Smith ripped the drawing into shreds. "Fischer, I don't want the army boys up my ass!"

Under the authority of the Army Signal Corps, censors were charged with quashing news stories and cartoons judged contrary to American interests. The censors were practically billeted at the New York offices of the seven telegraph companies that received wires from the theater of war.

"Your shenanigans almost got you axed."

I did something with my lower lip—bit it, chewed it, tugged it, licked it—I don't recall.

"But . . ." Had that word been an ax, my head would have rolled—it felt that sharp. "I'm sending you to Key West. You can use your poison pen against the Spanish."

Pontius Pilate might have gazed at the scourged Christ as Smith did me (or if you don't care for blasphemy, as an angler might a fish before he guts it).

I heard Jessie Mullins's warning ringing in my ears: "Don't let them sucker you."

"Do you want the job or not? It's always a tooth pull with you, Fischer!"

"Yes." Sometimes we don't fall into the lap of Fate so much as get shoved into it.

"Okay. Pearson will be going with you." Smith pointed to a pair of sleeve protectors. "He tossed them in the can, tipped his hat, and said he'd mail me a postcard from hell." Smith smiled broadly enough to show his gold crowns. "He's a cocky so-and-so." Smith handed me a voucher. "Pick up your dough at the cashier's. Buy yourself a Sam Browne belt and a slouch hat—and look up Steve Crane when you get there. Look hard; he has a habit of disappearing. Tell him I'll pay top dollar for another *Red Badge of Courage*. I hear he's up to his neck in debt."

Robert and I spent our last night at home packing. We had decided to give up the room. "No sense paying rent for the dust weevils," he said as we stowed our things in tea chests stenciled CEYLON in black paint. He had arranged to have them stored at his uncle's trimming factory.

"I pray to the goddess of grain that the war will be short," he said, pouring whiskey into a dirty glass. He downed the drink in one go.

"You'll have a brick in your hat tomorrow."

"I'll have three days on the rails to sleep it off, Ollie, old chuff, old fistula. This war will take your mind off Iris's backside, which she smartly showed you as she said so long, good-bye. Say, where's the snickerdoodles your sister sent at Christmas?"

He drank as if oblivion were his destination, instead of Key West.

A knock on the door got his attention while he still had it to give. "See who's there while I pull up my socks." He leaned over and fell on the floor. I pulled up mine and discovered Harry Owens and Sarah Jenkins in the hall.

"Sarah! What brings *you* here?" She was dressed like a fashion plate, in a deep blue tulip-bell skirt reaching to the tops of her Balmoral boots and a bishop-sleeve blouse sewn from pink-and-white-striped Liberty silk. (I was an expert in women's clothing, having sketched it for *The Press*'s advertising pages.) "I haven't seen you since last summer. Come in, you two."

"Gee rod, Robert's out cold!" said Harry as they settled their bottoms on a pair of crates.

"Don't mind him. As you can see, we're blowing town tomorrow."

"We heard as much and decided to drop by and give you bums a send-off," said Harry as he produced two bottles of beer from a paper sack. He cleared his throat in an exaggerated way and turned his gaze on the garish labels, as if insisting that I take note of them. I did, and to my surprise, I beheld the Shrimp's chromolithed facsimile.

"Gosh! It's you!"

"It's me all right, painted to a tee!"

The labels bore several belligerent motifs of the day: A bald eagle gripped a pair of thunderbolts in its talons, while a snake resembling a pig's intestine dangled from its yellow beak. Beneath a cyanide sky, Lady Liberty stood, haughty, between two palms. She wore the helmet that Bellona, Roman goddess of war, had on when she led the army of the Holy Roman Empire against the Ottomans. Her shoulders and the swelling of her breasts were shown to best effect by a carelessly draped Old Glory. ("Old Gory" Robert would have said had he not been rendered speechless by strong drink.) Portrayed by Sarah Jenkins and photographed by Harry Owens, LADY LIBERTY LAGER, as the label proclaimed her in Baskerville, was one step short of indecency, and a short one at that.

"Charlie Schmidt's cornered the Philadelphia saloon trade, thanks to this beauty!" said Harry, smacking his lips in appreciation either of Sarah's qualities or the reek of booze in the room. "Robert will be hopping mad he missed the show."

I poked him in the ribs to rouse him from stupefaction, and he began to hum the hymn the Baptists had been crooning before all hell broke loose in Croydon:

> Whoever steps in it will find a reward;
> They'll find peace of conscience and joy
> in the same,
> When they are baptized in Jesus's own
> name.

"Remember Giovanni Mosca?" asked Harry.

"The guy who paints miniatures of the Madonna."

"The same. He hand-tinted the photograph."

Harry replaced my Gustave Klimt etching with a calendar illustrated with Lady Liberty seated on a cask of Schmidt's beer. The year 1898 had shed its past, all of it up to May 27. On the morning of the twenty-eighth, Robert and I would depart for Key West. (No one could have known that, on one of the year's remaining pages, my friend's last day had been written.)

"I sold the photograph to four other Philadelphia firms," he said as he stood back to admire his handiwork. So boyish was his grin, so frank and guileless his manner, I hadn't the heart to express disapproval. (Besides, I hadn't a leg to stand on, my high horse having been hobbled.)

"Yes siree! Our very own Lady Liberty will soon be on tins of Armour hash, the lid of the Keystone Watch Company's Imperial model, the band on a belicoso made by the Theobald & Oppenheimer Cigar Company . . ." He held up his ring finger for me to admire a cigar band adorned with Sarah and the flag. "And this." He handed me two decks of cards manufactured by the Consolidated Card Company of New York and Philadelphia. Their backs featured Sarah in patriotic dishabille atop the caption AMERICA THE BLEST. "One for you and one for our scragged friend."

"The printing is out of register," I remarked, unnecessarily critical of the lithography.

"The hand of the pressman shook, as did the Almighty's when He created Eve."

"Sarah, you've come a long way since last summer's farce."

"I made an awful ball of things."

"It was the fault of the wasp."

"We'll leave you to finish packing," said Harry. "And the beer for when you're done."

Sarah gathered herself together. "So long, Ollie. Come back soon." She offered me her cheek. I turned her face toward mine and kissed her lips, which tasted of candy corn. I have not laid eyes on her since that night, except as she appears, candidly, on a pack of playing cards.

I put Robert to bed and, sitting by the window, drank both bottles of Lady Liberty Lager. I went out to the empty street, and in what I thought would be a last boyish act of rebellion, I relieved myself against a walnut tree. What happiness to bare one's secret part and listen to the plash! Standing in the yard of the Third Street house, I would picture Charles watching me from a second-story window and smiling, not in remembrance of the boy he had once been but to see me confirm his low opinion of my character by an ecstatic piss. I pushed him from my mind just as the bell tolled the latest canonical hour.

So it was that Oliver Fischer prepared to go to war, with every hope of finding plenty of trees to hide behind.

Finale

All for you if you let me come in—
Into the house of chance.

—STEPHEN CRANE

Key West, Florida

On the first day of June, in the year of the nation's grand imperialist adventure in the Caribbean, Robert and I arrived at Key West, 209 nautical miles south of Tampa, 92 miles from Havana and the Spanish army waiting across the Straits of Florida for the marines to land. We took a room in the Excelsior Hotel, and after a spicy meal of rice and frijoles washed down with a local beer, we set off along Duval Street to find Stephen Crane.

At a rum hole painted the color of a ripe mango, the Cuban barman knew Crane, who was not there, *"con pesar,"* but might be at the Green Parrot on Whitehead Street, which sometimes received the favor of his custom—unless, he said with a melancholy sigh, Crane was laid up at his hotel. *"El señor está enfermo."* In a pantomime of an asthmatic attack, the barman beat his chest with a fist and coughed, an awful hacking that brought to mind the late John Mullins near his end.

"Did you know Crane was sick?" asked Robert after we had regained the sidewalk and he had given me the gist of the barman's comments. Robert had acquired a smattering of Spanish after a summer of unloading banana boats from Puerto Rico while I loafed on the Asbury Park boardwalk.

"Smith never said."

We found the Green Parrot with the help of a gunnery sergeant stationed at nearby Fort Zachary Taylor. He insisted on standing us to drinks while we waited for Crane, who did not show himself. Rolling up a sleeve, the sergeant, by that time soused, would not let us leave till one of us agreed to an arm-wrestling match. Robert did the honors and beat the fellow hands down.

We returned to our hotel and sat on the veranda overlooking Duval Street. The evening preened itself in the iridescent colors at a pigeon's throat. Green and purplish rags of sunset are not exclusive to the tropics; I had seen them on North Third Street while waiting in the yard for my father's racing homers to come home and roost. The key's electric trolleys were of a darker green, which brightened as they passed beneath the streetlamps. The brazen gong to which their drivers frequently resorted to clear the rails of milling men, gaudily dressed women, and bronze-skinned Bahamian children lent the night a golden tone. Key West was, in the very color of the air, an artists' paradise, from which I had been banished.

Robert and I were lost each in his own thoughts. Mine were of an afternoon spent with Natalia

Mannino in a northern city that, in contrast to Key West, seems as drab as the common wren does to the red flamingo.

I walked to her house, not knowing whether I would stop or go on to my friend Whitey's. As I dawdled on the pavement, Mrs. Mannino knocked on the window, where she had been sitting in the rainy afternoon light, plying her needle on a satin shimmy for the daughter of the Whitaker family, which owned the gristmill on Tookany Creek. She was, at that time, and may still be, a seamstress. She nodded toward the kitchen, where I found Natalia kneading a ball of dough that, now and then, she sprinkled with flour.

"Hello, Natalia," I said, feeling my face flush.

"Hello, Ollie."

I watched her work until, ill at ease, I said good-bye and left the kitchen, thinking that I'd go see Whitey after all.

"Are you leaving already, Oliver?" She had followed me from the kitchen, wiping her floury hands on her apron. "You just got here."

"I thought I'd take a walk."

"Wait, I'll go with you."

She'd spoken casually, as a girl of fifteen would whose mouth had not been kissed nor throat burned with words impossible to speak. Nonetheless, a thrill passed through me like an electric shock. It was followed by Charles's warning not to consort with her, which I felt in my breastbone, as if a tuning fork had struck a tragic note.

And then, perversely, the thought of his lying beside my mother escaped the place where nightmares are stabled.

"Mein liebling."

"Schatzi."

No, I couldn't imagine endearments spoken in the bedroom of Herr Fischer and his frau, where, on windy winter nights, the sycamore tree outside their window waved the shadows of its bony branches across the wall papered in strange fruit, behind the hideous black-walnut bed.

"Ready?" asked Natalia, having put on a coat and tied a scarf under her chin, since the rain was still falling.

I said good-bye to Mrs. Mannino, whose needlework was as fine as a spider's would be if lavender thread could be coiled in its abdomen. Natalia and I went out into the rain. Her mother appeared at the front door, shaking an umbrella at us. Natalia went back for it, and in a moment, the umbrella had opened like a large black bird unfurling its wings above us.

We walked awhile, with only the noise of rain against the stiff black cloth overhead and the dashing of our feet on the wet and shiny paving. I could think of nothing to say and wished I had gone to Unionville instead. As is often the case, the girl is left to take the initiative. Natalia hooked her arm through mine. I had sense enough to leave it there. I took the umbrella from her and assumed the authority of an escort. I knew I ought to speak, but how, when I could scarcely draw breath? The air inside the little black tent seemed to have been used up. A particle of dust or a grain of pollen drew from me a catarrhal "Ahem."

The girl glanced up at my face, as if the noise were a nervous preface, but having cleared my throat, I went no further toward conversation.

"What's wrong with you, Ollie?" She scolded me with the readiness of one whose native tongue rises eloquently to any occasion. For a Sicilian, words could be counted on to pour out in a torrent of love or abuse impossible to stem.

"Nothing. I was thinking."

"Thinking about what?*" she demanded, putting a hand on her hip in a defiant way that produced in me a most complicated reaction, partly amusement, partly desire, and partly fear.*

Without a thought to confide, except for an inner turmoil I could not have articulated, I resorted to banality. "Do you like walking in the rain?"

"Sometimes."

"It's warm today."

"It's July."

"And it's raining."

"Plainly."

Young though she may have been, she saw, beneath my bumbling, a shy effort to make myself agreeable. She pressed my arm, and we walked toward Fifth Street, where the stores are.

Now and then, I'd glance at her, shyly, slyly, building a composite portrait in my mind. The curve of her dusky cheek, her delicately whorled ear, whose lobe held a tiny garnet, the pout of her lips, her slender neck, and the dark coils of her pinned-up hair—how they captivated me! How I wished I were old enough to know what words to say and what to do with my hand instead of putting it in my pocket.

We turned onto Tabor Road and headed west, walking under the dripping chestnut trees. We crossed the Philadelphia and Reading's tracks. At Third Street, I pointed north. "I live up the road in the house with the green hairpin fence." (But on no account must you call for me there.)

We reached Fifth Street and looked in store windows fogged by humidity. Underneath Woolworth's striped awning, I shook the rain from the umbrella and led Natalia inside, where I commented on eggbeaters, colanders, electric toasters, meat mincers, and a device that stamped patriotic motifs on pats of butter. She listened as intently as Lasthenia had to Plato, while on the wooden alleys of the floor above, bowling balls unwound in a lengthening rumble and clattered among the unseen pins. Although the Manninos had no piano, I bought her sheet music for Dave Braham's "Plum Pudding." At the lunch counter, she drank a chocolate soda, and I birch beer. The store's pent-up air smelled of cigars and roasting cashew nuts. We said little, satisfied to listen to the liquid gurgling though our straws. When we left Woolworth's, the rain had stopped.

"Let's walk to Hobson's Park," I proposed, as Napoleón might have invited Josephine to the Tuileries to poke among the flower beds with a stick.

"Won't it be wet?" She was playing her part in love's comedy, and I was grateful to her.

"I guess we can stand it!" If a voice could swagger, mine did.

We launched ourselves from under the awning, its scalloped edge beaded with rain, into the steadily lofting sky. Four blocks north on Fifth, we entered the park by a path bordered by maple trees. The wooden seats inside a gazebo at the bottom of a gently sloping lawn were dry. We sat and listened to spring water brimming in the trough and to frogs croaking unseen in the grass along a narrow stream that vanished at the margin of a sward made vivid and slippery by the recent rain—

The frogs! I said to myself, my thoughts having returned to the veranda of the Excelsior Hotel. The raucous frogs croaking in the salt marsh behind us had made me remember my first kiss.

From my overlook on Duval Street, in the sherbet-colored city of Key West, I fell back once more down memory's greased rails to that moment in the park.

A light wind blew through Hobson's Park and shook down rain from the heavy leaves. The air freshened. I lapsed into silence, letting in the evening light. My father charged from the mulberry trees, a stick in his hand, like a beater driving birds toward their doom. I shut my eyes to the Cyclopean eye burning on his lit cigar and gave myself to the odors of lilac, honeysuckle, mown grass, loam, and rain. Father vanished, leaving not so much as a cloud

*of tobacco smoke to tell that he had been there, if only in
my fancy. And then I kissed Natalia Mannino. So this is
love, I thought as I wallowed in the warm mud of self-
absorption. Sitting beside her, I all but forgot her, until
she began to bite her nails.*

"What're you thinking about?" asked Robert,
slowing his gallop on the veranda's green rocking
chair.

I shook off the recollection of that first, only, and
clumsy kiss I had shared with the dark girl who lived
on Ella Street. "My first love."

"Anne?"

"No, not Anne."

"Iris."

I shook my head. "Someone from long ago." I
spoke like a man looking back on a life of adventure
and romance, though I had not yet seen twenty-one
and, until that day, had been no farther from home
than Asbury Park, New Jersey.

We turned our heads at the sound of boots tread-
ing lightly on the stairs.

"I hear you boys are looking for me," said a young
man, whose thin face was sallow and unshaved.

"Stephen Crane?" said Robert, bending the two
words into a question.

"The same," he replied, sitting on one of the caned
rockers that, along with rattan planters sown with the
stumps of cigars, furnished the hotel veranda. "Welcome to what the cynics call the 'rocking chair period'

of the war." He took off his grease-spotted slouch hat, looked inside it, and put it back on. He appeared to be the nervous sort and coughed like someone with the croup. "Say, this ain't half bad! I'm paying five dollars a night for a cot in the hallway at the Key West Hotel. You can't turn around without stepping on a lizard or a journalist. Just arrive, did you?"

"This morning on a Peninsular and Occidental steamer from Tampa. I'm Oliver Fischer; this is Robert Pearson. We were told to look you up."

"*Who* told you?" he asked, his eyes narrowing.

"Mr. Smith at *The Press*, in Philadelphia."

"Harry Smith! Say, I used to give him jinks!"

Crane spoke like a man uneasy in his native tongue. The words came out in a deep drawl. Sometimes he'd stop in the middle of a sentence and wait for them to catch up to his thought. For a man who'd been proclaimed America's greatest living author by William Dean Howells and Hamlin Garland, his speech was full of stumbles and his clothes were shoddy.

"I'm on the *New York World* payroll, though my wallet is wheezy. This your first ball?"

He was twenty-six when I met him, and he'd already shown courage under fire during the Greco-Turkish War he covered for the *New York Journal*. "Courage is beside the point in a man like Crane," Smith had said. "Nonchalance is the thing that makes him different from other brave men. It's a quality you see in people who are all in the game. The flip of the coin, the turn of the card—the outcome hardly seems to matter."

Dressed in dirty ragged overalls and a shirt that flapped like a sail on his emaciated chest, Stephen Crane might have been one of the Almighty's botched attempts to make a man. He was, at one and the same time, less than a man and more than one. A constant reproach to the Creator, Crane could not be allowed to live much longer. (I didn't see it at the time, mind you. But a more experienced observer would have seen that his death sentence had already been pronounced and published on his face.)

"It's a cinch," he said, and then the awful cough gripped him. "What the bellows maker can't fix, the undertaker will."

The man looked frail! Yet only a year before, he'd been in Thessaly, traveling with the outnumbered Greeks. Not long ago, I read "A Fragment of Velestino," his account of the town's capture by the Ottoman Turks. I recall a dead horse lying amid bloodred poppies . . . a soldier holding a piece of bread to his comrade in the trench, who, moments before, had received his mortal wound . . . a crescendo of cannon fire sounding like an avalanche . . . a man fixing his garden gate knowing that the sledgehammer of his enemy had yet to finish falling on his village . . . the red fezzes of dead Turks sprawling in the road. (I remembered my own fez and felt ashamed.)

"My mouth is like one of Dante's Hells," said Crane, sticking out his tongue, as though he meant to look at it. "I was on a jag last night with Norris."

Frank Norris was another young novelist of the realist tribe. Not long ago, I came upon his description of Crane, as he had been at Key West: "His shirt was guiltless of collar or scarf, and was unbuttoned at the throat. His hair hung in ragged fringes over his eyes." *That* was the man who appeared to us on the veranda as the tropic moon hung in the sky like a scythe raised above the sea.

"God Almighty, I'm parched! What would you boys say to a drink?"

Crane, Robert, and I went to the Green Parrot, where he greeted the barman and a number of cronies and was, in turn, cordially welcomed. He had not been in town for long before he knew his way around the dives, wharves, tobacco sheds, coal bunkers, brothels, and billets, as well as the houses of several rags-to-riches types. That night he introduced us to Mr. A. J. Arapian, the "sponge king." He wore a glass reliquary around his neck, containing a piece of yellow sponge. "Kingdom: Animalia; phylum: Porifera; species: *Aplysina fistularis*," he said with the air of a connoisseur. "My good-luck charm." He kissed the glass-enclosed animal as reverently as if it had been the vinegar-soaked sponge offered Christ to drink by a Roman soldier at Calvary.

"What'll you boys have?" asked the barman, whose uncommon height and red hair made him conspicuous among the swarthy races exercising their forearms with bottles and glasses.

"A Florida lager," I replied. The Florida Brewing Company had opened two years earlier near a spring sacred to the Indians, who used to take their sick and wounded to be healed in it—a belief no more improbable than the restorative power of Christian baptism.

"Rum," said Robert. "A large one."

"Lemonade," said Crane. "I know what you boys are thinking: Why drink a distillation of the lemon when you can have the sweetness of life, its nobbling heat and darksome mystery in a glass?" He licked his chapped lips. "One jigger of the stuff, and I'll be on the floor with the butts, sawdust, and oyster shells."

He sipped his lemonade like a man dragged to a church social by his wife.

"Five years ago, when I was wading in my rubber boots through the gutters of the Bowery to wake up my ideas, I'd stop at Boeuf-a-la-Mode on Sixth Avenue, called 'Buffalo Mud' by the holey pockets crowd. A nickel would get me a beer and a free hot lunch. When I had a nickel, I felt blessed, which, for the son of hidebound Methodists, was evidence of heavenly election."

The door flew open in a sudden gust that brought

the smell of the street into the barroom. The barman shut it.

"Dick's from Duluth," said Crane, a dead cigarette between his nervous yellow fingers.

Key West had grown by happenstance. New Englanders came to salvage ships broken up on the shoals, followed by Bahamian "conches" who came to dive for sponges, and then Cubans to roll cigars—ten thousand in flight from José Martí's ten-year war with Spain, which, in the end, the island's rebels lost. After the fire of 1886 turned the key's brick walls into ruins, gaily painted buildings made of wood and tin roofs took root on the palmy avenues. The bright colors of the Caribbean island excited me, who had been raised in Lutheran gloom and in winters where snow turned black with soot and yellow with horses' stale.

Before the war could be said to have begun, Crane complained of our preparations. "The navy's made an awful balls of the coal! The bunkers at Tampa and Key West are low. How in hell are dreadnoughts, destroyers, cruisers, and torpedo boats supposed to cross ninety miles of open water with scarcely enough coal to fill Christmas stockings in a home for delinquent boys? The navy might as well go to sea in bathing machines and fart their way across to Guantánamo! Yesterday I squeezed Commodore Remey for the lowdown and got it on the wire this morning."

I took a pencil and a piece of paper from my pocket and began to doodle.

"Dick, make it beer this time; this lemonade's giving me a sour stomach. What about you grinds?"

"Another beer," I replied, glancing at the barman, whose face revealed nothing of his thoughts, which, for all I knew, might have been occupied by a problem in solid geometry.

Robert took a second large rum.

"Say, bud, you'd better lay off. This climate will turn your insides into a monkey house."

"I can handle it, Mr. Crane."

Crane shrugged his narrow shoulders and left him to get scragged.

"Not that empty coal bins will excite the Podsnaps and Mrs. Grundys slavering to read about Spanish beasts mauling comely Cuban girls. But by the time the newsboys hawk their extras, those empty coal bins will be filled with dead babies garroted by murderous Spaniards. As they say down here, 'If the news arrives at Key West as a mouse, it gets cabled north as an elephant.'" Crane looked mildly feverish as he held his beer glass to his forehead. "The story I want is at Fort Zachary Taylor."

"What about it?" I asked, looking up from my sketch.

"Clara Barton is what. I guess you mugs are not unfamiliar with the lady."

"Founder of the American Red Cross," said Robert, nodding his big head wisely.

"The Angel of the Battlefield," I said to show that I was listening.

"She nursed the wounded at South Mountain, Antietam, Fredericksburg, Charleston, Petersburg, Cold Harbor, and the Siege of Paris. She cared for the sick during the Florida yellow fever epidemic, for the starving during the Texas famine, and for the survivors of the Johnstown Flood. After the Armenian massacres, she sailed to Constantinople and persuaded Abdul Hamid II, chief butcher of the Ottomans, to open a Red Cross agency in Turkey. Mark my words, boys, someday they'll paint her name on a dreadnought." He raised his glass. "All hail Miss Barton!"

Robert drank a scalding mouthful of rum and commenced to cough and wheeze.

Crane gave him a contemptuous look that could have scorched the wings off a fly.

"This morning she stormed the fort, demanding to see the four hundred prisoners who had been taken there off Spanish ships seized as prizes of war. A slew of them had already died of fever during the months that they had languished out in the harbor, waiting while one gold-braided blockhead dickered with another over their fate." I waited for his glass to shriek as he ran a finger around its rim, but it stood mute. "At the port of Volo, I saw what happens when people are jammed into boats like cattle in a slaughter pen. I grant you that Fort Taylor is not an abattoir, nor is Florida Thessaly, but it's six of one, half a dozen of the other. The formidable Miss Barton has come to Key West to see that the Spaniards are humanely treated."

"I expect most people will say that they got what they deserved."

"Most people, Oliver, would rather watch a man get hanged than the New York Giants play a game of ball."

Robert got to his feet and went to the gents. His stagger was noticeable.

"Can your friend draw any better than he drinks?"

"He generally hits the mark."

"Meaning?"

"If he draws a jackass, it *is* a jackass and not a Republican senator from Vermont. I, on the other hand, tend to exaggerate."

I handed him the caricature I'd just finished, showing Assistant Secretary of the Navy Theodore Roosevelt sitting on the steps of a bathing machine. Through his pince-nez, he peers down the stack of a toy dreadnought named *North Atlantic Fleet* and, pouting, says, "I was told there would be plenty of coal for the fleet to steam to Cuba!"

"Say, that's not half bad! Except T.R. resigned and is coming down with his own bully regiment—the First U.S. Volunteer Cavalry. That, lambkin, is one story that editors who pander to the public's taste for gore and spectacle will eat up."

He scratched an unshaved cheek. "I was going to pair up with Freddie Remington, but he got tired of waiting and went home to paint more cowboys and Indians. As a wag said, 'To Cube or not to Cube; that is the Key Westion.' What would you lunkers say to illustrating my copy?"

"I'd like it fine!" I replied over the objections of Iris, Jessie Mullins, and my sister, Dot.

"Like what fine?" asked Robert, resuming his place at the table, a trace of vomit on his sleeve.

"Mr. Crane wants us to go along with him to cover the shindy."

"Let the idea soak in before you make up your minds."

We made noises signifying that soaking in was unnecessary.

"You shall have your wish, then. And don't call me 'Mr. Crane.' I'm not much older than you and am, I suspect, a lot more disreputable."

"The Dora Clark affair," said Pearson, who couldn't be counted on for discretion when he'd had a hat full.

"You know about that, do you?"

"I'll say!"

"Dora Clark was *not* a streetwalker—I'll bet my life on it. Her face was too pretty, her figure too stunning. Boys, she had the darkest red hair! She may have been only twenty-one at the time, but she was smart. She was kept by a Diamond Jim type living at the Waldorf, or so I heard said. The cops of the Nineteenth Precinct had it in for her after she told a dirty boot named Rosenberg that she didn't sleep with Negroes. Not that he was; she just wanted to give him the razz for trying to pick her up. After that, she couldn't go out at night without getting pinched for soliciting by some cop 'clubber' or other. Becker lied through his cigar when he swore that he'd arrested her for giving the come-hither to two guys walking past on the sidewalk. I saw the whole thing from across the street. She never so much as winked at the slobs."

A man on the pavement shouted something in Spanish through the open barroom door. Another man sitting at a table looked up from his stew, put down his spoon, and went outside. They got into an argument that they carried on as they walked down the street, out of sight and earshot.

"Earlier that night, I'd been at the Broadway Garden, a Turkish smoking parlor, chinning with a pair of chorus girls for one of my *Journal* sketches on 'Satan's Circus,' as the Tenderloin is known by those who relish its vices. Dora came over to our table to say hello to the girls, and I invited her to join us."

Crane drank some beer to wash the gravel down his gullet.

"When the Garden closed for the night, the three of us walked up Broadway. Dora and one of the chorus girls waited at Thirty-first while I took her friend to an uptown cable car stop. I got back in time to see Becker collar them for soliciting. Charles Becker is as crooked as Doyers Street! I went along with them to Mulberry Street police station, had my say, and both girls were let go. Later, Dora sued Becker for false arrest and got a taste of his fist for her pains."

He drank some more beer, this time out of habit.

"I testified against him at Jefferson Market police court and was slammed as a 'dopey,' a 'pimp,' and a 'liar.' When I called out the whole rotten bunch of cops, Roosevelt cut me, and the rags gave me a nosebleed in newsprint for being a fast liver and keeper of an opium joint. I was the main attraction at New York's Circus Maximus, and the lions were ravening."

He peered into his empty glass. Maybe he thought it would fill miraculously; maybe he believed that, if he looked long enough, he would discover the source of his bewilderment before God. "I swear I could smell the tar and taste the feathers! So I went to Jacksonville to do a bit of filibustering for Irving Bacheller's news syndicate. The story of the sinking of the *Commodore* and my swim through the breakers you've already heard."

He sat back in his chair and looked us in the eye. "I'm a good deal of a rascal, sometimes a bore, and often dishonest. And at this moment in my history, I'm famished as a rat trapped in a barrel. Eat up, you Indians. It's on me." It was always like that when we went out together during the ten days we spent in the key. He seemed bent on showing us a good time, spending money he didn't have.

We ordered a supper of black beans, plantains, pigeon peas, and pancakes.

"No meat?" asked Robert.

"There ain't a pig, goat, or chicken on two drumsticks left in Key West since the army boys came down and started bleating for grub. You refined types want to steer clear of canned horsemeat on a tortilla."

Robert commenced to sing "The Swell at the Front":

> At home he dined on terrapin,
>   And drank the fizz of France;
> And when the lamb had no mint sauce,
>   He made the poor chef dance.
> On canvas backs he surfeited,
>   On truffle patties lunched.
> He sipped his Mocha, puffed his "Turque"
>   And took his claret punched.

"So you dabbers hail from Philadelphia?"

Robert's squeeze box having emptied of every last atom of oxygen, I replied for both of us, "No sense in denying it."

"I set myself up there as a correspondent for *The Press*. I didn't take to it. Or it didn't take to me. Things fell kerplunk."

Crane lit another cigarette as Robert laid his

head, with admirable delicacy, on the tabletop and fell asleep.

"The times are fraught, Oliver." Crane shook off his melancholy, as a wet dog does rain, and said, smiling, "Who knows? God may wake up at the last moment and give us a fair shake."

Robert snorted, sat up, and said, "Amen."

"Pearson and I are going to waylay the Angel of the Battlefield." Crane looked me in the eye, which would have shown my disappointment at being left out of the scrum. "Nothing against you, Fischer. She may show her teeth if *three* rats rap at her door. Besides, Pearson's style is what Joe Pulitzer likes for the *World*. Why don't you slug around town and see what's doing?"

They got on a trolley headed to Southernmost Point, where Clara Barton was staying.

I let my feet have their way with the pavement, and after two hours of aimless plodding, I found myself in "Gatoville." After helping to finance the failed 1868–1878 Cuban Revolution, the patriot Eduardo Gato built one of the finest tobacco companies in the Americas. His *tabaqueros* lived in brightly painted tin-roofed houses, each with a front porch and privy. To the cigar rollers of New York's Tenderloin, his factory would have been a workers' paradise.

By 1898, Gatoville had become a barrio of two hundred tobacco companies. Many of them were owned by German émigrés.

I don't know why I chose to enter the Schumacher brothers' door. Maybe a twinge on the ball of my foot had set me in motion, or a particle of grit had got caught between the teeth of the universal engine that actuates human history. (Who can say what forces move or stay us beyond our power to resist, unless we're all skittering on a soap slide?)

A bald-headed man in his middle years was filling out a customs declaration. "The excise tax," he growled in a pronounced German accent, "was invented by fools who knew nothing of business!" He took off his glasses and polished the lenses on his cambric tie. "What brings you to Schumachers', young man?" he asked, looping the wire rims around a pair of ears that looked as though they could hear a rat gnashing its teeth in the wall.

"My name is Fischer," I said, standing stiffly before him like a Teutonic knight forbidden ever to stand at ease.

"Fischer . . ." he said, looking me up and down. "A German name—is that not so?"

"My father was born in Königsberg."

"A Prussian. My brother and I also. My name is Karl Schumacher." As if to verify this fact, he pointed to a brass nameplate on his desk. I read it aloud, which appeared to satisfy him. He gestured at a second plate on an identical desk placed beside his own, and announced, "My brother, Otto. We are the owners of this *tabaquería*." His voice could have scrubbed the ears of a jug.

Otto's desk was crowded with catalogues, sales prospectuses, and folded newspapers in varying stages of jaundice.

"Do you speak German?" asked Karl.

"Enough to command our neighbor Mr. Ziegler's dachshund to stay, sit, and roll over."

In the summers of my fifteenth and sixteenth years, Charles sent me to the Pennsylvania German Society on Spring Garden Street to learn the language of the Hun. (I had failed, he said, to learn enough German at Frankford High to hold a conversation with Kaiser Wilhelm II should the opportunity arise.) The society's professor Kopp, a graduate of the University of Heidelberg, however, was more interested in telling stories from the *Nibelungenlied* than in stringing nominal modifiers. I may not have become fluent in my father's native tongue, but my fancy grew fat and extravagant on tales of the bleeding corpse of Siegfried, the humiliation of Brünhild, and the beheading of Gunter.

My scant command of the language of Goethe, Schiller, Beethoven, and Brahms clearly pained Herr Schumacher. He became suspicious of my pedigree. "There are Englishmen named Fisher." His tone of voice expressed disdain for that green and pleasant island. "Perhaps you are one of them?"

I hurried to assure him. "My father reads the *Philadelphia Volksblatt.* My mother makes *Fasnachts* at Lent. I have a pair of *Lederhosen*!" A Swabian aunt had sent them, a present for my tenth birthday. The leather breeches are becoming to men who play in oompah bands, heft steins in beer gardens, and scramble up Tyrolean hillsides behind large dogs, but they made me a target for gibes and stones thrown by neighborhood boys. In any case, I proved myself deserving of the German cigar maker's notice.

The younger Schumacher walked into the room. "Otto, this young man is a Prussian!"

"Not by birth," I said, wanting to be accurate.

"You are a German and a Prussian by blood!" Karl pronounced it *blod*, as if the word had been phlebotomized.

Otto gave me his hand to shake. He wore an open-collared shirt, unpressed trousers, and native rope-soled shoes. If not for his Aryan pallor, he'd have passed for one of the *compañeros.*

Karl returned to the question he had put to me at the outset: "What is the reason for your visit, Mr. Fischer? Pardon me, but you look too young to be in business." He was being kind. It was not my youthful appearance that made him doubt me, but my ragged one. I resembled a tea planter whom misfortune had reduced to shabbiness. In fact, my clothes had once been worn by an actor who'd played Henry Morton Stanley in *Dr. Livingstone, I Presume* at the Walnut Street Theatre. Karl's face darkened. "You're not with customs?" A squint through his glasses assured him of the contrary. "Not likely. If you'll forgive me for saying so, Mr. Fischer, you do not look intelligent."

"I'm an artist."

"Did you hear, Otto? This young man is an artist!"

Appearing bored by the strange burlesque being performed among the desks and filing cabinets, Otto returned to his *tabaqueros*.

"Mr. Fischer, come; I want to show you something," said Karl, taking me by the arm.

He led me into a large office paneled in black pine and covered by a carpet "made by Qashqai nomads from the Zagros Mountains of southern Persia. Isn't it exquisite?"

I agreed that it was.

He took off his shoes and bid me do the same. He produced a pair of Persian slippers for each of us to wear. They were like those I had worn in Philadelphia, in my decadent phase. We stepped lightly to the middle of the carpet, where crimson medallions floated on a field of indigo, their spandrels enclosing ivory triangles. He smiled at me. "As the Qashqai tribe says, 'Where I am is my carpet. Where my carpet and I am is my home.'" He took a magnifying glass from his pocket and invited me to kneel beside him. "Can you imagine, Mr. Fischer? Thousands of

tiny knots tied by women, even children! We manufacture cigars. It's true they are fine cigars, but what
beauty is there in a tobacco leaf rolled by a black-bean
eater? I'll tell you where there *is* beauty, young man."

He led me to a cabinet made of Cuban mahogany
and pulled out a deep drawer. "Look, Mr. Fischer!
I have one of the finest collections of cigar bands in
the world! They are my pride. Beautiful, are they not?
You, an artist, can appreciate them."

Cigar bands lay flat in sky-blue velvet trays, like
the rarest of butterflies pinned through the thorax.
Hues of rose, gold, pink, lime, yellow, and indigo
reminded me of pastel drawings by Berthe Morisot.
More garish colors were like those chromolithed
onto circus posters. My eyes grew dazzled as Karl
opened drawer after drawer. Miniature likenesses
of gauchos, vaqueros, mustachioed bandits, cas-
tles, jewels, flowers, streetcars, fuming steamships
and locomotives, swans, wolves, speckled trout, and
the dark faces of Cuban women wearing mantillas
passed before me. One band made me grin. (I didn't
dare laugh, for fear of offending the connoisseur
beside me.) Wearing a red liberty cap, a ring-tailed
monkey judiciously sniffed a cigar.

Karl's collection could be viewed as a gazetteer.
Herman Melville may have slipped a band identical
to *that* one from a Dutch de Olifant onto the finger of
a lovely brown girl in the Marquesas. That *other* band,
taken from a Farel cigar, may have caught Stephen

Crane's eye in Macedonia before he bit off the end and smoked it.

Karl's cabinet (so different from any in the Mütter Museum) proclaimed the glory of the rolled leaf and its aromatic contents: Allegro, Aroma Rico, Buen Humo, La Carolina, El Coliseo, Corona Monarca, Doña Hermosa, La Dragona, El Ducado, Dutch Queen, Escamillo, La Flor de Antonio, La Flor de Manoa, La Flor de Natalie, Fragrante, Golden Flower, Henry Vane, La Inca, Jerome Bonaparte, José Valle, Mancenilla, Marca de España, Margarita, Puerta de las Antilles, El Rey del Mundo, Roman King, La Rosa Gloria, Rosy Posey, Sam Houston, Scarlet Crown, Schumann, Senator, Silk Tie, Sir Robert Peel, Sir Walter Raleigh, La Viola, Violetta Bouquet, White Owl, White Rose, William the Silent, Za Lora, Zarco, Zimbala . . . One by one, Karl intoned the names of the cigars to which the flamboyant bands belonged, as a philatelist would a rare issue, or a rabbi the Patriarchs.

Dazed, I turned away from Karl and his treasure, as sumptuous as any given by a Pope to a Holy Roman Emperor. I leaned against a wall to steady myself. La Flor de Natalie. Natalia, how lovely you would be now that you are in full flower!

"Mr. Fischer, you don't look well."

"I'm a little light-headed. I didn't have breakfast."

"In this climate, we don't always have an appetite. But you must eat breakfast—eggs and sausages, though they're hard to come by. You can't live on rum and fried plantains. And those black beans—terrible on the stomach!"

Eakins had said to me, "First, you must look closely, Oliver, as if you were not an artist, but an anatomist—or a land surveyor." And here you are now, Oliver, looking at cigar bands!

"Mr. Schumacher, I'd better be going."

"Yes, go. Where are you staying? The Excelsior? They make dishes that won't set your guts on fire." We traded our slippers for our shoes and went out into the factory, where a lector was reading to the *tabaqueros*. "The workers like to be read to; it keeps them placid; they forget the pain in their wrists. Listen, Mr. Fischer, he's reading from *Don Quixote* to them:

> *En efeto, rematado ya su juicio, vino a dar en el más estraño pensamiento que jamás dio loco en el mundo; y fue que le pareció convenible y necesario, así para el aumento de su honra como para el servicio de su república, hacerse caballero andante, y irse por todo el mundo con sus armas y caballo a buscar las aventuras . . .*

"I'd like to come back and draw them."

"They would resent it. Come, Mr. Fischer, it's time you went back to your hotel and ate. Nothing hot, not in this heat. And for God's sake, no beans of any shape or color! How I miss sauerbraten, spaetzle, and pilsner! Sometimes I think I will go back to Germany—sell my share in the business to Otto, if he wants it. God knows what will happen here! The Spaniards are not the weaklings Roosevelt thinks. They'll fight tooth and nail. Now I'll say good-bye. Wait! My compliments." He handed me a panatela from his case and a matchbook printed with the words SCHUMACHER BROTHERS FINE CIGARS. "I have to get back to my declarations. Mark my words: The excise tax will be the ruination of American business!"

Standing on the pavement outside the cigar factory, I felt as I used to when coming out of Charles's pigeon loft. I hated the rickety stairs, the stink, and the gritty floors where birds milled and gabbled and bobbed their heads. The dust raised by their stiff wings had made my throat raw and my eyes sting.

I recalled a sentence from the typewritten manuscript that I had read at Jessie Mullins's house—words spoken in defiance by the anarchist Louis Lingg at his murder trial in Chicago: "I die happy on the gallows, so confident am I that the hundreds and thousands to whom I have spoken will remember my words; and when you shall have hanged us, then—mark my words—they will do the bomb-throwing!" Had I a firecracker in my pocket, I'd have lighted it with a Schumacher Brothers match and thrown it into the *tabaquería*, so that the cigar rollers would remember the pain in their wrists and John Mullins would be avenged.

"Any scoops?" asked Crane as I walked up onto the Excelsior's veranda. He looked like a coat thrown carelessly over a chair. I didn't think he could survive the war. But I knew Crane was a scrapper, and though he might fiddle his expense account or play fast and loose with the ladies, he'd never cheat himself of an experience.

"No. Did you see Clara Barton?"

"We did, though it took coaxing. When I asked for an interview, she gave me a look that turned my hair to snakes." He ran his fingers through his greasy mop. "Pearson mentioned *Red Badge*, but it cut no ice with Miss Clara. She stood on the Axminster carpet and glared. Then a sharp-faced aide-de-camp in pants asked if I was the Crane who'd written *Maggie: A Girl of the Streets*. When I acknowledged the fact, Miss Barton warmed. She said Elizabeth Cady Stanton had spoken highly of it. They agreed that I'd struck a blow for women's rights. I got my story, and Pearson his sketch. Behold! The angel smileth. He's lucky; she can give you a look as if someone's milled red pepper down her dress.

"You walk the dog awhile, Pearson; my jaw's got cramp."

"She raised hell with the colonel, a fellow named O'Rourke, queer sort to be in charge of a fort—so you'd think to see him—big head, goggle eyes, just a tuft of hair sticking up when he took off his cap to mop his head. Miss Barton had him sweating, I'll say!"

"Pearson!" snapped Crane. "You're smothering it in lard! Find the spine, like I told you, and climb up bone by bone till you get to—not the blubbering heart, but the brain of the tale."

"Barton bullied O'Rourke into letting her see the prisoners. They're in a bad way, many of them. She demanded that they be taken care of 'at once!' O'Rourke tried to put her off with the old malarkey about 'chain of command'—said he'd have to take it up with Major General Shafter of Fifth Army Corps."

Crane, who'd been fooling with a tooth as if he meant to yank it from the gum, jumped in. "Battlefield Barton as good as told O'Rourke that she didn't give a fart in a hat for his chain of command and would make things hot for McKinley, the Pope, the Archbishop of Canterbury, the Patriarch of Antioch, and God Almighty if the Spaniards didn't get clean blankets, medical attention, and decent grub, pronto!"

"A bully woman," said Robert. "And on the square, too!"

"The censors will kill the piece, since it's a kick in the ass to the army and would madden the Spanish beasts running amok in Havana and Santiago. The Key West cable operator, a snake named Hellings, read my lede and told me—gleefully is how I'd put it—that it hadn't a whisker of a chance to survive the army censor's red pencil and shears. By the way, Filipinos, variously called 'slopeheads' and 'gooks' by our soldiery, use *amok* to signify a murderous rage. Which only goes to show."

"What does it show?" I asked naïvely.

"A people capable of rage are not the pusillanimous monkeys we suppose. Hellings wired my copy—after I stuck five dollars in his pocket—but he's right, damn him. The censors in New York will stick it in the stove. Tomorrow, I'll mail it to Pulitzer, along with Robert's sketch, and we'll see what a hash they make of it."

"Shafter will make you sing soprano," I said as I read a penciled note Crane had scribbled on his cuff regarding Miss Barton's "fine brown hair."

"I don't give a snap piss for the censors, and neither should you cranks!"

"Give us a shovel, and we'll dig up the truth!" declared Robert.

"Truth is a breath, a wind, a shadow, a phantom, and eludes all gross inquiry."

Telling the truth in court had made his life in New York hell. Some of his friends rejected him. Garland thought him a damned fool for not breaking off his bohemian associations. Readers of the *New York World* licked their chops over "a racy story with a Tenderloin girl" and, to sauce it, "an opium-smoking episode."

"Do you know what a newspaper is?" Crane asked me. Robert had gone to the other end of the veranda to admire the weeds.

I'd have given a ready reply had I not suspected a trap.

". . . a collection of half-injustices / Which, bawled by boys from mile to mile, / Spreads its curious opinion / To a million merciful and sneering men . . ."

"Then why do you waste your words on them?" I was suddenly exasperated.

"To earn my bitter herbs and crust of bread! Christ's sake, let's go get some grub!" His tough talk seemed, to me, a parody of street argot, although his unkempt, unwashed appearance was the real McCoy. Charlie Michelson, a *New York Journal* correspondent at Key West, later called Crane the dirtiest man in an army. I liked him. Most people did. I felt—how do I say it? That there was something not quite right about him. But I wanted to be in his company.

The three of us walked up Caroline Street to the Yellow Fiddler, not far from Key West Bight. We ordered jerk conch, tamales, and beer bottled by the Tampa Brewery.

Gnawing on a rubbery conch, Robert cried, "Damn it, this is hot!" as his eyes began to tear.

"I'd offer to share my tamales, but they taste like pounded firebricks from Hades," said Crane, whose teeth, I saw, were bad.

In our recollections of people, we tend to dwell on their spoken words; no one is likely to remember a clam. To understand Crane, however, one needs to acknowledge his silences, which were habitual and could be lengthy and embittered. That June night at the Yellow Fiddler, named for the marsh crab, Crane entered the valley of silence at eight o'clock and did not emerge until half past. Not that he withdrew entirely into himself, but his replies to our questions were terse, sometimes hostile, and his contributions to the parley few and listless. Mostly, he kept quiet.

Had it not been for the ghost of tobacco smoke given up by his clothes, he might not have been there at all. When he finally did speak, it was of a woman he'd been with in New York City.

"Amy Leslie—she also went by other names— lived in a flat house on West Twenty-seventh, a street jammed with opium palaces and brothels. The janitor at Amy's place enjoyed a flash of celebrity when he declared, with a smirk and a swagger, that I had stayed with her during the summer of 1896. On that rancid crumb of intelligence the public choked and, having done so, spat me out. What was the word of a fornicator against that of New York detective Becker and the entire Nineteenth Precinct? The dope layout the police found when they tumbled my room completed the picture of Dorian Gray and made me an object of spite and an outcast from polite society, whose morals were safeguarded by police commissioner Roosevelt and Hamlin Garland. I had nailed the tin tray to a wall in my room to memorialize an excursion into the Tenderloin, taken so that readers could be titillated by 'Opium's Varied Dreams.' With the exception of Hearst's *Journal* and Walt Whitman's old paper, the *Brooklyn Daily Eagle,* the gentlemen of the press bludgeoned me. I was afraid the cops might do likewise with their truncheons. I didn't go into the Dora Clark business, thinking of martyrdom. I don't care for martyrs. They stink of the match that sets light to the pyre."

Crane fell silent until the crack of Robert's knuckles set him running again.

"Amy and I left the city like Adam and Eve thrown out of Eden on their bums. She gave me to understand that she had conceived my nemesis. What business does a man whose fuse is getting near the cracker have being a father? I convinced her to get off the train in Washington and go back to New York. What would she have done in Jacksonville while I was in Cuba? You see how it was. Those last moments on the platform—I might have swallowed pins. You can see how it was. I gave a friend five hundred dollars from my Appleton royalties to see to her needs, the only time in my life I was ever flush." He dragged a finger across his lip. "I promised to see her right."

I suspected, from the sadness in his almond-shaped eyes, that he had failed to do so.

"Smith likely mentioned Cora Taylor. I met her in Jacksonville at the Hotel de Dream, a high-toned sporting house. Back then, she owned the place—posh it was, not for the horde. She was reading *George's Mother*! What are the odds? Cora's a How-arth, a well-heeled Boston and New York family of musicians, scholars, and naturalists. Her father is a painter; John Greenleaf Whittier was one of her mother's relations. A cousin wrote the biography of Darwin. Cora likes books and the people who write them. When I introduced myself as the author of *George's Mother*, she looked like Cleopatra would have the moment she laid eyes on Mark Antony—or the asp on her breast. Love like ours always ends badly."

I said before that Crane's language was colorful. I also said that he was no smooth talker. His manner of speaking was like a horse that's picked up a stone in its hoof. He'd get going and then grind to a halt. His sentences shambled toward conclusion. Nonetheless, he spoke his mind and made no bones about self-revelation.

"We took to each other right off. Frankly, I don't care what you two bandits think of me, but I won't stand for any slams at Cora. I'd marry her in a snap if her irascible husband would divorce her. He's a spiteful waster with a title, a disgrace to his father, who was once the British commander-in-chief of India. She was Lady Cora Stewart till she left him to his women, cards, and gin. She won't put up with a fool or anything tame."

He smiled, and I supposed that he was seeing her in his mind's eye, behaving in a manner that would embarrass all of her living relations, as well as the poet Whittier, who was no longer versifying.

"After the *Commodore* sank and scuttled my plans for Cuba, I sailed to Athens to report on Crown Prince Constantine's war against the Turks over who would lord it over Crete. Cora, calling herself 'Imogene Carter,' went along to cover that thirty-day spree for the *Journal*—'the world's first war correspondent who didn't stand to pee,' said one wit, who, no sooner had the words left his mouth, ate them. She stood up under the bombardment at Velestino, the retreat to Volo after the king's son lost his nerve once more and Colonel Smolenski wept for his country's humiliation by the Ottomans. We were together during the evacuation of Volo of eight thousand Greek refugees jammed in that Aegean port as the Turks advanced. She was at Domokos and at Stylidia when the women and children were taken aboard boats crowded with wounded soldiers, everyone hungry and wretched. She bore it all without complaint. After the war, we took a house in Surrey and hid from our American creditors and detractors. The place was always packed with people come to gape and mooch. Cora never kicked at the bad hand we'd been dealt. I've never met another woman to match her. Hell, she's got more spunk than most men I've known!"

He paused like someone who has come to the end of a rope, considers, and then, with a sigh, let's go. "I still think of Amy. . . . I never did square it with her, though I sent her money from Athens—twice."

At that moment, he looked as if he were gnawing on his own bones. God only knows what thoughts get into a man's head. (Not even He can read a woman's mind, else our kind would be in Eden still.)

"Gentlemen, shall we try our luck at the Eager Bird?" Crane scraped back his chair. "It is a fine short road to oblivion."

To hazard all the money in his wallet on a game of Five White Mice excited Crane more than any woman he might bed in one of the Eager Bird's upstairs rooms. A gambler through and through, he lived like a man convinced that the universe is reckless, and God a cheat.

I hear Eakins mocking me in a stage whisper: "Oliver, you were too young and callow to see into a human heart, especially one as tormented as Stephen Crane's."

"Crane wasn't much older than I."

"He was born a Jacob. Do you know Gauguin's painting of the biblical text 'So Jacob was left alone, and a man wrestled with him till daybreak'? The man turned out to be an angel, but he could have been a devil just as well. It would've been all the same to Gauguin—and to Stephen Crane. He was born with his heart in his mouth and told to chew."

Robert and I stood like sheep in the gilded abattoir, on a carpet the color of the spots on a bloodstone. The walls were papered in a botanical motif that, as I stared at it, appeared lewd. The crystal globes of an electric chandelier shed a lurid hue on customers sitting nervously or smugly on damascene-covered chairs and languid women parading in unfastened robes. One of the men took a slide whistle from his pocket and produced a slithering tone that set one of the girl's hips swaying.

"You should've seen 'Little Egypt' dance the couchee-couchee at the World's Columbian Exposition," said Crane. "She knew what she was about! I was twenty-one. Say, I bet you two tykes are about that age! I thought the eyes of her. Conchita was her name. I did think the eyes of her. Not that I was nervy enough to show her my boyish lust! I used to stand at the back of the room with the other besotted gringos."

"Play the banjo for me, Stevie?" asked a girl whose hair was dyed with Turkish henna.

"I'm out of tune, Maggie."

She crooned a snatch of the Willy Brown song "Dennis Reilly at Maggie Murphy's": "Come here, I've something I want to show to you."

Crane sang Reilly's reply: "Well, that's all right, I've seen all you have."

"Like hell you have!" And with a wink, the girl was gone.

"Take whoever catches your fancy—Joe Pulitzer's treat," said Crane. Choosing a young woman with a faint scar on her throat, he followed her upstairs. By some trick of reflected light, the shiny brass carpet rods were bloodred, a fantastic detail more likely found in a tale of Edgar Poe's than in life, but I swear that it was so.

Robert took the hand of the nearest woman

and pulled her up the stairs like a man in a hurry to get himself hanged. He never mentioned the business afterward. I've always wondered if he had been thinking about Anne. A skinny Cajun girl tended me in a bed sprayed with cheap perfume. I caught the scent of toil on the sheets, for that is what it was as I struggled to be done with it, and she with me. Ashamed even now to admit it, I thought of Natalia as she would have looked at twenty. After the day in Hobson's Park when our teeth clashed as we clumsily kissed each other on the mouth, I never saw her again. I was afraid of Charles, his anger and spite.

At the end of the ordeal, I thanked the Cajun girl as one would a woman behind a sweets counter who has sold him two bits' worth of lemon drops.

My two friends (it pleases me to call them so) were playing roulette. Crane's eyes were transfixed by the turning wheel. Robert gave me an odd look, which may have been intended as humorous or arch, but it fell apart before it could resolve itself into anything meaningful. Games of chance are absurd, which was the point for Crane. He was leaning across the baize table, his head cocked, as if waiting to hear the whisper of an intercessor who would tell him where to put his chips. His back expressed both anger and surrender before overwhelming odds. I think that it consoled him to have irrational, inscrutable forces reduced to a revolving wheel, which he could, if he wished, smash. A large painting on the wall might have been the work of Franklin Barrett, except that the woman held a fan of cards over her face. In a corner of the room, a Negro piano player was thumping keys and crooning what sounded like "La Pas Ma La."

Feeling sick, I went outside to purge my fumigated lungs of smoke from a score of fat Havana cigars and Turkish cigarettes. I had started to walk to the nearby bight, which appeared all the blacker for lying underneath the night sky, when something bulked out from the wall. Startled, I let out a cry. A man stepped into the yellow light that fell through the open window, along with the jangled notes from an upright piano.

"I'll be on my way," he said to me in a voice I recognized as belonging to a colored man.

"Stay," I said. "I'm nobody you need worry about."

He wore the uniform of a private in the Eighth Cavalry, an "immune" regiment that had arrived in the key for duty in Cuba. The African blood of Negro soldiers was said to be proof against malaria and yellow fever. It wasn't. "I was enjoying the piano," he said. "It reminds me of St. Louis."

"Why don't you go inside?"

He looked at me—at the damned fool that I was. "'Smoked Yanks' aren't allowed in a white man's sporting house."

"I was going to have a look at the straits," I said,

starting in their direction. He took my remark as an invitation to accompany me.

His name was George P. Garnet. His father was a job printer in the "Ville," the Negro section of St. Louis. He looked about my age—or what a man my age would look like had he been knocked about by ignoramuses until his gut was fit to burst from corseted rage. He joined the Eighth Cavalry, Seventh Immunes, raised in St. Louis. He learned to be a soldier at Jefferson Barracks on the Mississippi River. He arrived in Key West, only to be knocked about some more by ignoramuses.

"Not caring to have 'a bunch of monkeys in uniform' in their town, white people started in on us soon as we got off the boat. We couldn't set foot in a lunchroom or a café without them getting in an uproar over the niggers." Recalling what my father had said about Natalia, I felt my hands clench. "A drunk white man of the Ohio volunteers pulled a black child from his mother and—to show what a good aim he had—put a bullet through his sleeve. I tell you, Mr. Fischer, all the pent-up poison just spilled over. We went on a rampage, shot up the town, and smashed places that'd refused to serve us. 'City Gripped by Negro Reign of Terror' is what the papers said." Garnet gave a short bark of a laugh. "It took the Second Georgia Volunteers to stop us. Though plenty of white people in Tampa said the Negroes weren't to blame, we're confined to our billets till we ship out for Cuba. No sense wasting army bullets when the Spanish will likely shoot us. Jees, I'd go crazy if I didn't sneak off sometimes!"

We listened to water roll, sighing, onto the beach, the buckle of a wave fold over itself, the caw of a flannel gull up to no good. Then the wind shifted, and in an instant, neither water nor gull could be heard. With nothing to see in the dark, I closed my eyes and gave myself up to the sensation of being in a world of silence in which a man or a woman can be brought to grief too deep for words or tears. A world where hands are raised in anger, and cheeks left bruised by signet rings.

"My friend Willie Box got his head split open by an ax. He was all the time saying how he wanted to send his daddy a jar of Cuban tobacco. He's a tobacco sharecropper in Richmond County. Willie said that his daddy never so much as smelled a Havana cigar, much less smoked one. He was a nice young fella. Shame."

I heard George shift his weight on the sand. "What's your story?" he asked. (We all have one, though rarely so crowded with events as Crane's or, come to think of it, as that of the black man who stood in the dark beside me.)

I told him something of myself, even things that made me look a fool. He would grunt, moan, chuckle, or click his tongue. It was too dark for me to see his face. I suppose it was the same for him.

We were two faceless smudges in the night. After a time, we were voiceless, as well. Stock-still as we stood, we could have been mistaken for a pair of stone markers by anyone walking the beach. So immobile were we that the gull might have rested on one of us. But there was nobody on the beach except us. The truant gull had rowed the black sky homeward, upheld by its muscular wings.

"Out there is Cuba," said George. Whatever gesture he had made was swallowed by the dark.

In daylight, I would have seen him pointing to the turquoise water in front of us. The Straits of Florida don't care where their water laps—on a beach at Key West or one at Guantánamo. The gull wouldn't give a damn, either, so long as the tide brought it fish and turned up clams. I nearly asked George if he was afraid. But I couldn't find the words to put so monumental a question to another man, although if words could be found, they would come easier at night, when faces are concealed.

George walked up the beach and left me to my thoughts. They had not yet taken shape, when Crane stepped out from a thickset stand of pines.

"Did you hear?" I asked him, still moved by the other man's story.

"I did, though it comes as no surprise to hear that some men suffer and black men maybe most of all in these United States and territories, soon—if the war hawks have their way—to be enlarged by a few choice possessions."

He lighted a cigarette. I can't say that I recall him without one, lighted or dead, between his lips. Tobacco was his one vice; he drank, naturally, but mostly beer. At that moment, his chest was as noisy as a carriage spring. There was something he had to get off it. Whatever it was could not be hawked up like a ball of phlegm. He had to say it right out.

"In the spring of '92, they hanged a black man from a maple tree across the street from my brother William's house. Two thousand citizens of Port Jervis watched Robert Lewis leave the Earth behind. Evidently, the rope had been knotted by an idiot. They had to cut him down, redo the noose, then haul the fellow up again. He kicked awhile, till he was properly deceased. They said he'd raped a white woman. A lie. William begged them not to do it. If I'd been there, would I have stood beside my brother when they hanged Lewis a stone's throw from the school my father and mother had founded in the '80s for black children? Would I have been Joshua or Fleming, who skedaddled under fire?"

He meant Henry Fleming, the main character in his novel *The Red Badge of Courage*.

"You proved yourself on the *Commodore* and in the open boat," I said, half my mind on Crane, the other half on the *tabaqueros* who were read to like children, so that they would roll more cigars for the

Schumachers. I had no business going to Cuba. I should stay in Key West, I thought, and try to do something for the John Mullinses of this world, be they red, brown, yellow, black, or white.

"I proved that I loved myself. Do you see? I did not care to drown." Crane tossed his cigarette into the night; it blazed a moment, then went out. "Life, Oliver, is an ignoble haggle. Mine will not have been so long as some others', and I'll have no say in the final tally of my debits and credits."

He had no time to spare and, consequently, didn't spare himself. He was like a boy caught up in a game who forgets to go home to supper and to bed. Later, when we were about to depart, I confessed that I wanted to get clear of it—Key West, I mean, and what was to follow when we crossed the straits with the marines. "Jump into the game with all four feet!" he told me. That was his way.

"If you had one of Mr. Wells's time machines, where would you go?"

I nearly said that I would go back to Ella Street and tell Natalia to wait for me. But she belonged to a boy. The man needn't go so far back in time. He would return to the Philadelphia Automat and beg Iris to stay with him. "Where would you go, Stephen?"

"I'd be a boy again in Port Jervis. I was happy there."

I picked up a stone and threw it into the darkness that contained the ocean's immensity. Crane kept silent; perhaps he, too, waited to hear the splash. None came.

"We're like fish in a barrel," he said.

"God's?"

"If you like."

Later that night, I sketched the reflection of my face in a mirror placed above the dresser in my room. I used the mechanical pencil that Dot had given me at Christmas, which I carried in the leather case that John Taws had pressed into my hands. When I'd finished the drawing, I saw the face of a man who was afraid. For a moment, I believed that I had produced a caricature. The eyes were too wide, the lips too compressed; the face bore a look of distraction. Looking closely in the mirror, I saw that I had captured a truthful likeness. I remembered what Sam Clemens had told me: "Times being what they are, a man can't rightly tell where life leaves off and hyperbole begins."

I opened the copy of *The Red Badge of Courage* that I'd brought from Philadelphia. I hunted for a passage that had stopped me cold:

> A little panic-fear grew in his mind. As his imagination went forward to a fight, he saw hideous possibilities. He contemplated the lurking menaces of the future, and failed in an effort to see himself standing stoutly in the midst of them. He recalled his visions of broken-bladed glory,

but in the shadow of the impending tumult he suspected them to be impossible pictures.

I tried to draw George Garnet's face, although I'd only glimpsed it when he left the deep shadow of the brothel wall and stood a moment in the light of the window. Finished, I knew that it was a poor portrait—a caricature of a Negro man. I set it on fire and dropped the burning paper into the washbowl.

On June 10, 1898, Crane, Robert, and I went aboard the *Three Friends*, a steam tug owned by Napoleon Bonaparte Broward of Florida, hired by Cuban revolutionaries to carry arms to the rebels. We would be sending illustrated stories of Spanish defeats back to Key West on her or other boats like her. (The undersea cable connecting Havana and the key was in enemy hands.)

With his traveling case on his knees, Crane was writing the first of his war dispatches. Now and then, he would drink from a glass of beer pinched between his boots to keep it from toppling as the boat rolled and pitched. He was thin to emaciation. (I never saw him look any other way.) A hectic flush on his pallid cheeks spoke of a feverish excitement. His sunken eyes fairly glittered. He brought to mind Coleridge's Ancient Mariner, who, with glittering eye, was condemned to tell his story to anyone who would listen.

The cabin of the *Three Friends* was small and reeked of varnish.

"I wrote a piece two summers ago for the *New York World* about the electric chair at Ossining." He sniffed the tang, sharp in the close cabin. "I'm reminded by the smell. The room where the chair sat was paneled in wood that had recently been varnished. I could see plainly that my escort took pride in the 'works,' as if we were standing in a shoe factory, instead of a death house. I supposed that he didn't get many chances to show off 'Old Sparky,' as he called it. He wanted me to admire the setup, and I saw no reason to deny him the pleasure. Humankind is the damnedest thing imaginable and the most . . ." He didn't finish his sentence.

"A small window high up on the death house wall offered a view of the sky," said Crane. "Like that." He gestured toward a port light set into the hull of the *Three Friends*. "That night I dreamed I went to heaven, and the angels were rabid." He smiled. "Will you lobsters join me in a breath of fresh air?"

We went up on deck. Night had fallen. The sea clattered against the hull like slates blown from a roof on a stormy night. The roof of the world may make such a noise at the Apocalypse. I was afraid. Robert stood beside me, one hand in his pocket. Perhaps he was holding his "lucky card," embellished by an icon of Lady Liberty undressed.

"I wouldn't worry overmuch," said Crane, whose

instincts were keen (unless fear has a smell). "This is the first hand you've played, so the house will treat you squarely. The trick is to go all in one dash."

He looked out onto the black water. Did he see the seven men whose death sentences were beyond appeal, waiting on the deck of the *Commodore* as her topmast bent ever lower toward the ocean that was about to engulf her? Maybe he saw the white wooden ball atop her sunken mast, bobbing in the gray chop that covered the corpse of the steamer that would never again go filibustering.

The sky cracked open above us, showing the fire that lay hidden in the night. Moments later, I felt the blast like a concussion in my chest.

"That'll be the North Atlantic Squadron firing on Cervera's fleet. It's been bottled up in the Bay of Santiago de Cuba since the twenty-ninth of May. Wait and see; the blue blouses will bite it off and chew it up splendidly." Crane seemed happy.

Even dire portents can be beautiful, and tragedy is often accompanied by the picturesque. The color of a dead man's face is that of the cornflower. The molten gold of flames that consume an orphanage would be sumptuous to the Ming. Typhoid fever leaves calling cards the color of a rose. New blood shed on a battlefield shines more brightly than berries on a holly tree. The *Three Friends* is steaming toward Guantánamo, where the sea is spangled, as though the tropic night has thrown down its stars.

Oh, three blind mice of chance,
Shirts of wool and corduroy pants,
Gold and wine, women and sin,
All for you if you let us come in—
Into the house of chance.

My eyes are dazzled by phosphorus cascading down the black sky as Admiral Sampson's ships continue to pound the Spanish fleet. I am waiting for the blast to thud in my breastbone. In the moment between coruscation and detonation, the roulette wheel clicks, the cards have yet to be dealt, or the die cast. All is impending. The world holds its breath. The house may treat us squarely. My father may turn kind. Dorothy may leave home on the arm of a young man. Robert may escape the shrapnel, Crane the fatal hemorrhage. A condemned man's last breath may be of flowers instead of varnish. And I may do something that will satisfy Thomas Eakins and myself.

What happened after the *Three Friends* put us ashore at Guantánamo Bay does not belong to the story just told. This much, however, can be said: Robert Pearson went no further in *his* story than the beach. Stephen Crane distinguished himself at Cuzco, Santiago, Siboney, Las Guásimas, and, most vividly, at San Juan, where he reported on Theodore Roosevelt leading his Rough Riders up Kettle Hill. Stephen stayed in the game awhile longer, until the fatal card was dealt and his story ended on June 5, 1900, at Haus Luisenstrasse 44, Badenweiler, on the edge of the Black Forest, where he died of his sick lungs.

Oliver Fischer, erstwhile clown and scapegrace, showed a modicum of courage in Cuba by not hiding behind a tree. On August 13, once the armistice was declared, he took a steamer from Key West to New York City, and thence a train to Chicago, where he has lived ever since with Iris, in a marriage unhallowed by any church. Five years ago he traded his crayons for a Remington typewriter. Last year he wrote this book.

"Wait!" you say, holding my arm by the sleeve, as the Ancient Mariner did the wedding guest's. "The story may be over, but you can't go on with your life, until you've told us what it means, what we are to make of it."

Very well, if I must, then this: Our lives are suspended by a thread between radiance and annihilation, waiting for the scissors.

University of Chicago   *April 16, 1907*

Afterword

*Times being what they are, a man can't rightly tell
where life leaves off and hyperbole begins.*

I knew Stephen Crane as the author of *The Red Badge of Courage*, assigned reading for high school students of my generation, and of "The Open Boat," whose first sentence is, my literature professors maintained, one of the finest in American letters: "None of them knew the color of the sky." I knew that his prose and poetry would be a necessary inclusion in The American Novels series, undertaken by my recollection of having heard one of those professors, whose name I can no longer recall, assert that the seminal works of nineteenth-century American literature are the stories of Edgar Allan Poe; certain stories and novels by Crane; the poetry of Emily Dickinson and Walt Whitman; *The Scarlet Letter* and "Young Goodman Brown," by Nathaniel Hawthorne; *Moby-Dick*, by Herman Melville; *Adventures of Huckleberry Finn*, by Mark Twain; and the moral and natural philosophies written by Ralph Waldo Emerson and Henry David Thoreau. I added the political writings of

Elizabeth Cady Stanton and Susan B. Anthony and the slave narrative of Frederick Douglass because of their importance in shaping the polyphonic voice of our national literature.

Having died in 1900, Crane would serve as the closing parenthesis to a century of authors whose work has come down to the twenty-first century as our literary inheritance. But a series of novels that concludes with the eleventh seemed unfinished, and so I have written a twelfth and final book, where Jack London appears in a cameo role.

Stephen Crane's development from an author of amusing sketches of bohemian life to stories of unprecedented frankness, such as *Maggie: A Girl of the Streets* and *George's Mother*, was rapid. The consciousness of the man advanced with equal rapidity, as though he had a presentiment of the tragic brevity of his life. William Dean Howells, who recognized in him an American heir to the literary realism practiced by certain French and Russian masters, wrote to Cora, his common-law wife, after Crane's death, "I . . . admired his strange, melancholy beauty, in which there was already a forecast of his early death." Yet his short career was crowded beyond all expectations. You have only to heft Paul Auster's or Paul Sorrentino's biography of him to be amazed at a life story whose chapters are many and various. Crane died at twenty-eight, yet Auster's book runs to nearly eight hundred pages, Sorrentino's to five hundred.

As in the previous ten novels of the series, I have attempted to impersonate the voice of the historical characters that lie at the heart of each book. Of course, writers cannot know how their human subjects may have sounded in conversation in the days before audio recordings. I have tried to mimic the tone, diction, and style of their fiction or poetry, letters, journals, and diaries. I expect that the quality of speech found in them is more varnished than vernacular. In Crane's case, my effort was hampered by his use of "quaint idioms of his own manufacture," as noted by his colleague and friend Frederic Lawrence (Auster). My equivalents are, I hope, not inconsistent with Crane's own colorful improvisations. (I suspect that my imitation of a Stephen Crane poem, appearing at the start of this book, will not have fooled his admirers. If anyone was taken in, I admit that it is easier to emulate a style than to invent one.)

The prose of the first half of *The Caricaturist* evokes the parodic voice that Crane used in tales like "The Broken-Down Van" and "Stories Told by an Artist," as well as in his novel *The Third Violet*. Their exaggerated quality befits my dandified narrator, Oliver Fischer. The tone of the second half of my book modulates into the more serious register of "The Fire," "The Price of the Harness," or "An Experiment in Misery." Hyperbole is the dominant mode in my novel. Both the actual Stephen Crane and the fictional Oliver Fischer produced caricatures in the seaside town of Asbury Park, New Jersey, to earn their livings—Crane with words, as a correspondent for his brother Townley's news bureau there, and Fischer with crayons, as a quick-sketch artist on the boardwalk. (This novel's ultimate caricaturist is, of course, its author.)

I have tried to make my works of fiction obedient to the truth of characters whom I appropriate from the historical record, as well as the particularities of their place and time, while exercising the freedom to make limited adjustments to serve the story's intention, which is a serious one in spite of comic moments. I have made Crane more talkative than I believe he would have been in front of Oliver and Robert, for instance. Charles Michelson, a friend and fellow correspondent, reported that Crane was "destitute of small talk" and could be "tongue-tied" (Auster).

I should mention that Ralph Paine and Ernest McCready, newspapermen and friends of Crane, were with him aboard the *Three Friends* as she steamed toward Guantánamo Bay.

I adjusted the chronology of events in the life of the great American painter of the late nineteenth century, Thomas Eakins. He was forced to resign from the Pennsylvania Academy of the Fine Arts for the reasons given in the story (and a suspicion of his having had a homosexual encounter) not in 1897 but in 1886. The scandal that beset him was as public and virulent as that which drove Crane from New York City. Eakins taught painting and anatomy at the New York Art Students League, located in the Needham Building, *after* his dismissal from the Pennsylvania Academy of the Fine Arts. His encounter with the young Stephen Crane is my invention.

I appropriated "where the garrets are lofty and the cellars deep" from a letter written by Eakins to his father, quoted by William S. McFeely in his biography of the artist.

To cite another example of a temporal adjustment, I brought the Anti-Imperialist League to Philadelphia, to parade in August 1897, when, in fact, it was not established until June 1898. Likewise, the Women's National War Relief Association was not founded until May 1898.

A first-person narrator, like Oliver Fischer, cannot always be trusted to get at the truth of another character. In my opinion, it is a more honest voice than a third-person narration, which makes a pretense of omniscience. To the best of my knowledge, I (the true first-person narrator) have not presented Crane, Eakins, Clemens, or Carnegie in a way that would be contrary to their views and attitudes.

Burk, Mack, and Ortlieb did exist and were, in fact, friends of Franklin Barrett, who was my maternal great-grandfather. His life was as I have written of it; their lives are imagined. My great-grandmother did embroider the socks worn by the Philadelphia Athletics. Charles Fischer is an exaggerated likeness of Charles Hub, my mother's paternal grandfather, comptroller of the Western Savings Fund Society in Philadelphia, a Mason, and a pigeon fancier. (I have only my late mother's word for his unpleasant character. His daughter, Dorothy, my great-aunt Dot, who lived the life of a spinster in the house he left her, spoke of him as a good father and man. Who of us knows the truth of another?)

My rendering of the arguments and politics surrounding the Spanish-American War is accurate, if necessarily abbreviated. The headlines appearing in *The Caricaturist* were taken, in many instances verbatim, from actual newspapers of the day. I sometimes altered the dates of their publication and inserted additional exclamation marks in the spirit of caricature.

My representation of the streets, parks, squares, waterways, buildings, businesses, institutions, newspapers, and transportation systems of Philadelphia and environs is mostly faithful to the time of the novel. (A few adjustments of little consequence were made in the interest of the story. For instance: The Philadelphia Automat did not open until 1902, and the Philadelphia Athletics baseball club did not play its first league games until that year.)

One last note: I changed the name of the Key West brothel visited by Crane, Robert, and Oliver from Eagle Bird to Eager Bird, for the obvious reason.

I am waiting for the blast to thud in my breastbone. In the moment between coruscation and detonation, the roulette wheel clicks, the cards have yet to be dealt, or the die cast. All is impending.

If great truths partake of the Absolute, then none is revealed to Oliver Fischer at the end of the life I have written for him. The moment on the deck of the *Three Friends* is as close as he gets to an illumination, despite the appearance of one. (It is also as far as we can follow him on his way to Guantánamo.) The unsatisfactory truth he acquires is shared by Stephen Crane, as he is revealed by his biographers: Life is best lived in headlong flight toward a destination likely to be conditional. We are alive for as long as the roulette wheel spins, he would tell us. The trick is to hazard all, live in earnest, behave as though each act were the final one. Anything can happen—everything *will* happen, this much we know. But for a moment, which may be short or long, we can delude ourselves into believing in possibility, perhaps the grandest illusion of all. The wheel spins, and time is in adjournment. In that space, mistakes may be erased, a foolish word or deed turned into a graceful one. We live from one moment to the next, one accident after another.

Time, we know, cannot be adjourned.

In *The Caricaturist*, both Stephen Crane and Oliver Fischer are caught in the current of events. Crane swims, knowing full well that he will drown before reaching an end that, in all likelihood, will be inglorious. Under the impression that he is swimming, Oliver flounders. We know, from our privileged vantage, that he can neither predict nor reach his final destination. The first case is tragic, the second comic.

> *I was such an ass, such a pure complete ass—it does me good to recollect it.*
> —STEPHEN CRANE, 1896,
> in a letter to Viola Allen (cited by Auster)

Be kind to Ollie Fischer. The self is a tender animal, and one armors it against the expectations of fathers as one can. Persian slippers and Baudelaire may do a young man as well as any other absurd posture we may assume at one time or another in our lives. Absinthe and artifice are no worse than the booze and boorishness with which the yeomanly Robert Pearson confronts the hostilities of his age. What is art—high like that of Manet and Stephen Crane or low like that found on cigar bands—if not a carapace to protect the hypertrophic organ of human sensibility?

Events in the life of the nation at the end of the century put a strain on Oliver, as they would have on all who were conscious of the universe into which they were expelled at birth. And like anyone, his idea of himself was shaped and deformed by familial strains—in his case, those caused by an autocratic father.

Be kind to Ollie Fischer, who bears a passing resemblance to the author as a young man.

The Myrtle Jane on the Delaware River, circa 1908. My grandmother Helen (Barrett) Hub is the young girl sitting alone in the stern of the rowboat.

A boating party on the Delaware River, circa 1905. My grandmother Helen (Barrett) Hub, the youngest of the girls, is seated to the right of her mother, Gertrude.

Franklin Barrett (standing) and friends on Frankford Creek, in Philadelphia; his wife, Gertrude, mans the oars.

Watercolor by Franklin Barrett, 1954.

Acknowledgments

"This [book] is a work of fiction," as is stated in the boilerplate, in a thicket of small type, as if not to insist on its own fictionality. (Except for bibliophiles and media specialists, who reads a book's page of disclosures?) You, reader, enter the world of the novel and willingly believe in the author's arrangement of facts as they pertain to the artifice that he or she has constructed out of words. In a book such as *The Caricaturist*—in which people who once existed are resurrected so that I might "repurpose" them for the sake of a story (never mind my honorable intentions)—are you, reader, not entitled to know when I have fictionalized and when I have tried to cleave to the facts of their lives? To speak more broadly, is the space of fiction also a moral one?

For this reason and to acknowledge the difficult work of those who write the biographies and histories on which I depend, the later books in The American Novels series have included an afterword and the comprehensive citations usually found in biographies and annotated editions of fiction.

Primary Sources: *Crane: Prose and Poetry*, edited by J. C. Levenson (Library of America), and *The War*

Dispatches of Stephen Crane, edited by R. W. Stallman and E. R. Hagemann. Crane's preface to "An Experiment in Misery" ("Two men stood regarding a tramp. . . .") appeared in the *New York Press* for April 22, 1894. Paul Auster reprints it in full in his biography of Crane.

Note: In the stanza beginning "Oh, five white mice of chance[,]" I changed "five white mice" to "three blind mice."

Biographies.: *Burning Boy: The Life and Work of Stephen Crane*, by Paul Auster, and *Stephen Crane: A Life of Fire*, by Paul Sorrentino. Auster acknowledges his debt to Sorrentino, whose biography of Crane preceded his. And so must I acknowledge my debt to both of them. Stephen Crane would have been a sketch of a man in *The Caricaturist* if not for their books. (To cite my appropriations of Crane's own words quoted by Auster or Sorrentino would be impractical. Let this one note serve as an admission of my borrowing: "I am a good deal of a rascal, sometimes a bore, and often dishonest [Auster, 249].")

I relied, as well, on *American Painting of the Nineteenth Century*, by Barbara Novak; *Portrait: A Life of Thomas Eakins*, by William S. McFeely; and *Thomas Eakins: Artist of Philadelphia*, Philadelphia Museum of Art / Museum of Fine Arts, Boston (catalogue, 1982). (I found Eakins's advice to the artist, which I put in Franklin's mouth, in McFeely's book: "Get down your highest light, then your shadow, then work in between until you get them harmonious.")

City Directory (online): *Gopsill's Philadelphia City Directory for 1905* (Boyd's Philadelphia combined city and business, 1900), HathiTrust.

Historical Maps: David Rumsey Historical Map Collection, Greater Philadelphia GeoHistory Network (street, plat, and land use), Old Maps Online (Key West), and various railroad maps at the Library of Congress.

Miscellaneous (online): "City of Unbrotherly Love: Violence in Nineteenth-Century Philadelphia," by Kathryn Wilson and Jennifer Coval, Historical Society of Pennsylvania; *Encyclopedia of Greater Philadelphia*; fashion history timeline, the Fashion Institute of Technology, State University of New York; "The History of Cigar Bands," by J. Bennett Alexander, and a glossary of cigar terms, Holt's Clubhouse; "A History of the Pennsylvania Academy of the Fine Arts, 1805–1976," by Frank H. Goodyear, Jr.; Household Ads of the 1890s, VintageAdBrowser.com; and "The War Prayer," by Mark Twain, AmericanLiterature.com.

Newspapers (online): Chronicling America: Historic American Newspapers, Library of Congress, and *Cartoons of the Spanish-American War* (1899), Internet Archives.

Patriotic Songs (online): Music for the Nation: American Sheet Music Collection, Library of Congress, and *Spanish–American War Songs: A Collection of Newspaper Verse During the Recent War with Spain*, compiled and edited by Sidney A. Witherbee, 1898, OpenLibrary.org. Songs were the social media of the age, as the collection's 973 pages attest. One reason for the avalanche of doggerel was the number of newspapers. In New York City, eighteen English-language daily papers and seventeen foreign-language ones competed for readership. During the Spanish-American War, both Joseph Pulitzer's *New York World* and William Randolph Hearst's *New York Evening Journal* published dozens of daily extra editions and printed a million copies each day.

The Spanish-American War: "American Foreign Policy in the Late Nineteenth Century: Philosophical Underpinnings," by Michael Chimes, the Spanish-American War Centennial website; "Black 'Immune' Regiments in the Spanish-American War," National Museum of the United States Army; "Censorship Liberally Administered: Press, U.S. Military Relations in the Spanish-American War," by Randall Sumpter, ResearchGate.net; *Crucible of Empire: The Spanish–American War*, American Experience television series, PBS; "Cuba in 1898," by José M. Hernandez, Library of Congress; "From 'Dagoes' to 'Nervy Spaniards,' American Soldiers' Views of Their Opponents, 1898," by Albert A. Nofi, New York Military

Affairs Symposium; "October 10th, 1868: The Beginning of Cuba's Independence Wars," *Political Affairs*; "Official Report of the Naval Court of Inquiry into the Loss of the Battleship *Maine* (Sampson Board)," the Spanish-American War Centennial website; "Sketches from the Spanish-American War," U.S. Naval Institute; "Spanish-American War," *Making of America*, HathiTrust; and *The Spanish–American War, 1898*, by Albert A. Nofi.

Speeches (online): "Cross of Gold," delivered by William Jennings Bryan on July 9, 1896, *History Matters,* http://HistoryMatters.gmu.edu; "Imperialism: Flag of an Empire," delivered by Bryan on August 8, 1900, Voices of Democracy: The U.S. Oratory Project; and "March of the Flag," delivered by Albert J. Beveridge, September 16, 1898, Voices of Democracy: The U.S. Oratory Project.

Note: Carnegie's question to the crowd at the Anti-Imperialist League parade ("Is the Republic to remain one homogeneous whole . . . ") and his offer to write a twenty-million-dollar check are factual, although both were made toward the end of the war, during America's negotiations with Spain, concluded in December 1898 in the Treaty of Paris, whereby the United States purchased the Philippines, and gained possession of Cuba and Guam. (Cubans and Filipinos were excluded from the negotiations, even those who had led the rebellion.) I suspect that Carnegie's motives were more nativist than humanitarian.

William Jennings Bryan's speech ("There are many, today, who argue that the United States has come of age and can do what it pleases . . .") was delivered after the war, in the hope of shaming the American government into renouncing any claim to Cuba and the Philippines. (As we have seen, America is not so easily shamed.)

The words of anarchist Louis Lingg ("I am the enemy of the 'order' of today . . .") and those of the Reverend Johnson ("In this country the torch put to the factories . . .") are excerpted from actual speeches.

Art and Photo Reference (online): Courtroom cartoon (altered), www.widewalls.ch/courtroom-sketch-artists; "*Le Déjeuner sur l'herbe*—Looking at Manet's *Luncheon on the Grass*," Art in Context: Edouard Manet, Manet.org; "*The Luncheon on the Grass* by Edouard Manet," GalleryIntell; and "The Significance of Manet's Large-Scale Masterpiece *Luncheon on the Grass*," My Modern Met. (The original painting is in the holdings of the Musée d'Orsay, Paris, and is in the public domain.) The photo of Everett Stewart, "The Male Patti," is from the Library of Congress. (Birds on musical staff drawing is by the author.)

Notes: The sobriquet of Everett Stuart, "the Male Patti," alludes to the black American soprano Matilda Sissieretta Joyner Jones (1868/1869–1933), whom a music critic dubbed "the Black Patti" after the renowned Italian opera singer Adelina Patti. Trained at the Providence Academy of Music and the

New England Conservatory of Music, Jones made her New York City debut in 1888 at Steinway Hall. She would later sing for the British royal family, as well as Benjamin Harrison, Grover Cleveland, William McKinley, and Theodore Roosevelt. Roosevelt was the only one of the four presidents who allowed her to enter the White House by the front door.

The passage in Spanish that I quoted from the first chapter of *Don Quixote* is translated, in the Project Gutenberg text, as "In short, his wits being quite gone, he hit upon the strangest notion that ever madman in this world hit upon, and that was that he fancied it was right and requisite, as well for the support of his own honour as for the service of his country, that he should make a knight-errant of himself, roaming the world over in full armour and on horseback in quest of adventures . . ."

Thank you, Erika Goldman, Laura Hart, Molly Mikolowski, Joe Gannon, Carol Edwards, Elana Rosenthal, Alban Fischer (no relation to Oliver), Charles Giraudet, Eugene Lim, Jerome Charyn, and Helen.

BELLEVUE LITERARY PRESS is devoted to publishing
literary fiction and nonfiction at the intersection of
the arts and sciences because we believe that science and
the humanities are natural companions for understanding
the human experience. We feature exceptional literature
that explores the nature of consciousness, embodiment,
and the underpinnings of the social contract. With
each book we publish, our goal is to foster a rich,
interdisciplinary dialogue that will forge new tools for
thinking and engaging with the world.

To support our press and its mission, and for our full
catalogue of published titles, please visit us at blpress.org.

BELLEVUE LITERARY PRESS
New York